Battle Phoenix

By

Huckleberry Rahr

ISBN eBook: 978-1-959981-61-9
ISBN paperback: 978-1-959981-62-6

Editor: Weslee Imrisek
Developmental Editor: Angela Grimes
Cover Art: Getcovers.com
Formatting: Huckleberry Rahr

Books In the Ember Savita Series

1: Veiled Phoenix
2: Moonstone Phoenix
3: Battle Phoenix

Books by Huckleberry Rahr

- Jade Stone Chronicles
  - Wolf Healer
  - Epsilon
  - Alphas
  - Traitor
  - Pack
  - Battlefield
  - Pack Present
- Pebble Stone Chronicles
  - Xenagogue
  - Yugen
  - Zephyr
- Ember Savita Chronicles
  - Veiled Phoenix
  - Moonstone Phoenix
  - Battle Phoenix
- The Search – Short Story, eBook only

Acknowledgements

When I started writing, I always thought writers were a solitary group. That's how they're depicted on shows and in movies. Now, I've been a teacher for years and know that how educators are portrayed is often very wrong, so I don't know why I believed what I saw about authors.

I started off writing in a bubble. That didn't last long. As my group grew, so did my enjoyment of the art, as did my product, or so I believe.

Currently, there are several people who are the core of my writing group. We encourage each other, help figure out areas we need to expand details in each other's work, and are, at the end of the day, family.

Thank you Wes, Angela, Elizabeth, Lawrence, and Nikki. As for others who have made this story possible, Gavin, my eldest, read and gave input, and was a sounding board for all my brainstorming needs.

For me, each book takes a village, and few have one as great as mine!

To my readers

Ember Savita, the main character of this series, is nonbinary. They use they/them pronouns. As I wrote these books, I was excited to create this main character.

Writing a character with they/them pronouns is a challenge. I may have made some mistakes. If I did, I apologize. This book has been critiqued and edited by many people, but I'm sure some mistakes still found their way through.

Thank you for joining me on this journey. I appreciate all of you.

Chapter 1 - Welcome To The Fold

Ember

The three griffins landed in the Phoenix Forest late at night. Ember shivered, remembering the last time they'd been close to this exact spot. The trip with Felix and Aunt Monte had started off well, but being kidnapped in the end brought awful memories. Mom squeezed them from behind. "Don't worry, love, everything will be okay."

"I know, Mom. I just ... I have mixed feelings about being here. And where will we stay? It's so late. Can we get a hotel in town?" They thought about the letter demanding the family return to Serafina Landing to meet with the Elders.

Though Ember didn't like being told what to do and where to go, part of them vibrated with excitement to be in a city of phoenixes, a lineage of theirs they'd thought gone from this world; another part feared the reason their family had been summoned

Aunt Nuri laughed. "Serafina Landing isn't the kind of place that strangers visit. There aren't hotels or bed and breakfasts. I know a lot has happened, but did you miss the part that your dad and I each have a house in town?"

Ember groaned. "That's right. So we'll each go to our respective ... homes?"

She smiled wide. "I think we'll all hole up together. For now, we need strength in numbers."

The group bowed their thanks to the trio of griffins and Ember giving each a hug. Mom requested they return on Saturday and then the group watched as the majestic creatures flew off. When the trio was out of sight, they started their march into town. It was late enough that the streets were deserted as they wound their way to the house that made Ambrose's mansion look like a starter home.

"Gods above, Dad, this place is huge."

He grunted. "It's walls and windows. Now, get in and find a room. Up the stairs, turn left."

I wonder if Aunt Nuri's house is as big? Maybe it's bigger, because the community seems to like her more. It's like she's the preferred twin.

Ember's eyes widened at the huge double door entry that led into a foyer. They marveled at two sets of stairs that lined the sides of the entryway, meeting at the top at a small sitting area. From there, hallways led off in both directions.

"So just pick any room?" they confirmed, hefting their bag on their shoulder.

Mom gave Ember a squeeze, but Aunt Nuri answered. "Any at all. The house is yours as much as Ash's. Drop off your bags and come back for a quick tour. Then we'll eat."

There were at least a half dozen rooms, and they all had private bathrooms. The third one on the right looked over the woods, not the private swimming pool. It was painted a light cream on all the walls except one, which was painted a dark purple. Ember decided it felt right.

A third of the room was taken up by a huge bed. The frame's wood matched the dresser and side tables. After the long trip out, Ember wanted to flop on the bed, but instead they dropped their bags and headed back to get the rest of the tour.

On the main floor, to the left of the stairs, was a sunroom followed by a huge library. To the right was a living room. It all reminded Ember of a house in a fairy tale. All it was missing were vines covering the outside for a prince to climb.

I wonder what Felix and Daisy would think? I bet one of Daisy's books has a castle like this with a prince that has climbed it to save the maiden ... or a powerful princess who saved herself. Felix would probably just be too excited at the idea of all the phoenixes and try to find a library or center for historical documents.

An arch under the stairs led to a dining room. Ember didn't find the kitchen because once they got to the dining room, Dad showed up with food and they all dug in.

Once they finished eating, Dad, Mom, and Nuri needed to check in with the town officials and Elders.

Ember headed back upstairs and sat on a bed ... their bed. They thought about the clothes Felix had magicked, adapted from a lesson Mrs. Howel had taught on capturing magic proficiencies in glass balls before winter break. Ember decided having more protection was a great idea. They pulled out a pile of their clothing and began the process. Their boyfriend, Felix, was better at the spell, but he wasn't there.

As they worked, their mind wandered. A few weeks ago, they thought they and their dad were the only two phoenixes left in the world. Then they learned their dad had a twin, Aunt Nuri, and she was alive. And now ...

Would it be bad of me to wish my previous misconception was right? Life was boring, but so much less hectic. How much trouble are we in?

Gazing around the room, Ember contemplated the fact that they'd never had an inkling of this house's existence before—any permanent residence. *All those years of running, moving whenever I died and rose from the ashes, and all along Dad had a permanent home sitting here in the phoenix compound, empty and unused.*

Apparently, the house sat waiting for Dad's banishment to be lifted. It had been over two hundred years, and according to Dad, this was faster than he expected.

That all changed two nights ago when the Elders, having heard news that Dad and Aunt Nuri had revealed the fact that phoenixes weren't extinct to the general public, had left a note on Ember's front door. Mom and Dad had debated what to do. Aunt Nuri had suggested everyone come and discuss with the phoenix leaders the fallout of the new exposure. Ember had a few days left of their winter break. They probably wouldn't even miss any school.

Though the phoenixes said they'd allow the witches to come, Aunt Monte stayed behind to run the Fire Bird Coalition, FB Coalition. Infinite WISDOM was still out there, and they couldn't be left unchecked. The group had already kidnapped Ember and spent days trying to kill them. Who knew what their next insidious plan would be? The only good thing that came out of all the madness was now Ember's closest friends knew they were a phoenix.

Thinking about their friends, Ember pulled out their phone. They needed to let them know they'd made it. They started a group text with both Felix and Daisy.

Dad's house is bigger than Ambrose's!

Did you make it safely through the woods this time? How many times were you stopped? Felix followed his text with a skull emoji.

Not with Dad and Aunt Nuri. No one would dare! Ember laughed to themself.

OMG! Did you make it? What is it like? Are there phoenixes flying everywhere? Ember could practically feel Daisy's exuberance through their phone.

Ember smiled and rolled to their back. *No, it was pretty quiet when we arrived. Dad has a house. I'm waiting for the adults to check in. I'm bored, there's nothing to do.*

Felix just texted 'lol.'

I love that I'm here, Ember replied *but I want to spend some of my break with you two. I'm conflicted. Do you think it was the right decision to come back here?*

The bubble showing Felix typing immediately started. *I do. I believe it's important that you learn about this side of your nature. I also think that it's really cool.*

Felix's fascination with phoenixes had not diminished now that he'd learned Ember and their Dad were firebirds. If anything, it'd gotten worse.

Before Ember could type more, there was a knock at their door. They sent off a message saying they'd get back to them later.

"Yeah?" The only people it could be were their parents or Aunt Nuri.

The door opened and a teen walked in. She had hair the same color as Ember's, but curlier and longer. She wore a green, knit sweater that matched her eyes and jeans. Ember pushed the clothes they'd been working on to the side. The bed was plenty big enough. They were curious who would be in their family home. "How did you get in here?"

A smile stretched across the girl's face and she sat on the far corner of the bed. "Hi, I'm Fotia, and I'm your ... cousin? We share great-grandparents, I think. Anyway, I heard you'd come and I wanted to meet you. Declan said he'd already met you, you know, when he tried to stop you on the way to the cave, and that's not fair, he isn't family, and he can be an arrogant jerk. You agree he's a jerk, right? Everyone thinks he and I will end up together since there aren't many phoenixes our age, but gah! Can you imagine?"

One of Ember's eyebrows slowly rose as Fotia's avalanche of words just kept on rolling from her mouth. "So, you aren't a fan of Declan?"

"Gods, no! Why? Did you like him when you met him?" Fotia's eyes widened.

Ember smiled. "Not really, but I didn't get much of an impression except as someone who wanted me and my friends out of the woods."

"Oh, he didn't want you to leave, just your friends. He's really all about the rules. Well, he is now. Not when we were young and he pulled my ponytail, but I burnt his homework, so I got him back."

Holding up their hands, Ember laughed. "Stop. Enough."

Fotia smiled back. "I know, it's just, I've grown up here. I've never really had anyone new to talk to. And you're family. This is so fun."

"So, you grew up here. Have you ever been anywhere else?"

"Outside of Serafina Landing?" Fotia shrugged. "Sure. Whenever I'm on patrol."

"No, further. Have you ever traveled?" Ember tilted their head, not sure why this wasn't obvious. "You know, visited other places?"

Fotia's eyes widened. "Outside the Phoenix Forest? Are you kidding me? Gods, no. But I guess you live beyond our land, don't you?" She leaned forward. "Tell me what it's like; tell me everything."

"Everything?" Ember laughed and shook their head. "I don't know that I can tell you everything."

"Well, where do you live? Have you always lived in the same house? Do you have friends? Are they human? Witch? Do you go to school? Does everyone really have cell phones? Do they really rot your brains? Are all the popular kids mean? Why do they hang out together if they are? Are they all dumb too, or can they be popular and smart? Do schools really have a king and queen? Have you been to a prom? Oh! And how long were you at each stopping point?"

Is it possible she's talking faster? Goodness, my head's going to explode!

Ember threw their hands up to stop the questions. "Whoa! Wow. Really? You have a lot of questions."

"Sorry." Fotia rubbed her hands on her legs. "I babble. And I've never met anyone new. It's ... it's kind of scary and I talk a lot when I'm nervous." She began to pat her legs back and forth as she smiled at Ember.

Biting their bottom lip to stop themself from laughing, Ember just nodded. "Okay, let me see what I can do with your list of questions. To start with, my family moved a lot. It mostly correlated with my stopping points."

Ember just recently learned that phoenixes had ages they developed at before they 'died' and moved on. The dying helped their body finish its growth and was required to continue aging. When a young phoenix got to these ages, they could be at a stopping point for days or years, it all depended on how careful everyone was or how unlucky the phoenix kid happened to be. Despite just learning this, Ember wasn't going to let this stranger know it was new knowledge to them.

"I was five for ... I think two years. How about you?"

Fotia's smile widened. "A year and a half. I was out with Afi, you'll meet him later, and we were climbing a tree in human form. Anyway, I fell. Afi felt so guilty because he thought it was his fault. He lasted a few more weeks."

"Are you two the same age then?"

"Afi? No, he was watching me and was at his thirteen-year-old point. He was there for like ... I dunno, almost two years." Fotia squinted at the ceiling as she tried to figure it out.

"What about ten?" Ember asked. "How long were you at that point?" The conversation seemed so weird. The idea of stopping points was wacky but discussing it with someone who both understood and was their own age was kind of fun, if not trippy. This was all new, but it was exciting to have someone to share stories with who understood.

Fotia flopped onto her back. "Like, not at all. Two months maybe. It was awful. There's some prestige in being able to be at a stopping point for a super long time.

Declan talks about being thirteen for two and a half years. He gloats about it. I sometimes want to slap the smirk off his stupid face."

"I was thirteen for a few hours," Ember admitted and immediately regretted it as Fotia's jaw dropped wide open. "I received a new bike for my birthday. I took it out for a ride and as I followed a path, a part crumbled under me, and I went with it ... down a cliff." Fotia slapped her hands over her mouth, eyes wide. "I walked home naked. We were in a pretty private part of the city. After that Mom and Dad explained I should fly, invisible, in those situations. A naked female isn't really safe."

"Oh, a bike. I've seen pictures of those in magazines. Was it with training wheels? Was it red? Did it have a horn and a basket? Did you honk at people like a goose? Geese are mean! Have you ever been chased by a goose? I was once, they're terrifying! I wasn't in my bird shape, and it honked. Is that what a bike horn sounds like?"

Ember curled their lips in. *I will not laugh.* At Fotia's giggles, Ember lost it, laughing exuberantly.

A tension released in Ember. Again, in so few days, their family grew, and again the person was fantastic. "So, you were thirteen longer than my few hours?"

There was a twinkle in Fotia's eyes. "Yes, I was thirteen for just over a year. Good and proper, as my dads let me know. Do you know, I don't think my dads have 'died' and changed since my birth. I mean, one of them was female when I was conceived and born, but in my memory, I've always had two dads. What about you?" Before Ember could answer, Fotia waved her hands. "No, wait, ten, you skipped over ten. How long, Ember?"

In the few minutes they'd been together, Ember decided Fotia was good people; she was fun and non-judgmental. With a meek smile, she shrugged. "Well, I guess about four years or so."

"What!" Fotia demanded. "That's impossible. No one makes it that long. You have got to tell, well, everyone. That's fantastic. Forget thirteen for a day, who cares? Four years? That's it, you win! This may be a new record."

Ember laughed as Fotia went on and on. Finally, they broke in and tried to fill Fotia in on some of her other questions. "Yes, everyone has phones. I don't know about all schools, but yes, a lot of them have dance kings and queens, but not otherwise. As for popular kids, they are mean at my school, but I can't speak for the others. And some of them can think their way out of a paper bag, but not all of them."

Fotia's smile grew. "Amazing! Now, parents, friends, a boyfriend? A girlfriend?"

Ember ticked things off on their fingers. "Dad has been my second mom a couple of times. I'm glad. It helped me to understand everything going on with me. I was homeschooled until thirteen when I started public school. Two amazing friends; one is my boyfriend."

"Now, your mom isn't a phoenix. So, you can do magic? Are you a witch and a phoenix?"

"Are you always this curious?"

Fotia blushed. "I don't know. Like I said, I've never met someone new. Not to mention a person who's a family member. And look at you, we could be siblings ... maybe even twins."

A thought flitted through Ember's mind of Daisy and Fotia together. It would be either terrible or fantastic. Everyone would need earmuffs. "I can do some magic. It's helped me to hide. I attend a school for witches. There, I mostly do air magic. I can't dumb down the fire magic enough to present as a witch."

"Of course you can't. We *are* fire. That would be impossible. But air magic, that's great. I bet it helps to understand air since you fly in the stuff."

"It does."

Her head tilted. "Why all the clothes on the bed? What were you doing before I got here? Some secret thing people do when traveling I should know about if I ever travel?" As she spoke, her eyes got bigger, and she shimmied her hands.

Ember scrunched up their face and debated, then decided to tell Fotia a bit about what had happened to them. When they got to the part about finding a magical way to make their clothes not burn to ash, Fotia leaned forward, a small smile playing across her face. But once she heard about the kidnapping and repeated deaths, her face morphed, hardening into a mask of anger and determination.

"Holy Gods in the clouds! If I could find those people ... I would, well, I don't know what I would do." She sighed. "So you're making your clothes so they won't burn up?" Fotia's jaw dropped and her ire shifted back to her happy-go-lucky nature. "Can you do that with some of mine? That's so cool! I mean ... I have some outfits I love."

A chuckle bubbled from Ember. "Sure, I can try. I'm not even sure what I'm doing will be successful. I figured I'd work with Mom to perfect everything. But, yeah, once I have it figured out, sure."

After a beat, Fotia's brows knit. "Okay, but I have a question. I get that your clothes survived while you were in that place." She patted the comforter next to her thigh. "But what about the bed and blanket? Why didn't they burn up every time those jerks messed with you?'

Shock and confusion flowed through Ember. *Why didn't I even think about that?* They opened their mouth to say more, but Aunt Nuri's voice cut through their conversation. "Ember, it's time to be introduced as the newest phoenix."

Chapter 2 - Fighting For A Future

Ember

Ember and Fotia headed down the stairs. Dad, Mom, and Aunt Nuri stood with two men who looked about the same age as Dad. *I guess with phoenixes that doesn't mean much.* They both had short auburn hair and sparkling green eyes. Wide smiles welcomed Ember and Fotia as they came down to the first floor.

The shorter of the two men started to chuckle. "They could be siblings, practically twins. How long ago was Ember born?"

It amused Ember how close to Fotia's words this man's words were. *Is this Fotia's Dad?*

Dad shook his head. "Vatra, you know that doesn't matter. They're both sixteen right now. Stopping points are the great equalizer. You sound like Ember when they found out."

Fotia hugged the one who spoke ... Vatra. "Oh, my gods, Dad, Ember was ten for four years. I can't wait to tell Declan. He can stuff it. He's no longer the belle of the ball." She turned to Ember. "Ember, these are my Dads, Vatra and Feu."

Fotia's other dad, Feu, shook his head. "Fotia, why don't you let Ember decide if she—"

Mom gently made the correction. "Ember goes by they/them. They decided at a young age that it was easier than switching pronouns with every 'death.'"

Searching the faces of the people in the foyer, Ember saw Fotia's mouth hanging open. After a few beats, their cousin snapped her mouth shut. "That is *brilliant.* I mean, most of us don't switch that often. Like I said, I've had two dads for a really long time, but, yeah, smart."

Mom tilted her head. "Well, all of you have a lot of catching up. I'm going to go get dinner started while you sit and talk."

Vatra held up a hand. "You don't have to do that, Sadie. We can call in some others to cook for us. There are enough people around who would happily prepare us a meal. Do you know how long people have awaited the return of the Savita twins?"

Dad shook his head and grumbled. "Some things never change."

Vatra smiled at him. "No, nothing around here does. The royalty of Serafina Landing have finally come home, and they've brought family. People have been dreaming of this day. The idea that they could come in here and make your homecoming meal. Heck, if the community had known you were coming back today, there'd already be a feast in your honor, I'm sure."

Ember narrowed their eyes, not sure if he was teasing them or telling the truth.

Aunt Nuri rubbed her eyes. She looked tired. She placed her hand on Vatra's shoulder. "That's why we didn't tell anyone. We're just two more phoenixes. Yes, our parents, your aunt and uncle, helped create this place, but so did your parents."

"Yes, but mine didn't have the fire power yours did. Did you know that after Declan came back, he whined to the Elders that Ember stole his fire?"

Dad's eyes widened, and he turned to them. "You did what?"

Ember sighed. "I didn't *take* it, like, make it so he couldn't use fire. He threw a fireball at me to test if I was really a phoenix, a jerk move, by the way. I caught it and tossed it around."

Fotia and Feu gaped at them. Finally, Feu said, "You did what?"

Dad shook his head. "That isn't taking his fire, it's protecting themself, and having fun with a projectile. If this Declan was stupid enough to throw the thing, he was lucky Ember didn't do a counter strike. Feu, you knew Nuri and I could do that, why does it surprise you that Ember can as well?"

Ember wanted to smirk, but thought maybe it would be disrespectful. They looked over at Fotia whose face beamed with a huge smile. It looked like they wanted to rub Declan's face in all of this. *Maybe smirking is okay, at least when I'm with her.*

Before Feu could answer, someone knocked on the door.

Dad snarled, "We didn't tell anyone we were coming because we wanted our first night to be quiet. I can only imagine who's here." He moved to answer the door.

A woman and man stood at the double doors with a small, wheeled table behind them. The woman had dark hair, almost brown, pulled back in a neat ponytail, but Ember guessed under bright light it would have red in it. The man's hair was long, straight, and also pulled back, but low against his neck. His hair was strawberry blond. *For years I was teased and mocked for my auburn hair and now everywhere I turn it's all I see. It's odd not sticking out, but in a good way.*

The table between the two strangers was full of steaming hot food. Despite the good smells, Ember was cautious of strangers bearing food. Their gut told them to tread carefully around these two. The slight tensing of the others didn't help their wariness.

Aunt Nuri plastered a smile on her face. "Vuur, Apoy, exalted Elders, to what do we owe this unexpected intrusion? We've already checked in with you and promised to bring Ember around *tomorrow.*"

Vuur? Apoy? Elders? I do not like the sound of this. Ember's belly flipped. They tensed their muscles to hide their apprehension.

The woman's face contorted in what Ember thought may be a smile, though it looked insincere. "Nuri, we are acting as the welcoming committee. Since you didn't warn us you were coming, the house isn't prepared. There isn't food, not even anything you could make from scratch. After you landed, a group quickly got together and made you all these dishes. Apoy and I graciously offered to bring them by."

Under his breath Dad mumbled, "Graciously, yeah, right." Louder he said, "Vuur, Apoy, thank you for your consideration. Be welcome in our home." He waved his hand towards the dining room. "Would you like to join us for dinner?"

Though Dad said the right words, Ember could hear the strain in his voice that told them he hoped they'd drop the food off and leave.

Vuur's face contorted more. *Wow, she needs to work on her smile if that's what she's doing.* "Why, thank you, Ash, we'd be delighted."

A boulder formed in Ember's gut. They'd had enough stress over the last week. They'd just met Fotia and her dads. They didn't need the Elders here changing the atmosphere of the evening from light and fun to ... well, whatever it was they planned on bringing. *It's just not fair! Isn't it enough they demanded we come? Can't they give us tonight?*

'Just breathe, sweetie,' Aunt Nuri's voice said smoothly in their head. *'We're all here, don't forget that.'*

Twin phoenixes have the ability to speak mind to mind. In their first flight as phoenixes, Ember, Dad, and Aunt Nuri realized that somehow Ember could sometimes communicate with Dad and Aunt Nuri as well. It wasn't as consistent as what they could do, but right now their aunt's words helped.

Everyone headed through the arch under the stairs.

With Fotia's help, Ember found the plates and flatware, and the two of them got to setting the table. Feu placed the food dishes down the center of the table and Mom found serving utensils.

Everyone sat and started serving themselves from what was brought. Chili con carne with different toppings, cornbread, and a winter squash medley. The chili was spicy and for a moment Ember hesitated, remembering their last chili meal, but then they saw the Elders digging in and knew they wouldn't be invited here to be poisoned.

Though, that would be one way to test if I were really a phoenix. But if they poisoned me and Mom, Dad and Aunt Nuri would level the place ... they have to know that.

With that final thought, Ember dug in. Their stomach grumbled its approval. It all smelled wonderful.

Vuur put her spoon down and turned to look at Ember, her ponytail swinging. "So, Ember. Your parents told us that you are half witch and half phoenix. Is that true, child?"

Everyone in the room stilled.

"Vuur, we already—"

"Ash," her voice snapped out. "I'm speaking with Ember, do *not* interrupt us."

Ember clamped their jaw and willed their face to not show their frustration at how Dad was being treated in his own home. He'd already stated they wanted a night of peace after traveling all day. This intrusion and now this ambush was so like the mean crowd at school. *Well, if I can handle the bullies at school, then I can handle them here, too.*

Dad shut his mouth with an audible snap. His eyes darted to Ember and his mouth quirked up for a moment as if he'd heard their thought. Then he narrowed his eyes at Vuur. Ember wondered if he could kill with a look. He looked ready to boot Vuur from the house.

Shaking themself from the thought, Ember realized everyone was staring at them. *Oh, yeah, I was asked a question.* They cleared their throat before shooting Dad a quick glance. Face tight, he gave a curt nod. He was okay with Ember talking. "No, I don't think you're correct, and I doubt that's what Mom and Dad would've told you."

Vuur's eyes widened, and Dad smirked. In a small whisper, Ember heard him echo in their head. *'Good for you, dear.'*

"Are you calling me a liar?" the elder asked in a silky voice. "As the first and only half breed, it is your duty to help us understand what the cross breeding of a phoenix with a," she shivered, "witch, creates."

All around the table, the adults bristled. Aunt Nuri was the first to form words. "Vuur, I don't remember you being so crass."

"Like your brother, Nuri, I'll expect you to let the fledgling speak."

Why are bullies always so ... obnoxious? "I'm not calling you a liar," Ember's voice hardened. "I'm just clarifying. I'm fully a phoenix. I don't think there's such a thing as being half phoenix. I can shift and manipulate fire with the best of them ... best of *you*. I can fly and turn invisible. I'm not sure what half a phoenix would even mean. I've had my stopping points, and when an accident happens, I rise from the ashes of my death. So, no, Elder, I am fully a phoenix. As for me being a witch," Ember shrugged, letting their voice lighten, "yeah, you're probably right about that."

Before Vuur could respond, Aunt Nuri laughed. "Gods above, I love this kid. Do they remind you of me at their age as much as they do me? Ash was always respectful, but then there was me. Not that Ember wasn't respectful, but so damn smart."

Vatra chuckled. "You're not wrong. Are you sure Ember isn't yours? Ash snarls and growls more or is completely proper and appropriate. You're the one who throws around logic and well thought out arguments."

"Enough." Apoy, the male Elder said, a serpentine smile on his face. "So, Ember is fully a phoenix. We'll have to test them tomorrow." His eyes bored into Ember's. "What does it mean to be half a witch?"

Dad opened his mouth.

"No, we want the child to answer. We've heard from you and Nuri. It's time for the fledgling to speak."

Dad grumbled. "We told you we'd bring Ember around tomorrow, after they had some time to acclimate.

But you had to come tonight. What, did you think we'd slink away in the middle of the night?"

Apoy's face hardened. "No, we just want to make sure we know the right questions to ask to put Ember in the best light in front of the panel. The more we know, the better it'll go."

Dad slumped back in his seat and crossed his arms. "Fine."

Despite what they said, Ember wondered if they really had Ember's best interest at heart. Nothing yet felt that way.

Once again, everyone turned to Ember. They licked their lips. "Well, most witches have three proficiencies, magical skills, they can master, fairly easily. More than that, most witches can do most if not all of the other magics to some extent. I mean, no one can do spatial magic, but, like, almost everyone can light a candle or blow it out. Small things. Well, I can do fire, obviously, and two other magical proficiencies decently well. But I can't really do anything else at all, like most witches can. So, yeah, I do have the three proficiencies, just not the ability to diversify."

Vuur leaned forward. "Is that the end of your magical bag of tricks?"

Ember forced a smile. *What do these people want? I just gave enough of an answer for being half a witch.* They took a sip of their tea, debating on what more to say. A buzzing in their head told them that either Dad or Aunt Nuri was trying to talk to them. They wished they knew how to make that kind of communication easier. Not actually being one of the twins, it was faulty at best.

They quickly looked over and saw Dad shaking his head. *Did that mean to not hold back or to not say more? I wish I could phone a friend, or just text Dad.*

They put down their tea and were about to answer, explain to the elders about their ability to see magic, a skill their parents thought was a combination of their phoenix and witch abilities, when they finally heard. *'Ember, don't tell them anything they don't specifically ask for. Ember, don't tell them anything they don't need to know. Ember—'*

'You can stop, Dad, I got it.'

Ember saw him slump, rubbing his forehead. "I mean, what I can do is pretty good. Like my fire, when I do something, I do it well, but yeah, I'm basically half a witch. I mean, I've never quantified what it is to be a witch, and I can do magic, but I'm not as flexible and apt as the others at the school I attend. I guess I would ask what do *you* know of magic? It would help me to know how to answer you."

Both elders gazed at Ember with blank stares. They didn't think they'd get an answer to their question, but it was worth a shot. Finally, Apoy leaned back and sipped his wine before asking, "And, how much do you know about phoenix lore?"

With a sigh, Ember shook their head. "I don't know how to answer that question. I know every bit as much as I know, but I don't know what I don't know. This is something you should be asking Dad. He knows way better than I do based on what he's told me."

A few people around the table laughed. Dad scoffed. "Ember's not wrong. You need to ask better questions."

"Fine," Vuur snapped. "Can we discuss how many times you've died?"

Chapter 3 - Heated Talks

Ember

Ember's jaw tightened as Dad snapped, "What does my child's number of deaths have to do with anything?"

Vuur sipped her wine, then glared at Dad. "I'm having a discussion with Ember. If you'd please let me continue."

If Dad had been a cartoon, steam would have started coming out of his ears and they'd have whistled.

Not that I blame him. These jerks have come into our home and are acting like they own the place. Personally, I want to kick them out.

After days in a cell under the awful care of Infinite WISDOM, Ember felt like they were getting flashbacks.

Ember massaged their temples. "Why is knowing this important? I don't understand."

The Elder smirked before she lectured to Ember. "The early deaths of a fledgling phoenix is very telling of the care, control, and development of the youth in our supervision. The time we spend at our stopping points has always been important, not only for our growth, but to show command of our surroundings."

The slickness of the Elder made Ember feel greasy. *She could be a politician.* Maybe that's what she was as leader of the phoenixes.

"Okay, but are you asking how many times I have died because of an accident or something else?" Ember bit the inside of their cheek. They weren't sure how much Mom, Dad, or Aunt Nuri had told these people about the circumstances around outing the phoenixes, but they were in the center of it all.

Apoy's upper lip twitched. He leaned forward to stare intently at Ember, as if this would help his words hold more weight. "Is there any other way? Or are you trying to shift your sex? That isn't unheard of with our kind, but it *is* frowned upon."

"Gods above, you two are awful! My child has never intentionally died. I told you their story in detail when we got here," Dad bellowed, his patience obviously gone. "Again, I ask you, what is your purpose here tonight? It obviously isn't to bring us food."

Both Elders slowly turned to bland faces at him. Vuur's eyes narrowed. "Sovereign—"

Aunt Nuri scoffed. "He's no sovereign. Phoenixes don't have sovereigns."

"You two are royalty. You must take up your titles," Apoy said, sounding strained.

A chill ran down Ember's back. *If Dad is a sovereign, what am I? Nothing, that's what I am. Stop being silly, Ember. You know the answer.*

Dad growled. "We don't need to do anything of the sort. We commanded the human-witch armies two hundred years ago and you threw us out. From where I stand, that strips away any titles we may have held."

"Poppycock." Apoy waved a hand. "Those titles are yours, and you know it. They can't be taken from either of you, and your child is the royal heir. But that isn't the issue right now. Right now, we need you to let us speak with Noble Ember, not you."

I wonder what I'm heir to? Is it more than this house?

"But why? You're asking questions you know the answer to," Dad said, voice low and dangerous. "We're here, and tired. You wanted to see us and meet them.

Both things have happened. What reason do we have for not leaving?"

Vuur glared. "We need to see what your fledgling is capable of. You know that."

"Yes, and I agreed to the testing tomorrow, as ridiculous as the set up is. But why all the questions tonight?" Dad persisted.

The quieter he got, the more worried Ember felt. He would blow soon.

Apoy leaned back. "Ash, I expect you to let Ember speak. You'll sit back and listen, like the rest of us. Do you ever just listen to your child, or do you spend all your time speaking over everyone at home, too?"

Ember locked their jaw shut. They couldn't believe what they'd heard. They pretended respect one minute then threw malarkey accusations the next. These two Elders were awful. No wonder Dad didn't mind staying away.

"That's it. We're done here. I'm asking you two to leave. You can test Ember tomorrow." Dad pointed towards the door.

"No," Vuur said, eyebrow raised. "We're not done."

"Yes, you are."

Apoy stood. "I don't think you understand. You live in this house at our behest."

Dad slowly stood. A smile spread across his face. "I do, do I? Well then." A fireball appeared above his hand. "I guess we'll have to take care of the house being here."

The ball disappeared, and Mom slow clapped. "Are all of you done? I mean, the theater with dinner was spectacular. I don't even remember buying tickets, but really, too much more and I'll not be able to contain myself."

"Witch. You overstep," Vuur snapped, eyes glowing.

"No, you overstep," Mom replied, a calm wind to the growing fires of attitudes in the room. "You come into our home and cause nothing but strife. You question my child—*my child*—without consulting us if we'd be okay with it. Well, we're not. When we ask you to leave, you refuse. Well, if you won't leave, I'll remove you from my house myself, and if you don't think I can, try me. You've played with young witches, but I'm over two hundred years old. You have no idea what I'm capable of."

Fire erupted from Vuur, and Ember's uncles leapt to their feet. Dad just held up his hands. "Let Sadie do her thing. She's no wilting lily. And if she gets in trouble, Ember will help, or Nuri, or me. We have everything under control."

Dad put me on the list of Mom's saviors? Whoa! They couldn't help the smile that spread across their face.

After looking around, the two men gave a hesitant nod and sat.

Vuur took a step towards Mom and then Mom waved her hand, and the phoenix was gone. She just ... disappeared. Mom chuckled, then turned to Apoy. "Are you going to cause any trouble? Or are you going to leave via your own two feet?"

"Where is she?" he demanded. "What did you do witch?"

Ember had had enough. "She has a name. No one came here calling you phoenix, or bully, did they? No. You can call her Sadie." They knew they'd probably crossed a line, but they didn't care.

Apoy's mouth dropped open. "How dare you speak to me like that, you are a fledgling—."

"And they're right." Aunt Nuri's voice was calm. "Not to mention, you've seen spatial magic before. We're all old enough to have lived when the proficiency was, if not common, at least seen more widely. Though, I admit moving a mug of tea was something more common than moving people."

Apoy's eyes narrowed. "But she didn't touch Vuur. You don't need to touch a cup to move it, but people ... there has to be touch, and time to create the portal." He sounded so sure of himself.

Mom's eyes narrowed, the only sign of her rising anger. "Last chance. Leave now, or I'll send you away. Do not test me, Apoy. I've had enough of all of you and your arrogance."

With a huff, he got up and stalked out. "Do not be late to Ember's testing tomorrow."

Once the door shut, Mom slumped. Dad quickly filled her plate. "By the gods, Sadie. How did you not pass out?"

She shook her head. "I don't know. I'm just glad he didn't call my bluff. It's been a long time since I've portaled someone without touching them." Her hand trembled as she started to eat the food Dad served her.

Across the table, Fotia gaped. "How was that possible? Is Vuur alive? What did you do to her?"

"Vuur is fine," Ember confirmed. "Mom just moved her out of the house. My guess is to wherever they spent the day talking. When I do spatial magic, I need to have a clear vision of where I'm sending something."

Mom beamed at Ember. "Very good. Though portaling living beings is a bit more than basic spatial magic, it has to do with condensing space and pushing an object only a small distance. It's the next thing you need to learn if we're to have every advantage in the upcoming battle." Mom sighed. "Because I doubt Infinite WISDOM is done."

Chapter 4 - Home Sweet Home

Ambrose

The summer house was never meant to be lived in during the winter, especially over winter break. Ambrose wasn't sure why they couldn't go home. Then again, they'd been cut off from the internet and social media, so she had no idea what was going on. Ever since they took the hidden passage from the basement— and who *had* hidden passages from their house, much less holding cells? —Father and Mr. Shade had demanded she, and everyone else, keep their phones off.

The family, along with Mr. Shade, Cress, and a few of guards, had been in their new location for a couple of days. No one even knew of the outcome of what Ambrose thought were Ember's people coming to rescue them. *Did those people burn our house down? Did anyone get hurt? Die? Did Ember get saved or did they survive?*

School would start on Monday, so the family would have to head back to Feniks soon and hopefully she'd get all the answers to her questions.

After a full day stuck indoors, Ambrose came out to the bench that overlooked the ocean. She needed time away from ... everyone. The men were all acting sexist and arrogant. *Before Mr. Shade came with his power-grabbing scheme, Father treated me with respect. Now, I'm barely better than a servant. This is not what I thought I was signing up for.*

Her mother, gods above, she just melted into the background, seen but not heard. *How many times has she told me that? I can't imagine living my life that way, a wallflower! Gah, how annoying. Why can't she grow a spine? I will never be like her!*

Ambrose was made to be more than the wife of someone powerful. She was smarter than any of them. Her destiny was to be the leader. She bristled that the men treated her as anything less.

With a huff, she pulled her phone from her pocket. Just because she couldn't turn it on, didn't mean she'd leave it somewhere it could be lost or taken 'by accident.' She crossed her legs and hunched her shoulders against a cool wind. Checking over her shoulder, she made sure no one had followed her out, then she turned the phone on.

At first, she'd followed the rules, believing that if people had attacked their home, safety was needed, but then she saw other inconsistencies and knew it didn't matter. Anyone looking for them would've found them days ago. Mr. Shade, Father, and Cress—especially Cress— were idiots. If they didn't realize the number of ways they gave away their location, Ambrose wasn't going to tell them. She was being proper: seen and not heard. *At least I'm trying to. At this point I care less and less and now just want to find out what's going on back home.*

A massive number of texts from everyone she knew flowed across her phone like a ticker display. *What could be this important over the last two days? Nothing is that vital.* She rolled her eyes. Most of the texts came from Josie ... of course they did.

OMG, Ambrose, are you okay? Your house, the fire? Ambrose could almost hear the girl's frantic voice.

Who are the phoenixes? They came from your house. What have you been holding back? I can't believe it, are they part of your family? Are you a phoenix?

There was a time break before the next text—just after midnight. Then a smattering of messages, each more frantic than the next.

Ambrose!!!!! Where are you? Where is Cress? Is he a phoenix?

Everyone is saying you and your family are phoenixes since you disappeared. What happened?

Call me. Text me. Where are you?

The texts just kept going.

Ambrose switched to a web browser and started searching. She found the articles on the fire in her house. First she read about the people rescued. *At least that's one good thing. It sounds like most of the staff were rescued. I'm glad there wasn't more death in my home.*

After a few more links, she found grainy images of three phoenixes flying from the roof. *Three phoenixes? Who were they? Were they part of the people coming to rescue Ember? Phoenixes are extinct. How is this possible?*

It frustrated Ambrose that Father assumed that since Ambrose was female she knew how to prepare a meal. *'You and your mother need to have dinner on the table at six o'clock, Ambrose. Mr. Shade and I are busy, and you know Cress can't cook.'*

'But, Father, I've never been in the kitchen either. I don't know how to cook.'

'Your mother will teach you. Now, talk back to me again, girl, and you'll get my fist. We don't have any staff to cook for us, and we're all hungry. There are five of us, and we each have a role. Yours is in the kitchen with your mother.'

Mother did all the prep after the two had gone to the store to buy the groceries. Shopping was awful. There were so many people and kids with sticky fingers. There didn't seem to be any order to where the food was stocked. And to top it all off, the music playing over the speakers made her skin crawl. Once they purchased a bunch of mostly pre-made items, they headed to the self-checkout and used a credit card. So much for not being able to be tracked! Ambrose never wanted to go to a grocery store again.

She sat at the table. There was a large bowl of pasta, a bowl of heated up frozen meatballs, and warmed up frozen garlic bread. For dessert there was ice cream. Tomorrow, they'd have warmed up frozen pie.

Mr. Shade took a bite of the food, then washed it down with wine. "We can't stay here. We need to continue our fight. The kids need to be prepared to talk at another rally. The Saturday after school starts."

"School starts on Monday," Ambrose said with a sigh. She was less and less impressed with the leader of Infinite WISDOM. He was so ... limited.

Father's face scrunched up. "Ambrose, you weren't asked. You will speak when spoken to, otherwise stay silent."

She clenched her jaw. Before all this started, she was a respected, if not cherished, part of the family. Now she was barely tolerated.

Cress smirked. "She's not wrong. We do need to get back. We're adored there. We can't get our mindless admiring fans to follow us if we're absent. I bet if we turned our phones back on, we could start now."

"No!" Mr. Shade snapped. "We're here for safety reasons. Phones can be tracked. Leave all electronics off."

Ambrose worked at not rolling her eyes. *Anyone with half a brain cell could find us. Beyond paying for the food with our credit cards, how far afield is it to look for us here, in our second home? If he really wanted to hide, why not get cash and find a hotel? So dumb!*

Not to mention, who does he fear?

Father tilted his head. "Do you know that our main home is ruined? It may be fine to return."

"I know what you know, we've been stuck here together." Mr. Shade spoke as if talking to a toddler. "We sent the guards back with one of the cars yesterday after we all recovered from the trek here. They should be back with news soon."

Ambrose slowly took a bite of her pasta. It wasn't bad, which shocked her. She didn't think something that she and Mother ... well, that Mother prepared, would be decent. As she thought about the drive into town, it occurred to her they could head away from the house to check online. Didn't libraries have computers? She wanted to say something but knew that wouldn't go over well.

Cress lifted his glass of soda. "Ambrose, I'm low on soda, can you get me more?"

She raised an eyebrow. "You know where the soda is. I don't think you need me to get it for you. I'm not a servant."

Father pursed his mouth and narrowed his eyes at her. "Cress, Ambrose is correct. You can fill up everyone's drinks. Ambrose, why don't you get the dessert?"

She felt the fire in her fighting to get out. Her magic fed on her emotions, and she was livid. This was beyond unacceptable. *Can I get ice cream when I'm this hot?*

"Of course, Father." She got up and headed towards the kitchen. She finally decided she'd had too much. "I just hope my fire doesn't harm the kitchen the way the phoenix's fire burned our roof back home."

Chapter 5 - I Am Phoenix, Hear Me Roar

Ember

"Just remember, you're a phoenix and you don't have to prove anything," Dad growled out before gazing in his coffee mug and standing to refill it.

Ember finished their sausage and egg sandwich, then used spatial magic to call the carafe from the kitchen and filled both their mugs. Dad gave them a smile before picking up his own breakfast to take a bite.

"You do need to show them the extent of what you can do with fire," Aunt Nuri said, waving at Dad with her mug. "It's about moving up the levels and proving they're a power in their own right."

"No, Ember doesn't need to prove anything. They are a phoenix and don't need to show off. This whole thing is a farce. It shouldn't be done in front of everyone. If the Elders really wanted to know about Ember's abilities, it'd be done the way it's done with everyone else," Dad snarled back. "You know these things are done in private with a judging panel and parents."

Gods above, this is putting him on edge. He isn't usually this agitated.

Aunt Nuri shook her head. "Like every other phoenix? Ash, Ember isn't like the others. They'll need to be pushed through several tests at one time, not to mention, everyone is curious. Beyond them being the first phoenix brought up outside of our compound, no one has ever heard of a phoenix born to a witch; they're a curiosity. I don't know that if they tested Ember in private anyone would believe the final results."

Dad's face hardened. "I just want Ember to be given the same treatment everyone else gets, the same type of testing."

"Slowly, over the years, as they grew up in the school? Explain how that's possible, Ash."

"No!" Dad huffed. "That's not what I meant, and you know it. The testing panel should be a small affair. It isn't supposed to be this—" he waved his hand in a rotating gesture, "—circus."

Ember started to wonder if they needed to be present for any of this conversation. It was about them, but they didn't have any input.

Mom sighed. "Nuri, do you think Ember should stretch what they can do, or just stick with the basics? Can all phoenixes manipulate fire the way Ash and Ember do? What does Ember do that's beyond or below your average firebird?"

Dad scoffed. "There is nothing that the average student at the school here can do with fire that Ember can't do. They're better than the lot of them."

Nuri shrugged, then smiled at Ember. "I haven't seen what Ember can do, but I wouldn't be surprised if they're able to do even half the things me or Ash can, that they'll be marked high. Create fire, move it around, make it bigger, smaller, go away. These are the skills of all phoenixes. Beyond that, the finesse with which a phoenix presents each of these skills differentiates the levels."

"It's more than that, and you know it. It's also the ability to control fire you didn't create. Phoenix-created fire is a bit different than witch fire or regular fire. Any phoenix can snuff those fires out. But controlling another phoenix's fire is—" Dad's eyes shone, "—power."

Ember barked out a laugh, though a chill of apprehension zoomed down their back. Nothing anyone had mentioned was beyond their abilities, but to do it in front of a panel and audience all judging them ... judging Dad .... "Well, now that the three of you have made today's challenges clear as mud, and added no stress, I think it's time for us to head out. We're going to be late if we don't leave."

"They can't start without us." Dad smirked. "So, we're not late, they're early." He leaned back and took another sip of his coffee.

Mom shook her head. "Go get shoes and a coat and we'll head out. If Dad wants to stay here, that's his choice."

Ember stood in front of a panel with five adults, all stone-faced and ready to judge them. They only recognized two: Vuur and Apoy, the two Elders who had questioned them the night before. Vuur kept glaring toward the stands where Ember's parents sat, obviously holding a grudge.

Behind Ember were a group of people from town who were all phoenixes. *It feels like I'm standing in front of the full student body. No pressure, just perform in front of a hundred plus strangers—no worries.* They sat in what looked like wooden dining room chairs they must have

44

brought from their homes. A buzz of excitement emanated from the crowd. *Is that every phoenix from town?*

I still can't believe how many phoenixes there are in the world. This is mind boggling. Do they all go out flying together? For a moment, Ember got lost in the image of over a hundred phoenixes all filling the skies.

"—your abilities." Apoy said. "This will determine your level and where we may place you in school when classes start up a week from Monday."

Ember's heart stopped. *Classes ... here? When was it decided I'd go to school here? I have a school and friends. I don't want to go to school here.* It took all Ember's determination to not turn and gape at their parents.

"—normally test in front of this many people, but everyone is excited your family is back at Serafina Landing." Ember realized they'd missed more of what Apoy said, but they could figure it out. Apoy continued talking about the family's return. He made it sound like it had been Dad and Aunt Nuri's choice to stay away, not that Dad had been banished and Aunt Nuri strongly told to stay away.

It took years of practice keeping secrets not to show their annoyance. "And with their return, if Ember shows the skills their family claims they have, we'll welcome them into the school as one of ours."

The words stopped Ember's breath. *Do they really think we're lying about who and what I am? But if they find out the extent of what I can do, what then? Is my current life over? If I don't show I'm a phoenix, can I go back home?*

'No, dear.' Dad's voice penetrated through the murkiness of their mind. The connection didn't often work, but apparently their faulty WiFi was online. *'It's important that they know what you can do. Secrets here would be dangerous. We'll discuss what school you'll attend later. They don't have as much control over the situation as they think. Be brilliant.'*

Able to breathe, Ember nodded slightly and gave their dad a tight smile. They were never sure if what they mentally thought to Dad got to him, and they knew he didn't know what of his thoughts got through, but he'd understand the gestures.

Vuur stood. "We have a series of tests to explore a student's strength and control with fire. Being phoenixes, we all have fire at our control. The questions we have are: one, being a half phoenix," Ember couldn't stop the sneer from forming on their face. They'd explained the previous night that they weren't half a phoenix. Apparently, the Elder didn't believe them. "How strong is Ember's fire? Next is, if they have control over their fire? And last, if they are qualified, what level would they place with our instructors?"

The electric buzz that filled the audience grew. Ember didn't want to do any of this, but they didn't see they had a choice beyond shifting to bird and flying away. And even then, with this many birds, the group would probably catch them and bring Ember back. Taking a steadying breath, they did what they'd never done in two and half years of school: they prepared to show off their fire.

"You can do it, cuz!" Fotia's confidence made Ember smile.

I hope she's right.

Vuur stepped around to the front of the table where she'd been sitting. Ember wondered why they didn't introduce the other three people. Not that it would matter—they'd already learned too many names to remember—it just seemed rude. Ember just wanted to be done with this public exhibition.

"We have several different tests. Basic control is, of course, our primary concern." She paused to let her words sink in. "This is about safety, not putting Ember on display." She smiled sweetly at first Ember and then the crowd behind them. Her eyes came back to Ember. "Ember, please make a fireball."

Ember wanted to say, *'Of course it's only about safety. It has nothing to do with embarrassing my dad or my family.'* Instead, they decided to wipe the arrogance from the Elders' faces and prove why their family were royalty.

Ember held out their left hand and created a fireball about two inches in diameter. Easy peasy.

"Good, can you create two?" Vuur's condescending tone washed over Ember as she leaned back on the table and stared intently at the small ball of fire.

"Do you want two in one hand?" Ember put action to words and had a second ball appear atop the first like a fiery snowman. "Or one in each hand." They dissipated the head of their fireman and created a new ball hovering over their right hand.

Vuur's jaw tightened, but she nodded once. "Very good. How many can you create and control?"

That was an interesting question. Ember had never considered that. "I don't know, Elder." Ember knew they sounded respectful since the question intrigued them.

"So, are you at your limit?" Vuur's voice dripped with cool amusement. This was apparently what she'd been hoping for.

Annoyed, but with a blank face, Ember tilted their head to the right, and two dozen fireballs popped into existence surrounding them like a cloud. Once the titters from the audience quieted down, Ember said, "Would you like more?" Two dozen more appeared. With so much fire surrounding them, the air warmed and they knew they presented a strange image. Maybe a person in an inverse snowball fight?

Suddenly, Ember felt someone trying to dissipate several of the fireballs. With a sigh, they easily kicked the interloper away from their fire. Then they had the forty-eight balls start to circle them. "I can create more if you'd like. But I'd suggest the people trying to snuff them out ask me first; it's rude and getting annoying. I *will* fight back. Don't you think my dad taught me how to control my fire?"

A chuckle from the sidelines told them Dad was enjoying the show.

Face hard, Vuur scoffed. "So, you can create fireballs, but can you do more than have them move in formation?" One of her brows rose in challenge.

A couple of weeks earlier, a student at school asked Ember to help her "fix" her magic. It had been happening ever since Ember decided to stop hiding their proficiency in air magic. A display with their mom quickly led to them helping in Air Magic class. It was then that Ember learned they had an ability not even their parents had—they could see the magic witches controlled. With an instinct they couldn't explain, they could even help students manipulate their magic better, opening up the flow from practitioner to end-product.

This led Ember to a student who needed help with her fire magic. Though Ember didn't let on that they *had* fire magic, they did help with the advanced challenge the teacher had assigned. At the time Ember had thought the test looked fun, but in the intervening time, hadn't tried replicating the assignment.

With a small push, Ember dissipated all but five of the fireballs. They turned so they'd have more room to work. This task was complicated, so they took a calming breath before getting to work. They started with the center ball, getting it going in a circular pattern, perpendicular to the other four. Next the fireballs adjacent to the rotating ball began to move up and down, about two feet total in distance. And finally, the challenge.

Ember moved the outside balls under the bouncing balls when they were at their highest point. From there, they slid the two fireballs going in opposite directions past each other through the center of the circling middle ball. Next they floated them above the bouncing duo when they were at the lowest point. And finally, Ember set them at the ends, having reversed the positions.

Once done, Ember dissipated the fire with a smile. Gods, it was just as fun as they'd thought it would be. They may need to put together other fire obstacles. "Was that active enough? I can do it again, maybe have two going at the same time?" They turned to face the judging panel. "Or do you need something else?"

Standing next to Vuur, Apoy held a fireball almost two feet across. He smiled and threw the ball. "Catch!"

Chapter 6 - Pushing Boundaries

Ember

Ember was momentarily stunned at the audacity of attacking someone with such a large ball of fire. Then they were amused because what would that much fire do? Burn them? No. Maybe their clothes. *Which reminds me, I need to fireproof the rest of my clothes. Mom can help.*

Ember waved their hand, collected the ball when it was about two feet from them, enlarged it a pinch, and tossed it up. "Do you want me to dissipate it, grow it, change it, or play with it? What's the challenge? You really didn't give me the rules of this test." Ember held the ball high above the testing ground. They felt Apoy's pull but refused to give it up. He had attacked them; the fire was theirs now.

There were gasps from the crowd behind them. Ember heard someone whisper, "Did she just catch the fireball and manipulate it herself? Can teens do that? I don't know if I can do that."

What kind of a jerk throws a huge fireball at a person they don't think can control it? They really do want to humiliate me. Ember could almost hear their parents and Nuri thinking of ways of teaching the town about their pronouns. But to them it was a worry for another day.

Someone else snorted. "I bet Apoy's doing that, trying to make us like the girl."

"This whole thing's a farce!"

Behind their back, Ember created the words, *'Nope, it's all me'* in fire.

There were a few gasps. Looking over their shoulder, Ember saw most people were focused on the large ball above them, not the words they'd created. *Oh, well.*

Both Vuur and Apoy had their eyes on the ball. Annoyed, Ember made a fist, and all the fire snapped out.

Dad stood. "Are we done? I think Ember has shown their control. That's what you wanted to see. I don't know what you could teach Ember beyond what they already can do."

Vuur glared at him. "We are not done until we say we're done."

Ember tried to keep a blank face. They weren't sure what the point of all this was, but if Dad was correct, then all of this was a power play. Well, if the Elders wanted to play with power, Ember would show them what they had.

Vuur's gaze bored into Ember. "Our next set of tests will determine your power and level. I'm going to create a fireball. You and Apoy will each vie for control. We're going to see who is stronger."

A surge of excitement shot through them. Ember didn't think anyone except Dad and Aunt Nuri could beat them in a game of fire tug-of-war. Their bigger battle was not smiling like a kid in a candy shop.

One of the other men sitting at the table stood. "Vuur, why are we starting with Apoy? He's level eight." He faced Ember. "Most phoenixes are level four to six. Some achieve level seven. This test is used to figure out your level and starting with a level eight makes no sense."

Ember suddenly understood. The elders wanted to embarrass Dad and Aunt Nuri, not just them, by displaying their failures to all the other phoenixes. Vuur didn't know about the battle they'd already had with Apoy over the last fireball. With so many people watching, there was no way for anyone to communicate.

Ember plastered a huge smile on their face. "It's okay, if Vuur thinks this is best, who am I, a mere teenager, to object?" They blinked as if everything being discussed was beyond their comprehension.

If Felix or Daisy were here, they'd be laughing.

Vuur pushed off the table, not seeing Apoy's annoyed expression, and created the ball. Ember relaxed their shoulders and let their hands hang loosely by their side. If they could, they wanted to look vapid and uninterested during this bizarre game of tug-of-war as they could. They wanted the Elder's goal to fail miserably.

That's what you get for treating my parents so poorly!

After creating the fireball, Vuur said, "Okay, on the count of three, the battle for the ball will begin. The challenge will be to push the fireball towards the other person. If the fireball gets within a foot of one of the competitors, the challenge is over." She stared at Ember, probably the only person there who didn't know the rules. It would have been nice to have been told before this all started.

"Okay, so reverse tug-o-war, got it. Don't let the fire near me." They gave a small shrug like they were mostly disinterested. *After this, I want to add this to ways Dad and I vent our frustration.*

Apoy nodded curtly. "I understand the rules."

Of course, he does. How many times has he done one of these competitions?

Vuur smiled smugly. "You may begin."

The fireball, this time about one foot across, jumped a few inches towards Ember. They dug deep into the heart of the fire. They felt the personality of the fire. At first, Ember coaxed it to just ... wait. They watched as the fire froze in place, not moving one way or the other.

Ember continued to keep a blasé look on their face. The fireball tugged on their hold, trying to move towards them. Ember looked over to Apoy whose face was twisted up in a soundless snarl. They could see his jaw was locked and his upper lip twitched.

The side of Ember's mouth tugged into a smirk. *He's really working for this.*

Finally, they gave a small push. The fireball slid quickly towards the Elder. The crowd gasped, and Ember stopped the motion, still out of reach of a win.

Vuur sighed with a smile. "It looks like it's still a competition."

Apoy shook his head. "No. Ember stopped it, not me." Face neutral, he gave them a slight bow. "For the first time since—" He shot a look at Dad. "For the first time in a long time, I've been beat."

Without any discernible action, Ember dissipated the fire. "Are we done?" They tried to sound respectful, but they were tired of putting on a show for so many strangers.

"We have two more tests," Vuur said, frustration coloring her words.

The man who'd stood before, stood again. "No, we don't. We have what we need to know. Ash has taught his child enough."

Amused, Ember made a bouquet of multicolored fire roses. They walked up to Vuur and picked out the yellow one. "A flower to end the testing?"

Vuur waved her hand at the flowers and Ember felt the push to dissipate the bouquet. They blocked and clenched their jaw at the arrogance of the action. Vuur turned to Dad. "You need to teach your child respect, Ash Savita."

"No," Dad said. "I don't. They were put on display in this song and dance. Just because they performed to their own tune doesn't mean they're not respectful, it just means you don't like that they're also clever."

Chapter 7 - Just Add Water

Daisy

"**D**aisy, you have an hour and a half and then dinner will be ready. Do you want to go shopping with me?" Mom called from the bottom of the stairs.

"What type of shopping?" Daisy closed her book and sat up. She'd been lounging in her bed, relaxing. There were only scant hours until school started, and she wanted to make the most of the time remaining of winter break.

"Groceries, though I could be convinced to go other places. Ice cream, bakery. Is there anything you need?"

"No, I'm good." She stood and stretched. "Is Dad going with you?" She put on a sweater and headed down to the kitchen. It had been several chapters since she'd let herself get lost in *Legacy Bound* by Elizabeth Daly. If she didn't stop now, she'd be reading all night. It was time for a small snack and a soda.

She saw Mom getting her purse. "No, just me. Why, were you hoping to have a party while we were gone?"

"Ha, figured it out. I was about to call up the masses on speed dial."

Mom left, chuckling.

Once Daisy had her spoils from the kitchen, she headed to the backyard instead of back to her room. She hadn't played around with her magic in several days, and she wanted to try mixing her proficiencies again. Part of her hoped both her parents would be gone in case of a big mess up, but Dad was probably lost in some project.

Since she'd begun playing around with this, she hadn't asked any of her teachers or her parents if it was a thing seasoned witches did, but Daisy wanted to get better at it before she asked or demonstrated it to anyone. She loved the challenge and didn't want help ... or to be told it wasn't done.

She filled her practice tray with water and set it on the backyard table. She placed an empty one next to it. As always, she began with a warmup. With a tiny push of magic, the water formed a perfect arc, flowing from one tray to the other.

Gods above, I wish I knew how to change the color of the water. Maybe make it shimmer as it traveled. I wonder if I could work with Ember on that, something with air and the bending of light? If I could master putting air into my water, that would be amazing.

A tiny thrilled energized her. She loved learning and figuring out more things.

As soon as the water had fully moved from one tray to the other, Daisy created two tiny air twisters and had them fly across the backyard along the grass, passing back and forth, swapping paths, in a playful manner. To her, they looked like toddlers racing, and she chuckled.

She smiled to herself. "That's it, Daisy. All warmed up and ready for something harder."

Trying to not overthink things, Daisy shook her hands and imagined each of her muscles relaxing. Then she lifted her hands, palms to the sky.

The water in the dish formed a perfect sphere. Daisy imagined a well of gravity in the center of the ball pulling the water in.

Next, in the center of her sphere of water, she created a tiny air twister. As it spun, the water moved and swirled within the confines she held. It took more magic to enforce the shape she held, but the final product was worth it. She once again marveled at the colors and images that played along the shell of the ball of water.

Her hands trembled as she held the two proficiencies of magic together.

Once she knew she could hold them and control the magic for longer than twenty seconds, she released first the air magic and then the water back into the dish. If she wasn't careful, the water would explode all over the backyard ... like the only other time she'd attempted this.

She danced in her seat with a squeal at her success, then pumped her hand into the air. "Yes!"

Next, Daisy moved on to creating arrows with a push of magic. She'd struggled with this exercise every time she'd practiced it. This one she'd done several times. A failure didn't result in having to change her outfit and shower.

With a lift of her hand, five water arrows rose from the pan. She flicked her free hand and used air magic to thrust the first arrow. It flew past the tree across the yard, disappearing into the woods behind her home.

"Gods above and below. Well, at least it made it *to* the tree this time."

Daisy took a calming breath and tried again. The second arrow wobbled and dropped just short of the tree.

"Gah!"

The third one hit the tree, but the impact was weak. *Well, that would certainly terrify my greatest enemy into falling over with excessive peals of laughter.*

The fourth and fifth followed the third, but she didn't think her show of magical strength would scare anyone.

Sitting hard on the chair, she shook her head. "I really should bring Ember in. Maybe they could see what I'm doing wrong. They help everyone else, why not me?"

She closed her eyes, trying once again to relax. Then she ate the nuts and raisins she'd brought out. Time for the last challenge. Something new.

Twelfth-year earth magic is about the healthy growth of plants, but I've been doing it for over a year with Mom. But ... what if I add water? Would the plants become healthier?

She went to a table next to the house where Mom had a collection of seedlings not yet ready to be transplanted into the ground. She'd been helping to maintain the herbs since she'd proven her skill to her parents. "Mom has been taking good care of all of you, hasn't she? Look at you, thyme, you're growing like a trooper, aren't you? Oh how about you, basil? You're just waiting for the next Italian dish? And look at you, parsley, aren't you the big plant? And who's the super star? You are, tomato, aren't you? Yes you are." She reached and touched one of the delicate leaves.

All the plants would be ready for the ground in the spring, once the temperature and soil warmed a bit.

Daisy searched through all the seedling. A pepper plant was wilting. *The weather is probably too cold despite Mom's care.*

Daisy brought the wilting baby out to the table. She closed her eyes and used the steps Mom had taught her over a year ago. She calmed her mind, then looked into the center of the pepper to see what it was missing. Why wasn't it thriving?

Once she found the heart of the plant, Daisy began encouraging its health. Then, as a secondary magic, she pulled water to the dirt and towards the roots.

As she watched, the bush grew, and pepper flowers began to blossom.

A burst of pride exploded within her as she saw her success. She may not be able to defend with water arrows, but she could grow a garden, and a big part of her was happy about that.

Chapter 8 - The Future

Ember

It was Saturday morning and Ember lay on the couch, arms crossed over their eyes. As much as they'd spent their life dreaming of meeting other phoenixes, now they just wanted to be away from this circus.

They weren't sure what they thought meeting other phoenixes would be like, maybe flying together, campfires, telling stories. Ember didn't expect to be in the fire of said event.

"Ember, you okay?" The couch cushions dipped with Aunt Nuri's weight.

"When can we leave?" Ember knew they were whining, but exhaustion flooded their body.

Dad's voice came from another room. "Soon. Our plan is to get you back in time for school on Monday."

That perked Ember up. "So, we'll leave tomorrow?"

"Probably." He sounded as tired as they felt.

Aunt Nuri scoffed. "You did really good, Ember. You showed the Elders you're not half a phoenix. That was what we wanted. You also showed, well, everyone, that you don't need any of the trainers here to have control. That was important."

Annoyed, Ember pushed themself up to sitting. "Why didn't you tell me it was so important? Why didn't you tell me about anything that could happen? You two sent me in there blind."

"Would you have done anything different?" Dad asked as he walked in. He held two plates with tuna steak, rice, and corn succotash. He handed one to Ember, sitting on the loveseat with the other. Mom came in with two more plates, handing one to Aunt Nuri.

Ember sighed. "Probably not. But it would've been nice to know what all of you expected."

"We didn't expect anything, love," Mom said. "That's just it. We wanted you to decide what you wanted to show. This is your future."

"But what does that mean?" Ember said. Frustration laced their words. "If I'd held back, would they have insisted I go to school here? Are they going to insist anyway? Are we moving here? Are we going into hiding? What's going to happen now? I know you wanted to avoid ... well, everything."

Dad laughed ... laughed! Ire taking over, Ember tucked into their food. "So many questions, dear." Dad smiled. "I don't really care what the Elders demand. I wouldn't have cared no matter how you performed. As for moving home, to *this* home, that may be in our future, but not this week. You do need to learn about our people, but there's a war brewing, and we're not going to run. We didn't last time, and we won't now."

Mom rubbed Dad's leg. "If the Elders really think about it, they'll figure it out all on their own." She sipped her water. "Despite how they've been acting, they can be intelligent."

Aunt Nuri's eyes widened in excitement. "And now that people know about phoenixes—at least three phoenixes—being still around, we can go make big waves. Infinite WISDOM needs to be put in its place."

Ember was equally excited and apprehensive. After a life of hiding, they were tired of making big waves. That said, taking Infinite WISDOM down sounded like a solid plan.

After lunch, Ember went back to reading. With the stress of the day, they really needed the comfort of one of their favorite book series, one that reminded them of Daisy, since they discovered it together. They'd brought *Wyldling Trials* by A.R. Grimes, the second in the *Wylding Dream* series.

A knock came at the door and Fotia bounded in. "Is it true? Are you staying around? Going to school here? We can hang out this week, I can show you around, introduce you to people, then we can start classes together next week. It'll be amazing."

Ember put down their book, happy to see their cousin, though not thrilled with the reaction they predicted would come from their response. "No. At least not right now. There's too much happening back home and my parents aren't going to leave me behind with strangers."

Her shoulders dropped, then a steely determination came over her face. "I'm not a stranger, I'm your cousin!"

Laughing, Ember gave their exuberant relative a hug. "True, but I still want to be with my parents."

Fotia flopped onto the couch next to Ember. "Fine! Be that way. But I want to get to know you better. I also want you to show me how you did that flower thing. Different colors? And then you pulled one out? I've never seen anyone show up the Elders before, and you did it to both of the oldest of the Elders. It was ... I don't know, holy Gods in the clouds, it was just beyond."

"I was annoyed. Not only were they testing me and telling me I was disrespectful, they never told me what to expect at each step. They also didn't introduce the panel, something I'd have expected as the first step in that travesty of a debacle." Ember smiled ironically at Fotia.

Their cousin slumped. "Huh. Growing up here, we all know everyone. It didn't even occur to me that you didn't know the others." She shook her head. "From the audience it all looked amazing, but I guess I didn't think of it from your point of view. Did they tell you your level at the end? Mine is level four. As a teen that's really high. Declan always brags that he's level five, but he's older than me."

Ember shook their head and shrugged. "No idea."

"It has to be high. Did you really pull the fireball from Apoy or was that part of the show?"

The question was so insulting, Ember couldn't believe Fotia asked it. "I guess you'll have to decide for yourself."

From the other room, Ember heard one of Fotia's dads say, "Then it's decided. I'm going to go tell Fotia."

Both Ember and Fotia looked up as their parents and Aunt Nuri walked in. Dad smiled warmly. "We'll be leaving tomorrow, Ember. Nuri and I will explain to the Elders that you'll not be attending school here ... at least not right away. You can finish your eleventh year at Feniks Secondary School, but that may be the end. We feel you're learning interesting things in Potions and Magical Creations. The connections you're making with your friends and potentially in the FB Coalition are also important, but we're not going to make any promises about next year."

Joy filled Ember, followed by wariness. They really wanted to spend their last year at Feniks but knowing that they could at least end the year there was a good start.

They couldn't wait to text Felix and Daisy and let them know. Home tomorrow. "Will I be able to see my friends tomorrow, or will I have to wait until I get back to school?"

Mom laughed. "You don't know when we'll get home or if they're available, but you're already making plans?"

"Yes?"

Dad shook his head. "We should be back early afternoon. You can text them later." He shifted his gaze to Fotia. "But we're not done with our news."

"I'm going with them." Vatra leaned forward, intent on his daughter. "What's happening is too important and Ash, Nuri, and Sadie need more help. Dad's going to stay here with you, Fotia. It's only going to be me going with them."

Fotia drooped and her mouth fell open. She looked devastated, like she wanted to argue.

Aunt Nuri cleared her throat. "Pat and Lesly may come with us as well. They don't have any younglings to care for and they've always supported us. That will be three more phoenixes to help in the war."

A warmth spread through Ember. This was the camaraderie they'd hoped to find when they'd heard there were other phoenixes still alive.

Mom sighed. "Let's not call this a war yet. I'm hoping we can tamp it out before it gets that far."

Next to Ember, Fotia had been sitting tense. She took an audible breath. "I want to go with you. If three extra phoenixes will help, why not four?"

"No," Vatra and Feu said at the same time. They looked at each other and Feu continued. "You're too young and in school. Ember won't be in the battle. They're heading back for school, just like you'll be in school. You each need to finish the year."

"But I can go to school with Ember. Learn what life is like outside of this place. Isn't that important?"

Feu pinched the bridge of his nose. "Yes, but right now life outside of Serafina Landing isn't safe or 'normal.' You have a lot of time. Maybe you can join Ember during their twelfth year."

Fotia's face scrunched up and they crossed their arms before slumping back. "If they aren't here at that point. I heard what Ash said." Fotia huffed out a disappointed grunt. "Whatever."

Ember gazed at their cousin, wondering if she knew what she wanted to get into. Had she ever left Phoenix Forest? "Mom, Dad, could she come back for a few days? Her and Feu? They could help Vatra move in. Her school doesn't start for another week. Then she can see where I go to school and maybe meet my friends before coming back here."

They watched the array of thoughts and emotions play over the adults' faces. Dad and Nuri gazed intently at each other and Ember knew they were mentally speaking using their twin connection. Finally, Dad shrugged. "Vatra, Feu, this will have to be your call. Ember is correct on the timeline. If you want to all come for a few days, I can't see that being an issue. I mean, what could go wrong in a few days?"

Ember groaned. "Really, Dad? You know you should never say that! Haven't you learned anything from modern media?"

Chapter 9 - The More Things Change ...

Ember

"Ember, wake up, love." Mom shook Ember. They cracked an eye, but the sun wasn't up so they weren't sure why they should have to rise and shine.

"It's too early. Five more minutes." They rolled over, pulling the covers up over their head.

"If you want to stay, that's fine, but if you want to attend school with your friends tomorrow, we need to get going."

As if their mom has splashed cold water over them, Ember sat up, shaking their head, trying to clear the sleepy cobwebs away. "Are we taking the griffins back?" A big yawn obscured the end of their sentence.

Ember's family owned land north of the city they lived in. They had an agreement with three griffins, brothers, who patrolled the property: Roan, Tort, and Zorn. At times, they would agree to help the family in other ways. Roan, the leader, didn't love doing this because it left the land unprotected, but for the safety of the family, would begrudgingly agree.

"We thought we'd see how far you could make it flying. We have Roan, Tort, and Zorn with us as well. They can carry six. With the addition of Vatra, Feu, and Fotia, there are seven of us. That's why we're hoping all of you can take turns flying. The more you fly, the faster we can travel. I, of course, am stuck riding."

"I need coffee." Ember rubbed their eyes. "Could you do what you did with Vuur? You know, magic one or two of us back home?"

Mom sighed heavily. "Since I moved the Elder without touching her, I blasted out a lot of my magic. It will take a few days to really build it all back up. *Could* I make a portal back home?" She shrugged. "Probably. I wasn't kidding when I said I have a lot of power. Is it worth it? No, not even a little. We have other means of transportation, and I'd rather stick with that. I also prefer to stay with the lot of you." Her eyes narrowed on Ember. "Especially considering, if we end up flying together, we can start on spatial theory as well."

"Do you really think I have enough witch magic to make a portal like that?" Ember pushed out of bed and began gathering their stuff. They kept out one outfit for the trip and stuffed everything else in their bag.

"I don't know, but there's only one way to find out. And the nice thing is, if you don't now, you probably still could some day. As magic users get older, their powers grow. Maybe not a lot within the lifespan of most witches, but you Ember, have years, lifetimes even, to develop your abilities. Who knows, maybe one day you'll be able to perform more of the different proficiencies."

Ember gaped as Mom walked out of the room, saying over her shoulder, "Be down in five minutes. We need to eat before we leave. Coffee is ready whenever you want; there's a mug on the table."

With a bit of concentration, Ember thought about the table and what the mugs of coffee looked like. Then they envisioned the coffee moving to the top of the dresser. They pushed out their magic and a moment later the deep soothing scent of coffee filled the air.

"Thank you, Mom!" Ember sipped the go-go juice. After a taste, they ran to the bathroom and did their morning routine. Finally they got dressed, did a quick search to make sure they had everything they'd brought, and headed down for breakfast.

On the main floor, Ember found their parents and Aunt Nuri eating. A plate with eggs and toast sat next to a bowl of oatmeal covered in nuts and berries. Ember's belly told them how hungry they were as they sat and dug in. Dad filled their mug with more coffee.

The room was quiet as everyone ate. Ember figured their family, like them, was too tired to talk. In all likelihood, everyone was probably sleep-eating.

Once done, Dad collected the dishes to clean up and Mom and Aunt Nuri did a final walk through of the house. Then they headed out to meet Fotia and her dads.

The group walked out into the woods. Dad grumbled, "Thank goodness we don't have a parade to see us off."

"That's only because we didn't tell everyone we were leaving," Aunt Nuri said, quirking a smile at him.

He scoffed. "Not so. I told Vuur we'd be leaving today and as the arguments built, I walked away."

Mom laughed. "It's true. He didn't even raise his voice. Just shrugged and left. The others probably think we'll leave at a later hour, but we do need to be home in time to prepare for school tomorrow."

Fotia yawned. "I didn't know now was an awake time before Dad woke me up."

Ember chuckled as their dad called for the griffins. The three beautiful beasts—with red-furred bodies that looked like lions, heads of eagles, and snow-white wings—landed a few feet away. The three creatures assumed a battle stance when they saw strangers.

Ember ran up to the center one and bowed. "Roan, it is an honor to have you and your brothers here in Phoenix Forest available to aid our family." Ember turned to the left and nodded to Tort. "As always, your diligence in guarding us is forever appreciated." And finally, Ember gave Zorn a hug. "You haven't been misbehaving, have you? I've missed you, all three of you."

Behind them, Fotia gasped. "Did Ember just hug a griffin? I'm very confused. Are they shifters? Is this their boyfriend?"

Dad guffawed. "These are not shifters. They are full blooded griffins. Ember just has a connection with them. They've grown up with the creatures."

"But don't they know griffins are dangerous?" There was a quaver in Fotia's voice.

Vatra scoffed. "We're all dangerous, Fotia."

Mom came up next to Ember and introduced Fotia and her dads to the griffins. Ember wrapped an arm around their cousin to help calm her.

Once the beasts settled, the bags were distributed amongst the three. Mom chose to ride Roan. It was about a six-hour flight to Ember's family's private woods. All the phoenixes chose to start off flying.

Once in the air, Ember stretched their wings. They knew they had to conserve energy, but there was no such thing as being in the air and not having fun.

In the lead were Dad and Aunt Nuri, their white birds so similar, it was hard to tell them apart.

Fotia and her dads were a vision of blues and orange fire. Vatra was almost all night-sky-blue, but his head and the tops of his wings were fire orange. Feu was so dark blue, he was almost black. His wings and the end of his tail shone a fiery red-orange. In the sun, he looked like a campfire fighting for the last moments of life. The tops of Fotia's wings and her chest were a deep blue, as was her face, but the top of her head, the tips of her wings, her back and her tail burned with the fiery red and orange of a bonfire.

Ember marveled at the differences in colors. They knew that their feathers glowed an ombre from red to orange on their body, like the fire they controlled. Down their tail and the ends of their wings burned a deep purple.

Now they wanted to see all the phoenixes and the different color combinations.

As they flew, a chill of excitement and connection electrified Ember. They wanted to dive and spin and rocket to the moon. They'd never felt so energized.

'Ember, dear. You need to conserve all that energy. We've just begun the journey. We'll land in three hours, and you'll be tired. Don't waste the strength of flying with a venture.'

'A venture?'

Ember felt more than heard Dad sigh. *'This is one of the lessons we skipped. I never thought it would be practical.'*

Aunt Nuri snorted. Ember's mind nearly imploded at the realization they could have a group call while flying. Then their aunt said, *'How'd that work out for you, Ash? Now Ember, when there are fewer than ten phoenixes, it's called a venture, more than ten the group is called an odyssey.'*

'No, that cut-off is twenty,' Dad said calmly, as if speaking to a child.

A snort echoed over the line. *The line?* Ember thought. *Through my head? This is all too weird!*

'It's in the books as ten,' Aunt Nuri continued. *'This isn't a debate.'*

Dad scoffed. *'It depends on the books you read. The histories all use twenty, the schoolbooks use ten. I prefer to use the histories. I assume them to be more accurate.'*

'Of course you do. But you're the only one. Why don't you ensure Ember has current information.' There was a pause. *'And Ember, if you're getting all this. By current, I mean in the last few centuries, maybe a dozen or so. The use of ten is old. The use of twenty is ancient.'*

Ember laughed, a cooing sound erupting from them. The whole fight was ridiculous. *'Fine, but what do you mean by wasting my strength when flying with a venture?'* Keeping these two on topic was a job in and of itself!

An emotion, humor, traveled to Ember, and they shivered with the joy of it. *'Child, feel the connections. Use your air sense. You can relax into the waves we're creating together and use less energy and fly farther. It'll mean reaching the halfway point and not passing out.'*

Ember narrowed their eyes and focused on the air. Then they saw it, the phoenix magic, connecting them all. For the last few weeks Ember had worked to see witch magic, but this was different. It was like an iridescent web that they flew just above. If they just ... there. They were with the group. It was almost as if they could hear the others sigh at their inclusion. Then everything got easier. The wind resistance was there, but the group seemed to fly as one large bird, not individuals.

'Welcome to the venture,' Aunt Nuri said as Ember settled in to the larger flight, giddiness and joy filling them.

Dad's prediction was correct. They landed at the halfway point and had lunch. The town wasn't large, but it had a few restaurants. Fotia's eyes were huge, and they seemed nervous as they dressed, their gaze darting every which way.

"You okay, cuz?"

Her focus snapped to Ember. "Yeah. I've just ... this is my first time away from Phoenix Forest." A smile blossomed on her face. "It's exciting."

They nodded, then groaned. Every muscle in Ember's body screamed with every movement, but they were still standing. The well of vigor from the start of the flight was used before the end, and the last half-hour Ember flew on grit and the energy of the venture alone.

Aunt Nuri had found an all-you-can eat Chinese food buffet. The restaurant wasn't very busy, so they took two tables: one for the adults, and a small two-seater for Ember and Fotia.

Ember filled their first plate, sat, and started to eat. Halfway through, they realized they were sitting alone.

Searching the restaurant, they saw Fotia standing by one of the buffet bars, holding a plate, frozen.

With a shake of their head, Ember stood. They grabbed a second dish and approached. "Have you ever had Chinese food?"

"What? Um, no." Those were the fewest words Ember had ever heard their cousin say.

"Are you more nervous about the food or being away from Serafina Landing?" Ember placed a hand on Fotia's back, rubbing in what they hoped was a soothing way. It always helped when their mom did it.

"What? Um ... yes?" Her face finally broke into a smile.

"Okay, let's do this together." Ember led Fotia around, explaining what the different items were, taking the ones they skipped the first time because they didn't fit on their plate.

Back at the table, Ember finished off the food from their first selection before starting in on the second. "You don't have to worry about being out and about, you know. When you're in Phoenix Forest, everyone knows you. Here, you can just be, without everyone knowing you and caring about your business."

Fotia leaned in close. "Are the other beings in this establishment ... humans?"

Ember's eyebrows shot up. "Ah, yes. Most of the beings you'll see while out of the woods will be. Is that okay?"

Fotia's jaw dropped open a bit. Then her tongue darted out, licking her lips as she nodded. "Yeah, it's just ... I've never met a human before."

"There's nothing different between shifters, humans who can wield magic, and humans who can't. Two groups have abilities that the third doesn't, but in the end, we're all human. If you think about it that way, things are easier."

Fotia continued to eat, eyes widening in delight with each new item, as she contemplated Ember's words. She looked down at her hands and scrunched up her face. "Ember. I have to ask you something, but you're not going to like it."

"Not like it, as in, it's something small, or not like it as in, we should discuss over ice cream?"

Their cousin's head popped up and a smile spread over her face. "Oh, definitely ice cream. All serious discussions need ice cream."

The two headed over to a soft-serve machine and dished out swirls of vanilla and chocolate. Back at the table, Fotia took a bite, as if fortifying herself. "There are a lot of ... um, people here."

Ember looked around the restaurant. It was about half full. "Yeah. Not as bad as at my testing, but not empty."

Fotia slumped. "I knew all those people." She huffed out a breath. "The thing is. I'm tired, and everything is new, and, if I'm really honest, a bit overwhelming."

Reaching across the table, Ember placed their hand on Fotia's arm. "Are you saying you don't want to go to school with me tomorrow?"

"Oh! No. That's not it at all. I just think that when we get back to your home ... can I wait to meet your friends until tomorrow?"

Amusement filled Ember. "That's it? Of course. To be honest, I'm really tired, too." They pulled out their phone to text but saw that the battery had died. "It's not a problem. We'll just explain it to them tomorrow."

Fotia's face lit with a smile, and she dug into her ice cream with vigor.

Chapter 10 - Who Are The Phoenixes?

Ambrose

"Okay, class, create three fireballs in a row. They should all have a diameter of about two inches. We're going to build from what we did before winter break."

The teacher walked around the field, watching as the class stood spread out and created their trio of balls. Ambrose rolled her eyes. This part of the lesson was too simple for a break in the teacher's instructions. Everyone in this class had been making fireballs for years.

Finally, he said, "While holding the end balls still, make the center one revolve in a circle, perpendicular to the other two, with a radius of at least a foot."

There was another pause. It didn't take any time for Ambrose to get this step done. While her trio of balls did what they were supposed to do, she watched as over half the class struggled. *This isn't hard. This class will take forever.* She sat, leaning back on her hands and crossed her legs at her ankles. *Well, at least I don't have to deal with Father, Mr. Shade, and especially Cress. His head has grown to the point I'm shocked it fits within the school. And here, at school, I'm treated with respect.*

Next to her a couple of students who'd also completed the first step sat next to her. "So, Ambrose, we heard the phoenixes came from your house. Do you know who they are?"

The two students leaned in.

Ambrose knew this would happen. After Father and Mr. Shade finally pulled their collective heads out of the sand, the 'men' sat down to figure out what the group would say once they returned home. The story they'd come up with was ridiculous. Knowing she'd get in trouble for speaking out of turn, she offered an alternative cover up. She ended up losing her phone for the week for impertinence, but the family was going with her option.

"My family spent some time in our summer house over winter break. We wanted to get away from all the intensity of what's been happening around here. I'd even turned off my phone for a few days to enjoy the calm of the ocean." She smiled and laughed, the perfect actress. Then a shrug. "I didn't even know there had been a phoenix sighting until Saturday."

Both students narrowed their eyes, their disbelief strong. She heard one mumble, "No phone for a week, right."

Ambrose made a face. "What, you don't believe me? Go to the supermarket up in Kenmore, check the records. We were there. Why would I lie? I want to know who destroyed my house as much as you. My family returned and now we're staying at the Grand until repairs can be done." She huffed real annoyance at that. At least her room hadn't been destroyed and she had clothes.

The two smiled and one of them said, "Of course we believe you. I, for one, am just so curious who the phoenixes are and why they were there."

Ambrose opened her mouth to say something, but the teacher interrupted them, saving Ambrose from further explanation ... for now. "Okay, next step. I want you to swap the location of the fireballs on the sides. They should go through the middle of the circling center ball without colliding. Once you've completed this with my supervision, you're done for the day. I'm going to need to watch you do this individually to ensure no giant fire hazards. Who wants to start?"

Ambrose raised her hand, but someone else caught the teacher's attention. The person messed up three times before getting it right. Frustrated, Ambrose insisted on going next. The task was easy. Once done, she released her magic and waited, watching the remainder of her classmates struggle.

There were a couple of students who got through the task as fast as she did, and it surprised her that she rooted for them. *It would be nice to be challenged in Fire Magic class.* The idiots who couldn't even maintain the center ball still annoyed her. *How have they gotten this far without any basic skills?*

As she watched, she tried to figure out who else could be as strong in the fire proficiency as her. Before winter break, during the school outing for night plants, someone had taken away her fire magic. It was only gone for a few minutes, but apparently that was a high-level ability that not all witches could master. Ever since then, Ambrose wanted to know who had done it.

Is it one of these students? Most of them are doing very well; I can't imagine it. Was it one of the parents? Was it the phoenix who burned down part of my home? And why did they do it? There still wasn't a good answer, beyond saving the humans Mr. Shade had been sacrificing. At least he didn't have any more Everfire.

Leaving Fire Magic class, Ambrose plastered on a smile and lightened her step. She had a role to play. Not only did she have to maintain her popularity, she was the face of Infinite WISDOM. The other students and even some of the adults in the building had to adore her, look up to her, want to be her.

Ambrose sashayed into Magical History class and sat down. She had mixed feelings about this class. Mr. Elias fought against Infinite WISDOM. He knew the truth about what was going on, and on some level, she respected his intelligence. But, with Josie and Cress in attendance, it didn't matter. She had to push the agenda hard without getting in trouble.

Ember walked in with a girl that could have been their twin. *Another red-headed freak? Is that possible? There are two of them? Or am I finally losing it? And what has Ember told their parents or the authorities about being locked in my family's basement?*

Ember gave the teacher a small smile. "Mr. Elias? This is my cousin, Fotia. The school said I could have her join me in classes for a few days. She'll be heading home after that. If you're not comfortable with another teen in class, I can take her to the library for the period."

Mr. Elias's eyes narrowed as he gazed back and forth between them. He finally nodded slowly. "Okay, she can drag a chair near your desk, but no interruptions. If she's a distraction, Ember, today is the only day she's welcome."

The two moved off as more people entered and found their seats. Eventually the students from Earth Magic showed up, including Josie and Cress. Every muscle in Ambrose's body tensed. She didn't want to spend more time with her boyfriend. If it were an option, she'd dump him and leave him by the side of the road, but she wasn't sure that was still possible. Father seemed to like him more than her these days. Her stomach churned thinking about it. *He'll come back to me one day ... won't he? I am his daughter ... his only real child.* Ambrose lifted her chin, deciding Father was smart enough that he'd figure it out sooner or later.

Josie skipped over. "Oh, my gods! I can't believe those *things* destroyed your home and you have to stay in a hotel until your roof is fixed! That is so horrible! You know you're welcome to stay at my place, but, you know, my parents." Her voice dropped, letting Ambrose know that Josie's parents still didn't support the movement.

"Josie," Cress said, his voice slithering out like a cold snake. It gave Ambrose goosebumps, and she worked to not react. "We spoke about when you should speak and when you should ... well, not speak."

"Oh! Right. I'll go sit." She gave Cress a simpering smile. "I won't forget, I promise."

One of Cress's brows shot up and Josie made a gesture like locking her lips shut before spinning on a heel to move to sit.

"During winter break, I read over your assignments on life as a human when magic first comes out—before, during, and after the The War of Peace. For the most part, you all did well. A few of you struggled with what to write in the journal entries and you'll have a chance to improve your grades—"

"Do more work pretending to be human? Is that a punishment?" Cress drawled out, leaning back, stretching out his legs, and smiling.

Is this him being confrontational, or something Father and Mr. Shade told him to do? I hate being left out of the loop.

Mr. Elias took a slow deep breath and considered him. "Are we going to have a repeat of last time, Cress, or are you going to be respectful and appropriate in class?"

"I don't know, Mr. Elias, are you still a human-lover?" One of his brows rose in challenge.

"Ah, you're choosing the principal's office and another letter of apology, got it. Well, you know where the door is, Mr. Walsh. I'll be expecting the letter and a meeting with your parents this time."

A sly smile slithered across Cress's face as he stood, gathered his bag, and slowly walked from the room. "Later, loser." He turned in the wrong direction from the office.

This has to be intentional. Ambrose locked her jaw, unwilling to let her emotions show. If anyone knew she wasn't in on Cress's actions, their image would be done for. *But how can we play the perfect power couple if I don't know what's going on?*

Rubbing his forehead, Mr. Elias walked to the phone on his desk and called the office, quickly explaining the situation.

Ambrose gazed around the room, noting who looked happy at the turn of events, who smirked, as if supporting this charade, and who seemed nervous. When her gaze landed on Josie, the girl's eyes were wide. Her brows lifted, as if in sympathy.

Ambrose turned to the front of the room, hearing the words that meant Mr. Elias was near the end of his call.

He hung up the phone and stepped back to the front of the class. "Sorry about that. Today we're going to start studying the laws the Committee of Ten created in detail. I'm going to split you up into five groups and each group will take two laws. You'll have three weeks to study what you're assigned and put together a presentation. Then each group will present your findings, what life was like before the changes were put in place, how the laws affected our peoples, and why the committee created them. As a bonus you can give your opinion on whether and how the laws could've been improved."

He headed to the desk and collected papers to hand back. Ambrose looked over the sheet and saw it was a more detailed explanation of what he'd just said.

"Any questions?"

Ambrose's hand shot up.

"Ambrose." He sounded wary.

"Do you know who the phoenixes are and why they decided to come out to the public now?"

His face hardened for a moment then he shook his head. "As much as I enjoy this type of discussion, here and now isn't the appropriate time or place. Moreover, for all we know, it was all a hoax, Ms. Wells." His stare became intense. "A hoax your family created to cause more dissension in this anti-human movement *they* created."

Ambrose crossed her arms and shook her head. She wanted to push the idea that her family was connected to the phoenixes away from her. This answer did the opposite. *Darn it all to Hades and back!*

Mr. Elias stepped back and smiled at the class. "Now, do you want to select your own groups, or should I assign them for you?"

Chapter 11 - Welcome To My World

Ember

"Those balls were ... wow! And you made some with that other student, Olivia. She was so nice ... and powerful. It was amazing. And you hid your fire ability, but hers was strong. I just don't know how you do it." Ember stood outside Magical Creations with Fotia, who seemed to have found her voice.

Ember's cousin's eyes were a bit wild as she gazed at all the students zipping up and down the halls. They'd spent the last class on a lesson they started on prior to winter break.

Ms. Hewett, the teacher, had challenged everyone to create glass balls to contain the elements. Once everyone had mastered ... or successfully achieved that skill, the next step was to transform the glass of the balls so that when they broke, they morphed to a vapor instead of glass shards. This lesson would be going on within the class for a few weeks.

The ideas from this class had been the inspiration Ember had used to fireproof their clothes.

Trembling slightly, Fotia searched up and down the hall. "Where to now? Another class?"

"No. Lunch. We'll be eating with most of the people you've already met. Daisy, Tansy, and Felix from Magical History class, and Olivia from this class. It'll be great." Ember smiled encouragingly, then clasped their cousin's hand and headed to the cafeteria.

Fotia seemed to relax at the idea of food and seeing people she'd met. *Having a group project earlier in the day was a great way for her to meet my friends.*

The lunchroom was packed with students and Fotia paused in the doorway, gaping. Ember squeezed her hand to comfort her. "I know. Just stick with me."

"Right, where do we sit?" Her voice quavered as she searched the corners for an empty table away from the crowds.

"We need to get food first." Ember dragged Fotia to the lunch line.

Olivia stepped up behind them. "Hi, Fotia. Are you enjoying our school? Did you like last period? Is everything super different than back home for you?"

Fotia smiled then slowly stared over the mass of people in the room. "It is … um … my … than this? Um … yes. My school is much smaller." She shot Ember a quick, desperate look.

"What'll you have?" The lunch man's voice cut off their discussion.

Ember turned and grabbed two trays, handing one to their cousin. "I'll have pizza and fries."

Fotia's face blanched as she gazed at the food options. "Um … same."

Once they had their food, Ember turned to Olivia. "We'll explain everything at the table."

They headed to the al la carte options and selected drinks and fruit. At the cashier, Ember explained Fotia was a visitor, and that they would be paying for both.

Ember had never been so happy that they sat away from the masses as when Fotia sat and slumped. As excited as she'd been to join Ember at school, she was obviously overwhelmed.

Daisy dropped in across from them. "Hi, Fotia. I'm so excited you're here. We really didn't get to talk much in Magical History, having to do the assignment and all. Anyway, I'm Ember's best friend. Were you homeschooled like Ember? Are you like Ember was when they started? Like, totally unprepared for all this teen chaos? Are you ready to hide under a rock ... or this table?" Daisy's brows shot up at her suggestion.

There was a second where Fotia just gaped at Daisy, her jaw hanging open. Then she started laughing. "Oh, my gods, you talk as fast as I do. And you're ridiculous. I love it."

Felix sat down next to Ember. "What happened to us getting together yesterday? There wasn't time to ask you earlier." He kissed their cheek. "Are you trying to tell me something?" His smile let Ember know the last was said in jest.

Ember tilted their head towards Fotia. "We had family return with us, and everyone was tired and needed downtime. I decided I needed to spend time helping them acclimate to ... well, you know, our home. Also, my phone had died."

Felix held his hand out to Fotia. "Nice to officially meet you. You're a relative from Ember's dad's side, right?"

"Right." Fotia nodded. "Okay, I need to know how many people know what that means."

Ember checked around the room. So far it was only the four of them. "Just these two. They were there when I was rescued."

Daisy covered her mouth, eyes dancing. "So, everyone from that side is …, I mean, you're both—" She arched her hand over her food like a plane flying from point a to point b.

"Yeah," Ember confirmed. "Fotia came with her dads. She'll be heading back north after a day or two. She just wanted to see what my life was like away from the woods. And yes, Daisy, like me when I started here, probably more than me … this is a lot."

Olivia sat. "Three people cut me off at the cashier. They all had infinity signs on their bags and looked at me like I was dirt. It's getting worse around here."

Felix's face hardened. "After what Cress did in Magical History, I guess I'm not surprised. And did you see there's a city-wide event on Saturday. I wonder if they're worried about the phoenixes showing up."

Tansy finally made it to the table. "Did you hear the latest? Students are saying Ambrose's family created the phoenixes … it's all a hoax."

"Yeah, that happened in our class. Mr. Elias challenged Ambrose," Daisy said with a smirk on her face. "That class has gotten even more interesting. A great combination of the past and current events."

Fotia smiled. "It was so tense. That boy who talked back to the teacher. That would never happen at my school. Then getting kicked out. My parents would punish me for like ... ever. I just can't fathom being that disrespectful."

"He's one of the faces of Infinite WISDOM, him and the girl who asked about the phoenixes. They're both awful. We just try to avoid them," Daisy said.

"True, that's been our goal since I started in public school," Ember agreed. "But you don't need to worry. I don't have any classes with Cress beyond that one, and he just got himself removed, seemingly on purpose."

Tansy sipped her soda. "I just want the phoenixes to be real. I want to know who they are. Can you imagine it?" She gazed into the distance and sighed.

Daisy turned to her. "You too? I mean, Felix has always been obsessed, but you?"

"Well, not obsessed, but wouldn't it be amazing if not all the shifters we thought were extinct were gone forever?" Tansy smiled.

"I agree," said Olivia. "I'd love to see them flying through the sky, lighting it up with their fire."

Fotia bent her head, focusing on her food. Ember could see her smiling, a guilty look on her face.

Felix sighed. "You are talking my language, friend. A lifetime dream."

Before anyone could say anything else, Ambrose walked up to the table. "Ember, we need to talk."

"No, I don't think we do." Their body tensed as they worried what Ambrose would want to discuss. *Does she want to threaten me about telling her family secrets? Is she worried I'll somehow implicate her and Cress?*

Her face tensed. "Don't make me bring it up in front of everyone here. I will if I have to."

If Fotia wasn't here, I may just push, but I don't want to put any more stress on my cousin.

Searching the faces of the people around them, Ember stood up and followed the popular girl out to the hall. Once they were alone, Ambrose crossed her arms. "You were one of the people saved from my house. You know who the phoenixes are. Tell me."

"Bold of you to think I know, and if I did, why would I tell you?" Of all the scenarios Ember had considered, they hadn't thought about this. It was short-sighted, of course, but with everything else that had happened, Ambrose hadn't been high on their list of priorities.

Now they were in a quandary. They weren't about to out themselves or their family to Ambrose, but what could they say? They had to think of something.

"If you don't tell me, I'll spread it around that *you* are the phoenix and that's why you played human for so long." She smirked.

Damn it all, why is she smart? "Wouldn't that be admitting you and your family had been holding me captive?"

Her face scrunched up in frustration. "No, I'll say you were there to discuss the organization. You had begun to see the truth. That will only help us. But your family thought you were in danger. Then bam, flames."

"Right, how does that work with your cover story that you were at your *summer* home all *winter* break?" One of their eyebrows rose in challenge.

She made a guttural sound of frustration. "I won't explain, Ember. I'll just say that you and yours were trying to fight me and mine. That you are a phoenix. No one will question it. You know who I am, right?"

"Then I'll tell my story. Don't forget, I was unconscious when I was saved from your house, or did you forget Cress's last gift? How am I supposed to know who or what saved me?"

"Well, figure it out. You have until tomorrow's lunch." She turned, flipping her perfect ponytail, and sashayed away.

Chapter 12 - The Threat And The Resolution

Ember

Between them and Fotia, Ember wasn't sure who was happier for the end of the day. Back at Ember's house, they both headed into the living room and flopped onto separate couches. Mom followed them in with Vatra. He took his daughter's hand. "How ya doing, Fotia?"

She leaned her head on his shoulder. "It was ... a day."

"That bad?" he asked.

"No, just … there were so many people at that school. Each class had more people than my whole school—it was mind blowing."

Her dad chuckled. "So, more than four?" He rubbed her back. "I don't think that would be very hard."

Feu walked in and sat on Fotia's other side. He rubbed her leg. "Are you doing okay?"

"Yeah. Ember's friends are great. The classes we attended were interesting. The magic … gods, that was amazing." Her face lit up. "And fun. But I feel like my head is stuffed."

"Well, you can stay back here tomorrow if you want," Feu said, a glint in his eye.

"No Dad, don't make me stay back." Fotia sounded pitiful.

Ember slumped, then met Mom's gaze. "We need to talk."

Dad sauntered in. "That doesn't sound good, dear. What's up?"

After a moment to get their thoughts in order, Ember told everyone about their encounter with Ambrose.

Mom stood and paced the room. "We knew this would happen. It's all attached to those images of the three of you escaping their house. If I knew which of the volunteers snapped the photos … I tell you, I'd—"

"What?" Dad asked, sounding amused. "You're too gentle to really do anything." He pulled his phone from his pocket and made a call. "Hi, Nuri. Can you come over? We have an issue, and I think you should be here to discuss our next move."

It didn't take Aunts Nuri and Monte long to arrive. After the introductions and a quick rundown of what happened, the group started brainstorming.

"In Ember's class, the teacher said there's talk that the owner of the house made up the phoenixes. Could you push that?" Fotia asked.

"Unfortunately, no," Ember scrunched up their face. "Ambrose is one of the people who lives in that house. If her family had done the hoax, she would know."

"Oh." Fotia sagged. "This is hard."

Feu tapped his finger on his knee. "What about making up some person who doesn't exist?"

"No," Aunt Monte said, though others supported her answer, she went on. "It would be simple to figure out that sort of lie. And if a fake name was used that belonged to someone, we'd be ruining that person's life. Even if it were only for a short period, it wouldn't be fair or worth it."

"Can you just go with not knowing the phoenixes?" Aunt Monte asked. "If she tries to out you as a phoenix, lean in to the fact that you have magic."

Dad's head dropped back. "You know, when we went in as phoenixes, we knew what we were doing. We made a decision and acted on it. I'm tired of hiding, tired of pretending, tired of all of it."

"What are you saying, Ash?" Aunt Nuri asked. "Are we doing it? Are we really going through with what we told the Elders?"

His head dropped and he met the eyes of each person in the room. "Yes. I think we have to. It's time to let the world know that phoenixes are still around."

Fear and excitement surged through Ember. They fisted their hands as they felt themself tremble. A lifetime of hiding was a hard thing to mentally get over.

Vatra leaned forward. "All of us?"

Dad grunted. "Eventually. But we'll start with what was caught on camera."

Ember smiled. "As much as this is going to suck, it's better than any of the other suggestions. If phoenixes are coming out, it's only a matter of time that the truth about us comes out. There are only so many lies I want to have to apologize for or admit to later."

Mom gave Ember a hug. "You've lived a rough life, love. It's probably not been fair, but it was the only way we knew how to keep you safe." She sat next to Dad. "Now, as for coming out. How? When? And who?"

The room got quiet as everyone thought about the questions. Dad rubbed his face then locked eyes with Aunt

Nuri. The two sat staring at each other for a few seconds. Finally, Aunt Nuri started to nod.

With a long sigh, she turned to Aunt Monte. "How do you feel about calling in someone to record a video for us?"

She narrowed her eyes. "When?"

"Now. The video goes out tonight."

Feu shook his head. "Ash, I appreciate that you're taking this step, and as my sovereign—" Dad snarled, but Feu ignored it, "—as my *sovereign,* it's your right to make this decision. But I would like to take Fotia home before the backlash of the video hits. Can the video go out in the morning, and we'll take our leave at about the same time?"

Dad and Aunt Nuri said, "Yes." at the same time Fotia exclaimed, "No! But, Dad, I don't want to leave. We just got here. Don't make me leave."

He wrapped her in a hug. "We can come back after the dust has settled. We'll return when Vatra wants to come home. We'll come to pick him up and spend some time here before we all leave together. By then everything should be less dangerous."

"But, Dad—"

"No," Vatra said. "Your dad is right." He leaned over and kissed her forehead. "I don't want you getting hurt or put in a bad situation."

"I won't, I promise," she begged.

"Shh. I know you think you won't, but these people are awful. A couple of weeks ago, they put Ember in a box and poisoned them. And that was only their first attempt. They are not good people. I don't know the lengths they'll go, but I won't risk you, Fotia."

Ember stood and moved to their cousin, kneeling in front of her. "Fotia, your dads are right. I don't know what's about to happen, but it's not going to be a fun walk in the park. Go back to Serafina Landing. You'll come back and enjoy Feniks when it's at its best ... or at least not when it's at its worst. And I'll come and visit you for a longer time, too. It'll be amazing."

"Promise?"

"Promise."

Fotia held up a pinky and Ember wrapped theirs around it.

Chapter 13 - Smile! You're Live!

Felix

Felix sat at his desk in his room, finishing up some homework. With his extra-curricular activities, it was important to always have his homework done early.

He leaned back, taking a mental break. He thought back on the day. A smile crossed his face as he imagined Ember and their cousin, so alike, yet so different.

He liked Fotia. Not only was she nice and Ember's cousin, but another phoenix! *I can't believe the turn my life has taken.* But because Fotia was there, he couldn't get the story about what Ambrose wanted from Ember at lunch. After their talk, Ember seemed agitated. He debated texting them, but thought he'd wait until after dinner. He figured with all the family at their house, Ember would be distracted.

I miss spending time with Ember. Winter break was not the bonding time we'd hoped it would be.

He shook his head and went back to his math. There was an exam coming up despite winter break.

Looking ahead on the review, he saw a challenging question. He checked his watch and didn't think he had enough time before he'd be called for dinner. He packed up his math and debated. *I could send Ember a text and let them know there's no rush on the reply. Then they'd know I'm thinking about them.*

Having a plan, he picked up his phone and saw he had a text from Monte.

He laughed at himself for being oblivious while studying, and opened the app. *Can you head over to Ember's place? If you haven't eaten, you can eat with us. We have a need of your video skills.*

Felix shut his books and went to find his parents. "Do you mind if I have dinner over to Ember's? They want me to make a video of something. I'm not sure on the details. Monte sent a text."

Mom narrowed her eyes as if in thought. "Do you think it has to do with Ember or the coalition? Monte's been running it for the last week since Vi's been away." She shook her head. "Or are you calling her Nuri now?"

He shrugged. "No, she's still Vi at the coalition, so I'm still using Vi. Only her family uses Nuri. As for why they want me there, I'm not sure, but I'll tell you as soon as I get home."

Dad laughed and Mom nodded. "Go. Let us know if we're needed for anything."

"Thanks, love you both." He gave his dad a hug and his mom a kiss on the cheek then grabbed a coat. After texting Monte back an affirmative, he slipped into his old Toyota Camry for the drive over.

At the house, he walked to the door and knocked. Ember answered with a wide smile and gave him a hug. "Welcome to the circus. Are you ready for a long night of bizarro land?"

He laughed. "With your family? Aren't I always?" A lightness filled him at finally being back with Ember.

The two headed to the dining room. There were too many people to eat in the kitchen where the table would fit six, maybe seven comfortably. If there were more, the dining room was better, since it had a table that comfortably sat twelve. The smell of spicy meat permeated the house. "What's for dinner?"

Ember's mom placed bags of hamburger buns on the table. "Pulled pork, with a side of mac and cheese, and, of course, broccoli ... we need to be healthy."

The sight and smell of all the food made Felix's stomach grumble. He sat along with everyone else. He knew Ember and their parents, and of course Vi and Monte. Then there was Fotia and two men. He gazed at them, then at Ember, before filling a plate.

Ember smiled. "Oh! These are Fotia's dads, Feu and Vatra."

One of them had already taken a bite, but the other nodded. "Hi, I'm Feu. It's nice to meet one of the people I'm sure I'm going to hear all about."

Fotia blushed, then laughed. "He's not wrong. I had fun today."

Oh, my gods! More phoenixes. Two-thirds of the people in this room are phoenixes. Do not freak out ... do not freak out!

Felix clenched his jaw to stop himself from making a complete fool of himself with his utter excitement. The look on Feu's face told him he wasn't very successful. Then the man winked.

After that, everyone got to eating. The food tasted amazing.

Once he'd eaten about half his sandwich, he leaned back and turned to Monte. "So, what are we creating tonight that couldn't wait?"

Next to him, Ember laughed. "Ambrose told me today at lunch that if I didn't tell her who the phoenixes were, she'd tell the school *I* was a phoenix."

Felix's brows rose in astonishment. "Did she now? And was she going to use anything but her own popularity as proof?"

"That and my years of hiding my magic," Ember huffed out, laughing at themself. "Sometimes I can't believe what a waste she's made of her life. She really is smart, isn't she?"

"She is," Felix confirmed. "If she cared about studying and not being popular, we'd have a run for our money for top student."

"Well, we'd like to take the narrative back," Vi said. "The idea that Infinite WISDOM would control us is frustrating. So, we're going to out ourselves, so to speak, on the FB coalition website. We just need someone to make the video. And, as great as Monte is at programming and IT, her photography could use a bit of help ... not to mention her videos."

Felix barked out a laugh. "I remember. The last group photos she took for the volunteers were ... interesting." He smiled at Monte, who made a frustrated sound. "You kept on missing part of the group."

Monte huffed in annoyance. "But I spliced all the images together and the final picture was great," she insisted.

"Well, it was a picture, I'll give you that," Felix agreed. Everyone laughed.

After dinner, the group headed out to an open field. "So." Felix looked at all the people who were now so important to him, even Fotia and her dads, though he didn't know them very well. "How do you want to do this? An interview? A big reveal? What's the plan?"

Felix realized Ember, their dad, and Vi weren't in the group. He searched but couldn't see them.

Ember's mom came over. "Point your camera over there. Have me in the center. I'll start. Once I'm done, I think you'll know what to do. When Ash gets on screen, focus on him."

Felix's head started to hurt. This wasn't how it was done. As the camera operator, he should have a full script, or at least a better idea of what to expect, what to do, where to aim the camera. "Um ... okay. Anything else?"

She sighed. "I'm not really sure. I was just told to make sure you caught everything. I was told to do an intro and to cover the nudity. You were to not stop recording."

"Right, clear as mud." Felix rubbed his forehead with one hand, then took out his phone. It had a superb camera. He turned it sideways, set it to video, and hit record. Then he nodded and pointed to Mrs. Savita who stood, arms relaxed at her side. A peaceful smile softened her face.

"Hi, my name is Sadie Savita. There has been a lot of talk and speculation ever since a grainy photo came out of three phoenixes over the Wells's house a few days ago. Are the Wells phoenixes? Did they set up some elaborate hoax? Were the firebirds there to save humans from the clutches of the heart of Infinite WISDOM? The queries go on and on. And whereas I'm not here to answer all of what you want to know right now, I will answer the biggest mystery."

She turned and Felix panned out. He wasn't sure what was about to happen, but he wanted to get whatever it was documented.

A moment later, he saw Monte waving from his peripheral vision. When he looked over, she pointed up. Then he saw it, the phoenixes flying above. Ever so slowly, he panned the camera to catch them in play, two white beauties and Ember's fiery red and orange bird with purple feathers. They flew in figure eights above the yard, looking like fire swirling around clouds of feathers.

Then, as if they were given a signal, the three phoenixes lowered themselves to the ground.

Felix didn't miss a second once he had them captured on his phone. Unlike the previous image, his phone's picture was crisp and clear. No mistaking what was being recorded for the world to see.

As soon as the three birds stood tall and proud on the grass of the field, fire licking off their shoulders, Mrs. Savita turned back to the camera. "Here you can see the three phoenixes, in the feather. I'm going to obscure the air so you can see that it's them shifting, but none of the details. This is for identification, not a time to see anyone naked."

She turned back and raised her hands. The air in front of each of the phoenixes wavered. Squinting, Felix could make out the shape of the birds, but nothing more. As he watched, the images contorted, warping, and changing. After a minute or so, first one, then two and finally three humans stood obscured behind the distorted air. To him, it looked like they were putting on clothes.

"It's okay, Sadie." Ash's voice echoed across the field.

Felix saw Mrs. Savita's hesitation. Her shoulders rose and fell. Then she fisted both her hands, and the air cleared.

Standing where the phoenixes had landed were Vi, Ash, and Ember, all dressed.

Ash walked forward. "My name is Ash Savita. I was part of the Committee of Ten who created the laws that brought tranquility to humans, shifters, and magic users after the War of Peace. Vi here is my twin sister; she and I led the forces that ensured our side would win. As you can see, rumors of our death have been greatly exaggerated. And if you'd stop trying to undo all our hard work, I'd really appreciate it."

Chapter 14 - Blowing On The Wind

Ember

As Ember climbed the stairs to Air Magic class, they sent one more thought towards Fotia and Feu and their quick and safe trip home. The pair had left at seven this morning after a hearty breakfast. The two decided to fly instead of borrowing one of the griffins, knowing the worst that could happen was a night spent in the woods. Ember was impressed at how blasé both Fotia and Feu acted at the idea of a random night in a strange location, but Fotia explained that it was a training exercise all the phoenixes practiced in Serafina Landing.

I need to become tougher. Fotia may not be able to navigate the school as well as I can, but I don't know if I could sleep in the woods without a tent and all the extras we had when we went as a class assignment. And, come to think about it, I didn't really survive that all that well. Besides getting pretty beat up from the pranks, I did end up dying after getting bit by a camel spider. They thought about trees and sleeping out in the wilderness. *Maybe as a firebird ... but I don't know, I've never tried it.*

Ember shook their head and focused on the stairs. Felix said he'd upload the video at five in the morning. No one thought it would be seen until later this morning, or, more likely, this afternoon. Everyone just wanted it to be up well before lunch.

Once in class, Ember dropped their bag by the wall and found Mrs. Vintl in her office. Today was the tenth- and eleventh-year air magic class, their original class. Ever since the school found out how strong an air magic practitioner Ember was, those in charge decided Ember helping out was better than wasting time learning magic they could already do. It was weird being an assistant teacher to their classmates. "So, what's on the schedule for today?"

"Oh, hi, Ember. We've been working on lifting notebooks and keeping them steady. For anyone who's gotten that mastered, it's time to put something on the notebook." She held up some kids' numbered wooden blocks. "At the beginning, these should be placed in the center of the notebook. Then, as a challenge, off center."

Ember considered. "That's going to be hard. How long will the class be working on this?"

"A few weeks."

Nodding slowly, Ember imagined what the students would need to do to accomplish this task. "Sounds good."

Ember took a basket of blocks and headed back out to sit by their bag. Class would start in just under ten minutes.

It didn't take long for Daisy to arrive. She sat down, buzzing with energy. "Where's Fotia?"

"It has to do with something that happened yesterday and last night. A bit of a story I need to tell you. She, and one of her dads, decided to head home. It's going to get a bit too—exciting—"

"My gods, Ember!" Simon walked in and bellowed, cutting them off. "You're a phoenix? Why didn't you tell anyone?!" He stomped across the room, disrupting the small groups of students talking quietly.

Daisy looked first at Ember, who tried not to show how annoyed they were, and then at Simon. "And a good morning to you, too, Simon."

"Is that why you could fly on the platform? Because you're a phoenix?" he snapped.

They wanted to hit their head against something hard ... though, not as hard as Simon's head. "No, that would be air magic. Phoenixes are fire. I would think you'd know the difference, being as smart as you are. Haven't you studied all of this in the past?"

His brow knit for a second, then he shook his head as if dislodging Ember's argument. "Yes, but that's irrelevant. If you're a phoenix, why didn't you tell anyone?"

Daisy slowly blinked. "What do you mean, not tell anyone? I've known for years. Ever since we met. Maybe it isn't about not telling anyone and more about not trusting you. You are kind of a big mouth. Just look at how you entered class today."

Ember wanted to hug Daisy for supporting them even when she didn't know what was going on. They weren't sure why they ever thought they couldn't trust Daisy with their secrets in the first place.

Simon howled and stormed off.

Ember slumped. "Thank you."

"You're welcome." Her brows came together. "But how did he know?"

"It's what I was about to tell you. It's a video that went up on the FB website." Ember dropped their head in their hands and tried to relax as they told Daisy about their night.

It occurred to them that the day hadn't even started, and it was already too long.

Once done explaining, Ember heard Daisy stand. Their head snapped up as they watched their friend walk over to Simon.

Oh, no! This can't be good. The last time they were together over winter break, after Daisy left him, she ended up in the hospital. Ember moved to get up just as Daisy snarled, "So, you found out because you saw the video on this website, right?"

"Yeah, I monitor the lies that website pumps out. It's important to know both sides, Daisy." Condescension dripped from his words, and Ember wanted to roll their eyes.

Why did I think he was so smart?

"Heh," Daisy mocked him with a fake laugh. "So, how often are you checking out the 'lies' on this website?"

"I don't know, a few times a day. Why?" Simon's lip twitched as he gazed up at her.

"Because, if you're on this site, then you knew I was in the hospital for days after our coffee date, and you didn't even think to text me to ask how I was. But you knew I was there, didn't you? I bet you set Cress on me. Did you know he broke seven of my bones?" Daisy snapped back. "Was it all your idea? Did you ask him to break my bones?"

"What? That's a lie! That didn't happen."

"Are you calling me a liar, Simon Trahaus? Who are you to even *think* to say my words are anything but truth?"

Daisy's hands landed on her hips after poking him in the chest. Her face was set as if fire could fly from her eyes. "Do you think my bones weren't broken? Or do you think they spontaneously broke?"

Simon shrank into himself. "But Daisy ... wait, what? Seven bones? Really? It was him?"

Simon had always had a crush on Daisy, not that she'd ever noticed. Having the organization he'd started to support harm the girl he liked may have been the thing that broke his arrogant brain.

Before Daisy could answer, Mrs. Vintl started class. "If everyone is done with all the excitement, today we're going to separate into groups. For some, you'll stick with what you've been doing. For others, you'll be given a new challenge, something harder." She looked down at her attendance sheet and quickly checked off the names of the people in the room. "Okay, before I separate everyone, are there any questions?"

One of the tenth graders raised his hand. "Yes, Arti?"

"How can Ember be a phoenix and do air magic? I thought shifters couldn't do any magic." Everyone turned from staring at Mrs. Vintl to Ember.

Ember kept their eyes on the teacher, waiting for her response. They weren't going to disrupt class if they could help it.

"Right." Ms. Vintl said, "What I meant was, are there any questions about our assignment?"

Another hand shot up and Mrs. Vintl's shoulders tensed. "Yes, Rane?"

"Was that really Ember's mother who helped in that demonstration? Because if she did air magic like that, that would make her a witch, not a phoenix. And how can Ember be a phoenix if their mom is a witch?"

Mrs. Vintl shook her head then rubbed her eyes with one hand. "I'm sorry, Ember."

"It's not your fault." Ember sighed.

After Monte had sent the text to Felix, they'd all discussed how they'd explain how Ember could do magic, how their mother was a witch, and how they were a phoenix. The questions would come up. Ember hadn't expected them quite so soon, but in hindsight, they weren't sure why not. They kept hoping for a bit of time, but obviously time wasn't on their side.

They couldn't cover any of it up. There were hospital records of Ember's birth. There were years of Ember doing some level of magic. And though Ember had the red hair of phoenixes, they looked enough like their mom that there was no question they were related.

Ember turned to the class. "Yes, Sadie Savita is my mom. She's a witch, which is how I can do magic. My magic is limited to air magic because I'm only half witch." They shrugged.

Simon's mouth dropped. "Phoenixes can mate with witches? That's a lie. No shifter can have a kid with a witch. No cross breeding is possible."

"Well, then, I must not really be standing here. You saw the video. I am fully a phoenix. I love to fly, and you've all seen me do air magic." Ember tried to smile and keep things light, but they just wanted to throttle the toad of a boy. "But you clearly know more than me, so I'm just a figment." His level of obnoxiousness was growing exponentially.

"Prove it," Simon said with a sneer.

"What do you mean? Prove what?"

"Prove you're a phoenix."

"That's enough," Mrs. Vintl cut in. "I've let you ask your questions and even gave Ember time to answer. We have a lesson to get through and it isn't about harassing Ember."

Simon snorted. "They're just a witch. It was all a hoax."

Ember smiled and turned their back on Simon. Then, in the smallest letters they could, wrote, 'you are such a fool' a foot in front of his face in fire.

Chapter 15 - The Truth Comes Out

Ember

"Mrs. Vintl, can I head out of class early? I need to talk to Mr. Elias." Ember knew when he saw the video, there'd be some explaining to do. Even if he hadn't seen it yet, they needed to apologize for their parents deceiving him and warn him about the contents.

If they were to be honest, Ember wasn't sure how to approach him. Before winter break, Mr. Elias had been teaching and studying the War of Peace his whole career. When he learned Ember's parents' names, he'd wanted to meet them. At the time of the meeting, Dad spun a story about family names, hiding who they were.

Now that the video was out with Dad admitting his involvement, including being part of the Committee of Ten, Ember wanted to talk to Mr. Elias, one of their favorite teachers, and hoped he understood. They knew the conversation wouldn't be pleasant, but it had to happen.

"Sure. I think everyone is working well right now. I don't see any reason you can't leave early," Mrs. Vintl said, with a supportive grin. "I'll see you tomorrow."

"Thanks." Ember headed over to gather their stuff. As they passed Daisy, they gave a small wave and mouthed, "See you in a few."

Though they left early, it was only by a few minutes. They ran down the steps and got to Mr. Elias's class just as the bell rang. As the first period class shuffled out, Ember slipped in. They dumped their bag on their seat then moved over to Mr. Elias's desk, where he sat looking over some papers.

He looked up. "Oh, Ember, you're early."

"Yeah, I was wondering if you saw the video on the FB coalition website yet?" They checked over their shoulder to make sure they were still alone.

"No, not yet. I usually don't have downtime before my free period. Why? Anything I need to know about?"

Ember wrung their hands. "Yeah. I mean, well, do you remember that meeting with my parents?"

He sat up. "Yes. I still chuckle about thinking a witch could be two hundred years old. It's silly right? Wanting something so bad, we see things that can't be in the strangest places."

"Well, right. About that. Your assumptions may not have been exactly wrong."

He stilled and his look intensified. "What are you saying, Ember?"

Ember took a quick, calming breath. "Well, it's just that you were right, and I wanted to apologize before you found out from any other source." They shook out their hands. "You have to understand, we've been hiding ... well, I'm seventeen. But Dad, Mom, they've been hiding a long time. It's only because of recent events that it's become clear that hiding is no longer an option."

He held up his hands. "Both of them? But your mom's a witch."

"I know. And I want to explain ... *they* want to explain. But it's a longer story. You should know, Monte, from the coalition, was around during the War of Peace, too." Ember shrugged, realizing they were babbling. "And Vi. You know, since she's my dad's twin."

Looking dumbstruck, he leaned back hard in his seat. "Ember, I have to teach in a couple of minutes. You realize that, right? My head's spinning. They really are ... them?"

"Yeah, they are."

He huffed out a small laugh. "Can you come after school and fill in the missing pieces? Because right now I feel like I'm going to explode."

Behind them, Ember could hear the room filling. "I'll see what I can do, but I think so. Again, I'm sorry for the deception; so are my parents."

He shook his head. "I get it. I'm not happy about it, but I understand."

Ember headed to their seat. Felix slipped in behind. "What were you talking to Mr. Elias about? Are you in trouble already?"

They snorted. "Remind me at lunch to tell you about a parent-teacher conference I had a few weeks ago."

His head tilted. "Oh? Did you get into trouble and not tell me?"

"No, just think about what Dad said last night and what our teacher knows. You may figure it out." Felix's eyes widened. "Anyway, I wanted to apologize for the lies that were told."

Cress strolled in. Mr. Elias stood. "Cress, I haven't received your letter of apology or had a conference with your parents." Ember could hear a bit of exasperation.

They thought Mr. Elias didn't want Cress in class any more than Cress wanted to be in class. "Your assigned spot is in the principal's office. If you don't make it this time, you'll be suspended."

Wide smile on his face, Cress gave Mr. Elias a big thumbs up, turned on his heel, and sauntered back out of the room. This time, he turned the correct way to get to the office.

Chapter 16 - A Video Is Worth A Thousand Words

Ember

Ember sat at lunch. No one else had joined them yet and the moment of quiet in the chaos of the cafeteria felt like a dream, their very own eye in the storm of insanity.

They'd had a long conversation with Olivia in Magical Creations about being a phoenix and their affinity with fire. Their friend seemed more amused and amazed than anything else. Before winter break Olivia had gone to some extent to keep Ember from burning themself on glass balls filled with fire. Now she understood why Ember had been so cavalier with their own safety.

It had been the only calm conversation of the day, and it had felt good.

The family had woken early to see Fotia and Feu off, so Ember had time to make their lunch. They watched as Daisy navigated the line to get something greasy. As students moved around the room, they wished one of their friends would make it to the table to be a buffer from the attention Ember felt from different students they barely knew.

It took a few minutes, but Daisy arrived. "Have you been monitoring the video?"

Ember scoffed. "Why would I do that? I don't mind people knowing, I just want to be past the shock and to the point they know. I can't wait to be yesterday's news. Anyway, it's school; I just want to go to class and learn."

"Said no teen ever," Tansy said as she sat. She glared at Ember, but there was no heat in the stare. Despite that, a new wave of guilt washed through them. One more friend they'd been lying to. "I can't believe you sat here yesterday and said nothing! I literally said I wanted to know who the phoenixes were ... and nothing."

Felix and Olivia got to the table at the same time. Olivia grunted. "I need to start bringing my lunch. That line is getting worse, and the food isn't getting any better."

Everyone laughed.

Tansy waved her hands. "No, we're not changing the subject. Ember, talk."

Olivia took a bite of her hamburger and shook her head. "Give it up, Tansy. The phoenixes were in hiding for years. I'm sure it wasn't something Ember could just blab about."

Tansy draped the back of her hand across her forehead. "Fine, I'll back down."

"So, we're friends again?" Ember took a bite of their ham and cheese sandwich.

"I guess."

Daisy harrumphed. "Back to my question. Have you seen the number of views on your video?"

Felix opened up his phone and pulled up the video. His eyebrows rocked up. "Whoa, that's ... a lot. The video has only been up for like, seven hours. How is that even possible?"

"It's phoenixes, Felix." Tansy snorted. "What did you think would happen? Everyone has been secretly obsessed and now there's an answer. It's ... I don't know, but it's big."

"What's big? Ember's ego? Or is it Felix's? He thinks he knows everything." Ambrose stood at the end of their table. Ember couldn't believe with all that had gone on that day, they still had to deal with the popular girl.

"What are you doing here?" Ember's voice was flat ... they tried to not sound aggressive.

"We need to talk, you know that."

With an effort, Ember kept their face blank. "You're kidding, right? Are you the only person ... like in the world, who hasn't seen the video?"

"What video?" Ambrose snapped out the words like a whip.

"The video on the FB coalition website about the phoenixes?" Felix said. "You have to have heard about it. Like, everyone is talking about it. It's all anyone has talked about all day. How could you be so ... vapid?"

By the end of Felix's question, Ambrose's ponytail flipping back and forth was the only thing left in her wake.

Ember sipped their soda, smiling at her receding back. "Good riddance."

Olivia laughed. "That's why you and your dad and aunt did it, isn't it? Ambrose. Yesterday. Gods above she's a pill."

"This is—" Felix focused on his phone, started to shake his head. "There are so many ..."

Daisy leaned over the table to try to see what he was doing. "You have to finish one of those sentences, buddy, if you want us to know what you're trying to tell us. Can you use your words for us?"

There were chuckles around the table as Felix's head snapped up. "What? Oh, yeah, sorry. I'm just reading the comments—"

"Never read the comments!" Tansy snapped.

"What?" Felix asked, brows knitting.

"It's just, you're never supposed to read the comments." Tansy shrugged. "There are so many internet trolls that will make your head want to explode."

"No, it isn't that." Felix continued to read off his phone. "There are a lot of questions. Some that your mom asked during the video about the Wells being phoenixes or maybe being here to save us all from Infinite WISDOM, Ember. Some that are new. People are curious. It isn't trolls, just a lot of people who want to know. It isn't that they're mad or angry, it's just ... like me and Tansy, they feel like only half the story has been told."

Ember stared at him intently. "So, what do you think we should do?"

"I don't know, but I don't think your family's time in the limelight is over, my friend."

Chapter 17 - How Much Is Too Much?

Ambrose

"My parents are debating if they'll come in to meet with that human-lover teacher or not. I haven't missed going to his class." Cress stuffed half his burger in his mouth, smacking loud enough to be heard over the thrum of the people in the noisy cafeteria.

Ambrose wished she could sit anywhere else but next to him. The sounds he made—talking or eating—disgusted her. She thought when winter break ended and she could return to school, things would get better, but she still had to deal with Cress. Though he had a home of his own, a family of his own, and a life of his own, the hotel suite her family had secured included a room for him, so he spent most of his time there.

At this rate, she'd rather spend all her time with Josie, as obnoxious as the girl was.

"Wouldn't you just have to repeat the class if you fail?" Josie asked ... speak of the devil. She'd been the first to the table but had been awfully quiet. The only place Ambrose really heard her speak up this week was Magical History class. "Would you be able to move up to twelfth year if you don't pass *his* class?" She emphasized the pronoun as if she didn't dare speak the class's name.

"You're sweet, Josie, but remember what we talked about in Earth Magic class on Monday." Cress tilted his head and one of his eyebrows rose. His face was stern. He almost looked like Father when he was being authoritative.

Gah! Could anything be worse? Though she was curious, she was more annoyed that he was acting like a lord ruler here at school. Who did he think he was, anyway?

Ambrose watched as Josie's face tensed, then relaxed, then as the girl forced a smile to spread across her face, though it didn't reach her eyes. "Right. Only speak when you want my opinion. Otherwise I should be seen, not heard."

Stomach tightening, anger boiled in Ambrose's gut. *How dare he have the audacity to give such rules to a fellow student? That sexism can't be allowed to thrive!*

Ambrose flipped her ponytail over her shoulder as she worked to keep a blank face. "Really, Cress? And what makes you think you can determine whose opinions are worth hearing? We're at school. You can't silence people here. And, if I remember correctly, it's been my thoughts that have moved the movement forward, not yours." Her skin boiled at his assumption he could be as misogynistically dominant here as Mr. Shade and Father were at home. School was Ambrose's escape, not a continuation of her hell.

He slowly turned towards her. "You *know* who likes my thoughts, Ambrose. And you shouldn't push me, should you? *He* wouldn't like to hear about it."

"What, are you going to run to Daddy?" She raised an eyebrow in challenge.

It's ironic that he'll be running to my father not his own. I wonder if he even remembers where his own home is anymore.

With a small scoff, she rotated in her seat to face Josie. "We should hang out after school today."

"You can't, Ambrose," Cress snapped, his voice crawling over her skin like tiny scorpions. "We have to prep for tomorrow's event. Your father is picking us up right away."

Ignoring him, Ambrose smiled at Josie. "Tell me about your winter break." No one had asked her all week. Ambrose had almost forgotten about her, she'd been so quiet.

Before Josie could answer, Cress spoke loudly, "So, Brett, you want to move up in the movement, right?"

Eyes wide, Josie turned to watch the boys talk. It seemed she was unwilling to ignore Cress's order.

Setting her face, Ambrose lifted her chin to watch what happened next. She had to work to contain the fire within her or she may burn this place down. Cress didn't know the danger he was in with his arrogant idiocy.

Cress's best bro-pal, Brett, huffed out a laugh. "You know I do. This movement is great, man."

"Well, get this. At every assembly, there are these idiots who protest." Cress leaned towards Brett. "You know what I mean?"

"Yeah, right, man. The human-lovers." Brett didn't seem to know how to keep his voice down. The only thing that saved their conversation from being overheard was how loud it was in the room. "I don't know why the human-lovers even show up if they don't like what's being talked about." Brett's face scrunched up in confusion.

And just when I thought Cress was easily confused. How did he find someone dumber than him? I guess he'd have to, to find devoted followers. Ambrose used her years of training to hold her face blank, but she wanted to roll her eyes at their imbecilic antics.

Cress laughed and the sound felt like razor blades running down Ambrose's back. She realized she was starting to hate everything about him. "Well, stick with me, and I'll get you in tight with," he leaned in and lowered his voice, "Mr. Shade."

He's going to get us all suspended. We're not supposed to talk about any of this here outside of the assemblies, and he knows it. But if I mention it at home, I'll be the one punished, and I finally get my phone back tomorrow.

"Really?" Brett's eyes widened. "You can do that? You'd do that for me?"

"Absolutely, my friend. And I know exactly how you can get on the big guy's radar." Cress's smile was reptilian.

How did I ever let him kiss me? A shiver ran down her spine.

Brett's tongue darted out as he tried to wet his bottom lip. "What do I do?"

"On Saturday, once Ambrose and I are done with our presentation." Cress slid his arm around her shoulder. She tried not to shiver. They still had to be a power couple at school and if anyone knew how much she despised him, all bets would be off. "Find me. We'll find one of the interlopers at the event and have a long talk with them.

Depending on how you do—you're in!" Cress punched his words by pumping his free fist into the air.

"Yes!" Brett copied Cress's action, and then they both high-fived. Then his face crumpled in confusion. "But how?"

"Just think, twenty minutes after the event is over, in the woods south of the event, there's this great place on the walking path. It's private. We'll take the human-lover, 'talk' to him." Cress air quoted the word. "And then you'll be in. I'll tell the boss to situate himself there and watch so he knows how committed you are." Cress looked manic in his joy.

Both boys started grunting and making animalistic sounds. Josie watched, smiling. Ambrose didn't think she really understood what Cress meant by 'talk.' Or maybe she did.

The idea of harming people who disagreed disgusted her. The fact that they enjoyed it made her sick. She wasn't sure how her life had gotten her to this point, but she was beginning to hate every part of it.

Ambrose collected her bag and slipped out of the cafeteria. There were ten minutes left of lunch and she needed some down time.

The quiet in the hall sank into her bones. Having a few minutes to herself felt like a luxury. The calm of the hallway cleansed her mind, and she made a decision.

She navigated to the library.

Along the back wall were a bunch of computers. There weren't many students in the large room. Simon sat at the check-out desk, but she avoided eye-contact with him. The last thing she needed was another arrogant male. Even if he saw her, he wouldn't have the spine to approach her if she didn't summon him.

She selected the last computer in the row, with a monitor that faced the wall. Since it was a school computer, she didn't need to log in. She opened a web browser and stared at the school's home page.

Am I really going to do this? It could change everything. I'll be going against my family, my friends, my—she gulped—*my life.*

Making fists, she stared at the computer, numb.

"Five minutes, everyone. Finish up what you're doing, then you'll need to shut down and head to class." The librarian's announcement broke Ambrose out of her stupor.

With a final shake of her hands, she opened up a search engine and looked for the FB coalition, the site that hosted the phoenixes' video. Navigating to the site, she created an account under a dummy name. There was no way she'd use her own identity—not that they'd believe it, but she needed to be safe.

Once done, she clicked on the 'contact us' link.

One more breath to steady herself. She thought about Cress and Brett and all the people Mr. Shade had locked up in the cells below her house. All the innocent humans—her personal servants—he'd harmed and killed. Even Ember, a witch ... a phoenix, locked in a cell for days. This was supposed to be about the magical community supporting each other, not power for the sake of power, or sexism, or whatever it was Mr. Shade and Father were doing.

She started typing.

If this worked, Mr. Shade would be arrested, and Infinite WISDOM would get a black eye.

Chapter 18 - Interview With A Phoenix

Ember

On Friday, Ember walked home with Felix and Daisy. They smiled at their friends. "The week is over. I survived!"

Felix flung his arm over their shoulders. "The week isn't over yet, you know. We have more to do tonight. Are you ready?"

Ember leaned their head back on his arm. "Nope. There's no such thing as being ready for anything in my life; I am fully convinced of this." They all laughed. "Anyway, I'm just going to watch. I think Aunt Nuri would be the best. Have you heard the woman speak?"

Felix just stared at Ember for a moment. "I don't know, maybe once or twice."

"Is she a good speaker?" Daisy asked. She'd never been to any of the FB coalition meetings. Though she had joined on Sunday, Aunt Monte had run the meeting since Ember and family were traveling back from Phoenix Forest.

I can't wait for Daisy to hear her; she is in for a treat!
"The best." Felix winked at Ember.

When the three of them got to the house, Ember's parents as well as Aunt Nuri and Aunt Monte were all sitting in the living room. Dad gazed up at them from the couch. "Dinner will be here in twenty minutes. While we wait, why don't you head to the kitchen and get started on homework. There's a lot on the docket for this weekend."

The time slipped by while they worked on Magical History together. It was fun having Daisy and Felix there to work and joke with. Ember could almost believe life had settled back to the way it used to be ... except there were two aunts now sitting at the table who could tell them what it really was like during the time in history they were studying.

Once pizza came, everyone moved to the dining room to eat. As the meal came to an end, Mom leaned back. "Okay, tell me what you all are thinking for this new video."

Aunt Monte pushed her plate away from the edge of the table and crossed her arms leaning forward. "Have you been monitoring the website at all? Do you know how many people have seen the video we posted on Tuesday? How much interest there is? Questions?" She looked at each person sitting around the table. "Any of you?"

Daisy raised her hand. "I have. Since I learned about how popular it was the first day. I've been trying to keep Ember updated as well."

"Me too," Felix chimed in. "But you knew that. I've been taking notes. I can't read all the comments—no one has that much time or patience—but I've gotten a feel for the flow of questions and written down the important ones."

Aunt Monte smiled at him. "Perfect. Anyone else?"

Dad scoffed. "No. I'm leaving all of that up to you lot. I know I was the star of that video," he snorted. "And I did watch it after it went up to make sure we didn't look like utter fools, but after that I figured I'd let it do its thing ... and it has, right?"

"Yes, dear, it has." Mom patted his shoulder and shook her head. "The video got over five million hits on the first day and has grown exponentially since. I stopped watching after the second day." She turned to Aunt Nuri. "Is being anti-technology a phoenix thing? I mean both Ash and Ember act like they're allergic, beyond Ember and the normal teenage phone thing."

"Hey!" Ember protested. "I text. I watch videos. I even made one when I was practicing earth magic. I just don't want to think about this monumental thing that's changing the fundamental trajectory of my life."

Mom's eyes softened. "I know it's rough, but don't you think it's for the best? You can stop pretending and just be you. And I did say average teenage phone stuff."

Ember slumped after giving Mom a small smile. "Yeah. That'll be nice. And probably in a few weeks I'll be thrilled. I just ... I'm still at the point where people either don't believe it or are gaping at me. It's annoying."

"That may never go away." Aunt Nuri shrugged. "Phoenixes are unique enough that people will always wonder and be a bit in awe of us. Just ignore it and move on." She turned to Mom. "And yes, most phoenixes act like technology comes from the devil. Think of it like a charming quirk. It's easier that way."

Mom chuckled.

"Okay, people," Aunt Monte said, sounding exasperated. "It's getting late, and I for one will turn into a pumpkin soon. Remember, I'm old."

"Not as old as me," Dad mumbled.

Aunt Nuri reached over and punched his shoulder lightly. "Still not the oldest, brother."

He smiled at her warmly, his joy at having her back in his life obvious.

Daisy started laughing. "Are meals here always this boisterous? Your family is a hoot!"

Ember began to rub their temples. "Unfortunately, yes." Despite their groan, they too were amused by everything.

"Focus." Aunt Monte sighed. "As I was saying. There are a lot of comments on the video. Felix has been combing through them because a lot are ... well, awful. But there are some questions that could be answered in a follow up video. You know, a 'one and done.' Give the public some closure to their curiosity." She slowly gazed at everyone around the table. "What we need to determine is, one, which questions do we answer? And two, who do we put up for sacrifice?"

With a wink, Daisy turned to Aunt Monte. "I think it should be Ember."

"Wait, why? No!" It felt like they'd been thrown into an ice bath. "Mom or Aunt Nuri know so much more." Ember had a fleeting thought about Dad, but he'd probably spend most of the time just glaring at the camera. They bit back a smile at the thought.

Mom leaned back. "Let's hear her out, love. This is about brainstorming, not shutting ideas down."

"This should be good," Aunt Nuri said with genuine interest, her face beaming with amusement. "Tell us Daisy: why Ember?"

"Because they're using two teens as their spokespeople. This whole movement is about the youth pushing the messages forward. Wouldn't it make sense for us to do the same thing?" She leaned back and crossed her arms over her chest.

Ember slumped. "Why do I have smart friends?"

Felix reached over to squeeze Ember's shoulder in a small massage of support. "I think I agree with Daisy." Or *not* support! He winced at their harrumph. "At first, I thought Vi would be great. I've been to enough FB events to know how good a speaker she is, but Daisy's right, this battle is being pushed by teens. I mean, adults do speak at the events, but not until the teens push the agenda."

Ember huffed in annoyance.

Dad laughed. "You know, Ember? You were correct about your assessment. You surround yourself with too many clever people."

Don't I know it!

Ember sat in Dad's chair in his office. Someone had hung black curtains all around.. Daisy and Felix were the only ones in the room with them. They thought with anyone else around, they'd be too nervous ... and the area would be too crowded.

Earlier, while the adults prepared the office, Daisy dragged Ember up to their bedroom to change clothes and put on some makeup. Ember didn't have much, but Daisy made do with what they had. Just enough so that Ember didn't look washed out on camera.

Though Ember knew how to do their own makeup, they were currently a bit numb with everything going on.

The consensus was that their regular clothes—jeans and T-shirts—wasn't good enough for this video. Two months ago, that would've been a problem. However, just over a month ago, after the school field trip for night plants, Ember had been bitten by a camel spider, a creature venomous to phoenixes.

When a phoenix died, their sex changed. To help maintain their female presentation, Ember and their mom had gone shopping. Mom had insisted on some skirts and button-down shirts. She had said those were the type of clothes Dad wore when he tried to hide the shift.

Daisy squealed when she saw all the options. Ember had only worn one skirt to school. She quickly found a black skirt and dark green button-down. "I can't believe you never wear any of these clothes. They look great on you, Ember."

They shrugged. "If I survive all this, I'll consider it."

"Good!" With that, they both headed back down to where Felix waited.

Once Ember was back in Dad's seat, Felix held up his phone, then pointed at them. It was 'go' time. After a minute he lowered the phone. "You okay?"

"Yeah, I'm just not used to talking to a phone." Ember huffed out a laugh. "*On* a phone, sure, *to* a phone, not so much. This is just a bit ... you know." They pulled at the hem of their shirt nervously.

"I know, but the sooner we get done with this, the sooner it's behind you." He smiled encouragingly.

Ember laughed. "That was an amazing pep talk."

Daisy mock-punched Felix's arm. "Yeah, it was awful." She turned to Ember. "How about you look into the phone, but talk to me? Tell me what you want to tell the world. Chances are I don't know most of it anyway." She gave a sheepish smile. "I'm not mad, don't worry. I really do understand."

"Right, tell you. I'm just talking to my best friend. I can do this." Ember nodded and Felix lifted his phone again.

After tapping on it, he pointed it at Ember again.

They took a steadying breath.

"Hi, my name is Ember Savita. You probably saw me on a video with my dad and aunt shifting from phoenix to human earlier this week. Since the video went live, a lot of you—and I mean a *lot* of you—have asked questions. I can't answer them all, but I'll see what I can do with the most common queries. I'm here with the floating voice behind the camera who will prompt me when there's a question I forgot. Voice, would you like to say 'hi'?"

Felix rolled his eyes. "Um, hi."

Ember smiled. "Okay. I think I'll start with my story. I should cover a lot of what you all seem to be wondering about ..."

It took some time to explain about witches and phoenixes, magic and fire, but Ember tried to cover all the questions from the comments. A few times, when their mind went blank, they shifted their eyes to Daisy, who smiled and nodded encouragingly.

At the end, they blew out a breath. "Okay, does that cover everything? Are there other questions?"

Felix smiled. "Will you live forever?"

Ember's eyes widened. They didn't know all the questions Felix had. Instead of prepping, Daisy and Ember had gone to get camera ready. Again, they should stop being so shortsighted. "I don't actually know. I think I have the phoenix immortality, but I am half witch, so only time will tell." They smiled wide as both Felix and Daisy groaned.

Then, Felix bit his lip. "You don't have to answer this, but it's come up a lot. Have you ever died, and does it hurt?"

"Yes." Ember barked out a laugh. Felix knew at least part of the answer, but Ember didn't see any reason to not let everyone know the full truth. They were a phoenix, after all. "It hurts a lot. Zero stars; I do not recommend. I can be a bit accident-prone at times."

They didn't want to get into the idea that all phoenixes were accident prone—that they always ended up where trouble was—or that Infinite WISDOM had kidnapped them with the single purpose of trying to kill Ember to prove they may be a phoenix.

The only reason Mr. Shade and Mr. Wells hadn't put two and two together was because Ember never burned up. When a phoenix held a piece of moonstone, they died and rose, but not from their ashes. Ember thought the pain was worse, the healing was less, but the side benefits of not shifting their sex made it worth it.

During their time in Serafina Landing, they'd secured a new piece of moonstone. Mom had gotten it set into a bracelet that fit tight to Ember's wrist. They planned on never taking it off.

Now Felix's eyes twinkled. "In all the fantasy books, a bite from a werewolf turns a person into a wolf. Can you turn a person into a phoenix?"

Ember covered their mouth with their hands to stop from laughing and shook their head. "You wish. That isn't really a question, is it, oh floating voice of questions?"

"It is," Felix confirmed.

"Gods above. No. There is only one way to make a phoenix, and it isn't through biting. Please tell me that's the last one."

If they were getting into werewolf lore, wacky superstitions would be next.

"Well, there is one more, but I don't know if you want to answer it now. No, there are tons more, but I'll present you with one more."

Ember slumped. "What is it?"

"You haven't done fire magic in front of anyone who knows you. Will you do some now?" Tension grew palpable in the room. Ember realized it was Daisy watching her intently. *She's never really seen me do anything, has she?*

She'd seen small sparks when Ember started a fire at their campsite, but nothing more.

With a shrug, Ember created words in fire that read: *'That's all folks!'*

Chapter 19 - Best Seat At The Event

Ember

Saturday morning, Ember sat with Dad drinking coffee and having a bagel. "Are you and Mom going to the rally today? Is Vatra?"

Vatra came into the kitchen looking ready for the day. For the last week he'd been learning the lay of the land with Mom, Dad, and Aunts Nuri and Monte. The goal was to make him feel confident moving around town and get him caught up with everything that had been going on.

He selected a mug and filled it with coffee before sitting at the table. "I am. I didn't come all this way to stay on the sidelines. Since I got word that Feu and Fotia made it home safely and they're no longer a distraction, it's time I understand what this group is saying. From what I've learned online, this whole situation stinks. I can't imagine what anyone could say to sway a person with half a brain to follow along."

Ember agreed, but was glad Daisy wasn't there to hear those words. Though, it was possible their friend would've explained what the draw was without being hurt or offended.

"I agree," Mom said, coming in and pouring herself a cup of coffee. "But, Ember, I don't know if I want you going. You know everything they spew. There's no reason for you to put yourself in danger again."

Ember bristled. "There's always something new they bring up. I'll stay safe, I promise. And me and my friends, we have a plan. We don't intend to be seen."

Mom sighed and Dad's eyebrows rose. Varta chuckled. "The famous last words of every phoenix."

Infinite **WISDOM** had drawn a huge crowd. Bigger than any of the others Ember had seen. Though their whole family attended, Ember, Felix, and Daisy sat in a coffee shop across the street. With the loudspeakers set up all over the place, the three of them could hear everything that happened without being mistaken for part of the crowd.

At the beginning, the people running these circuses were obnoxious but contained to the school. Now they were dangerous and growing daily.

Ember themself had been attacked and 'killed.' If it hadn't been for being a phoenix, they wouldn't be sitting enjoying a double shot cappuccino and a prosciutto and egg breakfast sandwich. It was only by luck that Daisy had survived.

In the last couple weeks, since these productions had moved from the school to city-wide events, everything had shifted. Things seemed to be getting more charged and polarized. Not wanting to be in the mix, the three decided to play it safe.

The beginning of the show was much like all the others. Ambrose and Cress spoke about the values of witches versus humans. Though they couldn't see the stage, Ember could imagine the two prancing about, smiling, and gushing about the bigger picture.

"The humans outnumber us and want to bring *us* down."

"They're creating legislature to strip away our rights and make us slaves to their whims."

Daisy leaned forward. "You know, I spent several hours researching that one. Literally, there is nothing about that. Nothing. It is such a bald-faced lie."

Felix huffed out a laugh and sipped his coffee.

As the crowd cheered, Ember shook their head. "You'd think they'd come up with something interesting to say. They just keep repeating the same thing, over and over. I mean, there's usually something a bit different, but so much of it is the same. Especially these two. Maybe they don't think Cress can learn new lines."

The other two chuckled.

Daisy shook her head. "You know you've done it now, right? Now the group will say something to shock us all."

"What could they possibly say? Are they going to say something about phoenixes? Maybe our videos? What if one of those jerks calls me out by name? That would be a waste. I'm a nobody." Ember finished off their sandwich and debated a pastry.

"You never know, the videos are very popular, you know," Felix teased. He watched Ember eyeing the display and leaned over to kiss their cheek. "On it. A doughnut or a fruit tart?"

"Surprise me." They smiled.

Daisy narrowed her eyes. "Don't forget about me, lover-boy."

Felix laughed as he walked to the counter.

"And then there are the phoenixes. The firebirds." Ember jerked at the sound of Mr. Shade's oily voice as he called out their people. "Our long-lost shifters who gave us this future of human-loving peace. Without them we'd be in a better position. Because of them, the humans have spent the last two hundred years subjugating us, treating us not as equals, but as lesser creatures than we are, and soon, like slaves."

By the end Ember felt dirty as Mr. Shade's voice slithering over the field of his mindless followers, into the coffee shop, and to their ears.

"As Ash Savita said in his video, he was there, part of the *Committee of Ten*," he said the words like they left a bad taste in his mouth, "creating those shackles he calls laws that ensured our place as beings who would always have to bow down to humans." His voice lowered. "Are you content playing second fiddle to humans?"

The crowd roared. Ember couldn't make out what was said, but they could imagine them yelling in agreement. Ember and Daisy both gaped towards the stage. Ember's jaw dropped and shards of icy chills attacked their body.

Mr. Shade continued. "Are you happy knowing humans outnumber us and think they're better than us?"

Ember recognized this part of the speech. The questions, the responses. The new addition seemed to be over. But it was enough, and it was horrible. Though they'd expected phoenixes to be included, they still hated it.

Felix returned with the fruit tarts. "Don't worry. The people he's preaching to already know the phoenixes support humans. This shouldn't change much."

Despite his words, Ember thought a lot had changed. Phoenixes weren't an idea, they were them and their family. Their dad's name had been part of the presentation and that sent chills down their spine.

Ember's phone vibrated in their pocket. They were pretty sure it would be Mom or Dad telling them to head home. Things were too hot to stay out today, especially with how well-known the family had become. For all they knew, their pictures were being circulated—enemies numbers one, two, and three. Four if you included Aunt Nuri ... or would Mom be number four?

Gods above, we went from obscurity to complete notoriety in only a few days.

Pulling out their phone, they saw the text was from Monte. *Email from anonymous source. After the farce of an event, Cress and buddy will take a human-lover to bend in the walkway in south park for a 'talk.' Initiation for buddy. Can you monitor from above? Don't have anyone else. We need to know who 'buddy' is. Need to know if source is legit. We don't have time to get authorities in prior, but I'll call them in and hopefully they'll get there quickly.*

Ember shook with fury. They shot off a quick acknowledgement and stood. After showing the text to Felix and Daisy, they said, "I'm going to go and change. I'm going to spend the rest of my time during this horrible carnival in the sky. I'll talk to you two later."

Felix and Daisy gave Ember a hug before they headed out. Daisy followed. "Can I ... um help in any way?"

Ember started to say 'no' then stopped. "Yeah. Take my clothes. Then leave them in my backyard."

Daisy nodded. "Yeah, that makes sense."

Ember hugged their friend. "Thank you."

"What for?"

"For everything? For being you? Just ... thank you. I wish I could've told you sooner. You've been amazing." They hugged one more time. "I think you two should head home. Ambrose and Cress know you two are my best friends. I don't know that it's safe, even if you're at the coffee shop. I don't want anything else to happen to you."

Daisy nodded. "I'll let Felix know."

They found an alley and Daisy blocked the end while Ember changed. They turned invisible and shot up into the sky. Once aloft, they watched Daisy and Felix walk away from the event. They didn't know how much time they had so they circled until they could find Cress. He cheered and hooted. He was in a group with his friends, Brett and Jared. *Where are Ambrose and Josie?*

From this high up, Ember could ignore what the speaker said. At this point, they didn't want to know. As they flew, stretching their wings, a sense of peace came over them. They spun a few corkscrew twists and looptyloops. The pressure of the previous two weeks melted away. They wanted to fly farther, but knew they needed to keep close to the stage.

Finally, everyone below started to break apart. Ember was high in the clouds, but in their bird form, their eyesight was superb. They flew in a lazy spiral until they were halfway down, following Cress and Brett's progress. *Where is Jared? Maybe the initiation is only with one of them?*

The two merged into the massive crowd. It would've been hard to follow them, except for how happy they both were, waving their fists in the air and making enough ruckus that others moved away from them. They flanked some person, shorter than them, and hooked their arms in his. The man seemed to try to pull away, but Cress leaned down.

What is he saying? Whatever it was, the man calmed down.

As Ember watched, Cress and Brett got the man they'd targeted to the spot they wanted. They boxed him in and at first it looked like they just spoke to him. Then there was pushing, then punching. Ember watched as Mr.

Shade stepped out from the shadows of the trees and encouraged the actions of the teens.

Gods, I want to dive down and help, but that's not my role. If I get hurt I won't be allowed to help anymore.

It hurt Ember's soul to watch. They cried out, knowing that as high as they were, no one would hear. Shutting their eyes for a second, Ember pushed down the hurt of seeing the wanton violence. When they looked back down, Mr. Shade was no longer there. *Where did he disappear to? Back to the trees to watch? Did he leave?*

The authorities came, finally, but Cress ran. *Is he using earth magic to help his speed? Did he sense the police with his mental magic? Gods above and below, I wish he'd been caught.*

Ember saw Brett panic. He tried to choose a direction to scurry away, but the authorities nabbed him.

Their target was pretty badly beaten, but to Ember's relief, he appeared to still be alive.

Unfortunately, Cress and Mr. Shade went free.

Back at home, Ember wanted to scream. "It was awful. I haven't seen Brett working with the others. Was he auditioning? Was he trying to get in tight with Mr. Shade? Is this a situation where, to get into the organization, he had to prove he was willing to hurt someone? Beat them up?"

Dad wrapped them in a hug. "Shhh, it wouldn't really be that surprising. The whole organization is awful and a mess."

Hot tears ran down Ember's cheeks, soaking into Dad's shirt. "I just ... that man. Is he going to be okay?"

"Yes." Dad's voice sounded sure. "The authorities got there in time."

"But not in time for Mr. Shade," Ember snapped back.

"No, not in time for that weasel."

"You know, I could've removed his heart or put a fireball in his gut. No one would've known it was me." They hiccupped.

Dad rubbed their back. "No. I don't want you going down that path. You aren't violent, Ember. You did exactly what was asked of you."

In the kitchen, Aunt Monte typed on her laptop. "I just wish we'd gotten this information sooner. I don't know who this person is, but they definitely had the inside scoop."

Aunt Nuri's brow furrowed. "It didn't come from your normal source?"

"Normal source?" Ember pulled away from Dad and sat at the table. Too tired to stand, they pulled a soda from the fridge with a small push of magic.

Aunt Nuri nodded. "Can you grab one of those for me?" Ember did. "We have a person on the inside of Infinite WISDOM. They feed us information when it's safe. This is a second person. We know the first; we don't know who this other person is."

"Wait." Ember thought their head would explode. "You have a mole, and you know who it is?" Both their aunts nodded. "Who?"

Aunt Monte shook her head. "That is on a need-to-know basis, and as much as I may love you, Ember, you don't need to know. It isn't safe. The fewer people who know, the safer this person is."

Ember slumped. "Fine, I get it. So what are you going to do about this other person?"

Aunt Monte shrugged. "I guess I'll reply to the email and hope it wasn't a one-time thing."

Chapter 20 - There For The Taking

Ember

It had been a week, and it was time for Ember to expand their understanding of spatial magic. They sat cross-legged in the backyard next to a table. Around the table sat Mom and their Aunts Nuri and Monte. They were both interested in the magic and the lesson. Ember didn't mind the company.

"Okay, Ember, the theory is simple, the magic is challenging. You have to not only perform the skill, but you have to believe you can do it. I know that this is your hardest magic proficiency to accomplish. But I think you can do it."

They nodded. "Where do we start?"

"Well, we start with tacos."

Aunt Nuri chuckled. "Don't we all?"

"Um-hum," Aunt Monte agreed.

Ember smiled. "I like tacos ... are they for eating and energy?"

Mom waved her hand, and a platter of tacos appeared on the table.

Leaning over, Ember grabbed a pork taco and ate it. "So, how does good food explain this lesson? Because I assume it's more than energy I'm getting from this."

Both their aunts munched away as they looked between Ember and Mom.

Mom held up her beef taco. "If we think of the universe as being a tortilla—flat and mostly stable—then when we use spatial magic we pull an item to us across the flat surface. But there's another way. With our magic we can bend it, like this taco. If you can get the two points you want close to each other, adjacent, we can slip an item from point 'a' to point 'b.' Barely moving the item at all."

"Isn't that what we do with the magic anyway?" Ember asked, their brow furrowed. "When I pull an item to me, isn't that the theory? I mean, I've never really thought about it, but isn't that what it is?"

"No." Mom took a bite of her taco while she looked up at the clear blue sky. "Spatial magic in its most basic form is taking your magic, like an invisible hand, and grasping an item. That's why the farther away it is, the harder it becomes, and the more power you need to expend. When moving a single object, the magical hand is enough. The more powerful you are, the farther you can grasp something. The only limits are distance, weight, and ... well, if the item is alive. For some reason, the act of living adds extra weight to the object."

Ember ate their second taco as they listened to the lesson. "I think this all sounds familiar. You told it to me years ago when we started lessons in spatial magic, right?"

Mom smiled. "Probably. But then we moved on to air and fire magic. The lessons continued. It's possible I don't remember giving you the basic introduction." She sipped her soda. "If done right, this higher-level magic allows you to bend the space and move the object only a tiny distance."

"Okay, so how do I take a tortilla and make it into a taco? That seems ... hard. Like impossibly hard." Ember rubbed the back of their neck. "And when will I need to do that?"

"It's better to know and not need, than to need and not know, don't you think? I don't want you to be blind to one of your abilities. You've grown a lot in the last few years, and we've neglected your home studies. Well, it's time we get back at it."

"What do I do?" Ember wasn't sure about making the world into a taco, but they liked tacos, so they were up for anything.

"I want you to close your eyes and imagine something from your room is right in front of you. Maybe your desk. Try to construct as much detail as you can. Once you have the full image in mind, push a bit of magic out to create the passage to your room. Then reach out and grab something off your desk." Mom smiled after she finished explaining the exercise.

Aunt Monte's jaw dropped. "Is that even possible? You could store everything on your desk and never have to carry anything. It'd be amazing."

"It would, but you'd need to practice it to the point that it was second nature, and the energy output wasn't as much as it is right now." Mom looked at Ember. "Do you want to see me do it first?"

"Gods, yes! Right now that all sounds impossible." Ember's head pounded at the thought of doing all those steps.

Nodding, Mom sat still. After a moment, Ember felt the push of power. They saw a shimmer in front of Mom. Then she put her hand through the distortion. The image of Mom's arm truncated at the wrist looked weird.

When she pulled her arm out, she held a bottle of perfume.

Everyone gasped.

Ember licked their lips. Closing their eyes, they imagined their room and their desk. There was a laptop and a lamp. Their school bag was on the floor next to it. Three schoolbooks and two books for pleasure were on the top. *Come on, Ember, you were studying this morning. What else?* They couldn't think of anything else important.

They took a cleansing breath and pushed out their magic. After a few moments, they felt something happen, but when they opened their eyes, there wasn't a shimmer like what had appeared in front of their mom. Despite that they waved their hand.

Nothing.

The push of magic took energy. It had felt like someone had taken an ice cream scoop—a really big scooper—and stolen a chunk of everything that was them. With a shacking hand, Ember ate another taco.

Mom slid from her chair to sit next to Ember. "No one gets it on their first attempt."

Ember sighed. They started the sequence again ... and failed.

They kept at it for what felt like hours. In the end, Ember finally grabbed a book. Their head throbbed and their body trembled. "Gods above, Mom. What's the end game with this?"

"Isn't it obvious? Moving people."

Chapter 21 - Fired Up Mad

Ember

Ember got to school early on Monday. After their weekend, they happily arrived before the other students and escaped up to the Air Magic class to prepare to assist. Whereas they wouldn't mind seeing Daisy and Felix, who had Earth Magic class, they didn't mind *not* having class with Cress and Josie. Ember decided it wasn't a bad trade off. They were happy to not see Cress. Just thinking about the attack after the event turned Ember's stomach.

"Ember, you're early," Mrs. Vintl welcomed them to class.

"I just wanted to get here and relax before the students came, if that's okay?"

"Sure. I'm just finishing up my prep for the week. It was a long weekend. Some crazy things happened. You know, if you ever want to talk, I'm always here." She looked intently at Ember, as if trying to impart her support … maybe through telepathy.

Ember nodded and headed over to the wall to sit and wait for class to start. They appreciated the offer, but they were not lacking in people to talk to. What they needed was a place to decompress.

As students filed in, Xander, one of the ninth-years, came and sat down next to Ember. Before winter break, he'd asked Ember to help his sister, Zahra, with her fire magic class. Students didn't usually approach Ember before class, at least not in this section of Air Magic. On Tuesdays and Thursdays, Ember's old class, Daisy always sat with them, and often Simon was a pest. But in this class they were usually left alone.

Xander hugged his knees as he gazed at the group sitting in the center of the room. His shoulders rose to his ears, and he scrunched up his mouth.

With a sigh, they dove in. "Can I help you with something?"

Xander squeezed his legs in a bit tighter then clenched his jaw before saying, "When there's work time, can you help me in the private room?"

Ember let their head fall against the wall behind them. Xander thrived in air magic. He didn't need help. The class had been doing obstacle courses and he performed at the top of the class. What he didn't do well in was fire magic. When Ember helped his sister, he almost got burned by a fireball. Ember had to stealthily extinguish the fire so he wouldn't end up with third-degree burns. They were convinced that was what Xander really wanted help with today.

Ember wasn't sure why they could help people fix their magic. Ember and their parents figured it had to do with their unique combination of phoenix and witch abilities. They didn't know anyone else who could see the connection from witch to spell. Though Ember had tried to avoid helping anyone with fire proficiency, helping Zahra ended up working in the end. Initially, they'd used Olivia there as 'back up' to avoid someone getting hurt if there was another fireball. Now that everyone knew Ember's phoenix status, maybe Ember wouldn't have to avoid helping with fire magic ... but not during Air Magic class—now wasn't the proper time.

Hopefully, Xander wasn't going to ask about it now, but they worried that was exactly why he sat down.

"All right, class, gather over here so I can explain today's lesson," Mrs. Vintl said.

Seeing Xander's wide-eyed desperation, they nodded. "Alright. I'll come collect you in a few minutes."

He gave a single jerk of his head and headed to the mass of students in front of the teacher.

Once everyone got started on the task, Ember and Xander moved to the private practice room. After shutting the door, they forced a smile onto their face. "So, what can I help you with?"

His face contorted. He went from looking sad and desperate to scrunched up, narrow-eyed, and angry. "It's your fault I got burnt, isn't it?"

"What?" Ember couldn't piece together his logic. They'd stopped the fireball from burning him.

"Don't play dumb, phoenix." He sneered out that last word, like it was a swear. "All this time, first you act like you have no magic, then you suddenly can do air magic, and now, what? You're basically made of fire?" He started off counting off on his fingers, but the end, he threw his arms out to the sides. His eyes narrowed as his face contorted and his voice lowered. "What happened that day in the courtyard with Zahra? Were you the one who controlled the fireball and made me think it was me? Did you walk home laughing at what a fool the kid was for thinking he could manipulate fire?" His arms started waving around as his voice rose. "Were you hoping I'd get burned later? No wonder everyone hates you and all your human-loving friends."

By the end he was spitting mad.

Though Ember bristled at most of what he had to say, they had to answer some of his grievances. They lifted their hands in a placating manner. "I've never laughed at you, or anyone, for that matter. Honestly, you're doing well in fire magic ... but yes, that day in the courtyard I helped. Neither—"

"I knew it!" he snarled. "Mocking me and Zahra."

"No. It wasn't like that. I was trying to help." Ember tried to keep a level voice.

"Sure you were," he spat. "That's all your kind ever does, tries to help—to the detriment of witches. Why don't you stop trying to help and leave us alone? Can't you just disappear like the rest of your kind?" He stepped around Ember, glaring at them, and left the room.

Trembling, Ember took a few minutes to decompress. *It's only first period. How many more Infinite WISDOM followers will I have to battle before the day is done? Am I their main target here at school?*

They headed back to class, yearning for their days of anonymity.

Chapter 22 - Spying On The Enemy

Daisy

Daisy woke early and liked to get to school before the other students. Travel coffee mug in hand, she was ready to tackle the day and any challenge a teacher threw at her. Now that Ember helped out in Air Magic class on Mondays and Wednesdays, she no longer had someone to goof off with in the morning. She got to her locker to drop off her math and Spanish textbooks, then headed out to Earth Magic class.

She missed having Ember in the class, but at least Felix was there ... eventually.

The class met in a field, but there was a tree she could lean against while she waited for class to begin. Not wanting to socialize with the rest of the class, she sat on the far side from the school and pulled out her phone. No reason not to check out the videos on the FB coalition page and see how they were doing.

Before she even logged into her phone, she heard Cress's voice, and her body tensed. Her body trembled when she remembered his voice as he and his goons put her in the hospital. Daisy licked her lips and pushed against the tree to remind herself she was at school, and safe.

No one will attack you here.

With a quick glance, she saw both Cress and Josie.

She wasn't sure what had happened over the last few weeks, but Cress had started behaving worse, bolder in his slimy ways. Before, Josie had always grated on her, but lately she'd almost seemed meek compared to the jerk Cress had become. Daisy didn't try to hide, but she didn't attempt to get either of their attention.

"Tell me again, Josie. You definitely heard me and Brett speaking, right?"

"Well, yeah, of course I did. It was just the group of us at the table. After you tossed the others from where we sit, no one else dares even try. You made our space like royalty." Josie sounded like she wanted to please or placate him.

"Right, that's because we are, babe." The two stopped in the field, just within Daisy's line of sight, though they were apparently too wrapped up in their conversation to notice her. "Me and Ambrose, we're royalty. And anyone me and Ambrose invite can sit with us." He drew his finger across her jaw line. "Maybe one day you'll be royalty, too, babe."

Josie's eyes widened. "May-maybe ... ah ... me?" Daisy saw the other girl's chest heave as if Cress's touch were more than her tiny head could handle. *Gross!* And what was Cress doing flirting with Josie? Wasn't he in a power couple relationship with Ambrose?

Cress leaned down, looking as if he'd kiss Josie. "Now, Josie:, did you *tell* anyone about what you heard? You know you can tell me. We're friends. You can tell me anything."

No! Don't tell him anything Josie! It's a trap! Daisy wanted to jump up and shake Josie, but she didn't think it would help.

Josie gulped. "No. Who would I tell? My parents are human-lovers. They don't get any of this. I stopped talking to *them* months ago. I feel dirty even looking at them."

"And right you should, babe." Cress cupped her face. "I'm glad you didn't tell anyone. I just want to make sure. Nobody. You don't have any other friends?"

Josie looked like she would swoon. "No." The one word came out breathlessly. "Just you and Ambrose. Everyone else is a wannabe. You know, wants to be like us or hang out with us."

Cress straightened up, a reptilian smile slithering across his face. "Right you are, babe. Right you are."

There was the sound of murmurs from the direction of the school. Daisy looked around the far side of the tree and saw other students venturing out for class.

Before any of them got there, Cress leaned down close to Josie's ear. He could've spoken softly, but Daisy still heard every word. "It won't be long, babe. You know you're who I want, don't you? We just have to keep up appearances. For now. You keep listening to me and doing what I say, and everything will work out how it's supposed to be. How it should've always been." He gave her a small peck on her cheek, and she froze until class started.

Nausea slithered down Daisy's throat. The thought of Cress touching anyone made Daisy want to throw up. She'd never liked him, but after he'd put her in the hospital, the idea of his hands on anyone, especially a female, gave Daisy flashbacks.

Once Felix got there, things got a bit better, but she couldn't wait for class to end. Then again, she had another class with the two of them ... well, with Josie. Cress still wasn't coming to Magical History.

In third period, Daisy had Math class. Ember and Felix were in a stupid high math for brainiacs. She was in Pre-Calculus. It was still respectfully hard, just not as difficult. Somehow, Simon and Ambrose were in class with her. She'd've expected Simon to be in with her other friends.

The class was held in a potions classroom, so everyone sat at large lab tables. As always, Simon sat next to her. He leaned in. "Can I talk to you about your stay in the hospital?"

"I would rather not." Talking to him made her skin itch. Not as much as hearing Cress talk, but not much less.

"Why not?" His face hardened. He had such a bad temper.

"Because, Simon, you had plenty of time over winter break, and I don't want to fight. You don't believe me and facts are facts regardless of if you want to see what's right in front of your nose or not." Annoyed, she gathered her stuff and stood. She suddenly realized the only other place to sit was next to Ambrose.

Clenching her jaw, Daisy slowly walked and sat next to one of the last people she wanted to talk to. Ambrose barely gave her a glance.

The teacher presented a challenge problem they'd be working on during class. "If you want to work with your table-mate, go for it. It'll make your processing easier. You know what they say, two minds are better than one."

Daisy and Ambrose gazed at each other, then both started working on their own. The problem was hard, but fun. After ten minutes in, Ambrose sighed. "Have you gotten to this part yet?"

Daisy looked at her paper. Ambrose was just behind Daisy's work. *Damn, the mean girl has a head on her shoulders.* "Yeah." Daisy showed Ambrose her paper.

Ambrose narrowed her eyes and quickly read over Daisy's work. "Thanks."

The two began working together. Their approaches were similar, and they worked well as partners. It felt like a business arrangement. They each filled in the pieces the other missed.

When they were almost done, Daisy realized the incident in Earth Magic class had been niggling at her. She sighed. "Did you know Cress was flirting with Josie in Earth Magic class? Is this some joke in poor taste the two of you are playing on her?"

There was a moment Daisy didn't think Ambrose would answer. Daisy wasn't sure she'd have answered. "No, no prank." Ambrose sounded tired. "It doesn't shock me, but it also doesn't please me. Thank you for letting me know. Now, can we get back to this? I'd like to finish it before class ends."

Daisy rolled her eyes. *Is this what it means to be popular? I am so glad I actually like my friends.* "Whatever."

Chapter 23 - The Good, The Bad, And The Ugly

Ember

Ember got home from school on Monday and grabbed a quick snack. They sat at the kitchen table with soda, chips, salsa, guacamole, and a chocolate brownie. Smiling, they took a bite of the soft gooey chocolate first and shut their eyes to savor the treat.

The first step of the spell was to form an image of their desk. Ember breathed deeply and tried to include everything in their mental reconstruction. This morning before school they'd taken a picture with their phone and had been studying it off and on during the day. That level of detail hadn't been available during the first attempt at the spell, but Ember hoped it would help make everything easier.

With a final mental push, Ember created a portal and pulled their favorite notebook into the kitchen.

Applause told them they weren't alone. They looked up to see Vatra standing in the doorway. "Sorry to be watching. I didn't mean to interrupt. That was really cool."

Ember shrugged with a big smile. They liked their cousin and hadn't been able to spend much time with him. "No worries. Come sit. Are you enjoying your stay?"

"There hasn't been much going on. I've mostly been here or learning the lay of the land. Everyone has been busy."

Ember nodded. "Yeah, we all seem to get that way."

"Do you need to practice again?" He waved at the notebook.

Mom told them to practice whenever they had a moment so the process would get easier. Ember finished their brownie then nodded. "One more."

They repeated the process, imagining folding space like a taco and grabbing the pen that had been lying next to the notebook. *Now I'm hungry for Mexican food ... great.* The second attempt was both easier and harder. Getting the image set was faster; having the reference of the spicy food helped mold what Ember needed to do. However, since they'd already expended their magic for the notebook, the second push felt more like digging through sludge.

Once the taco magic was completed, they slumped. Then they dug into their snack, hoping the 'easier' Mom promised would happen soon.

It's only been a couple of days, and I've only done this successfully a handful of times. I have to give myself a break.

Vatra got up and snagged two more brownies, placing one on Ember's plate. "That was different from the regular spatial magic, right? You didn't just pull an object to you, the way you do soda at dinner, right? It's something more?"

"Yeah. I'm learning to move bigger things," Ember said as they broke off a chunk of chocolate. "Mom said one day I may be able to move people."

Vatra shook his head. "That's amazing." He stole one of their chips and dipped it in the salsa. "So, not to change the subject, but I'm going with Monte to see more of the town today. We're planning to visit the hospital. She's going to do some healing. Do you want to join us?"

Ember perked up. "Yeah, that sounds great! Just the three of us?"

"If that's okay." He winked. "I know you like hanging with your friends, but can you survive just spending time with us old folks?"

Finishing their brownie, Ember chuckled. "Old? Never! You don't look a day over a thousand."

Ever since Aunt Monte learned that the magical proficiency practitioners today were weaker than in the past, she'd considered doing more for the injured. Her abilities had been strong when she'd been young, but after two hundred years, like Mom, she was a powerhouse.

Once they arrived at the hospital, Ember was saddened to see how full the facility was. There didn't seem to be an empty bed available. The number of injured people had grown because of the last event. Before arriving, Aunt Monty had secured a list of the patients with the most need. She led their group to the first room, and after going in and getting permission, Vatra and Ember were allowed in to observe. The young woman lying in the bed, probably in her twenties, with light brown hair and brown eyes, stared at Ember. She had multiple broken bones, internal injuries, and a concussion. She smiled at Ember, eyes bright and mouthed 'phoenix.'

Vatra and Ember stood back while Aunt Monte worked. A glow seemed to cover both her and the patient as she performed her healing. Ember watched—using their magical vision during part of it—as the power moved from Aunt Monte to one of the injuries. The efficiency was breathtaking.

It took Aunt Monte about a half hour to repair the young lady's injuries. Once Aunt Monte was done, the woman sighed. "I was told the healing would take half a day, and at least two or three sessions. Thank you."

The people in the second and third rooms didn't want anyone but Aunt Monte to enter. Ember and Vatra waited in the cafeteria, drinking substandard coffee and eating monster-sized muffins.

After the third patient, Aunt Monte found them and collapsed into a chair with a sigh. "I'm wiped out. I haven't done that much healing in a while. I should practice more." She reached over to tap Ember's nose. "Like you with your desk." She raised an eyebrow with her cryptic comment.

They were in public, and Aunt Monte wasn't about to mention spatial magic or portals.

Ember smiled and nodded. "You're not wrong, though you're starting from a much stronger place."

As the three of them left the hospital, one of the administrators stopped them to speak to Aunt Monte. "Mrs. Doyle, what you did today with three of our most extreme cases was amazing. Most of the medics can only do one a day, maybe two for the very strong, or only less severe cases. We were wondering if we could get you on rotation. We are in critical need of healers."

Aunt Monte considered the man. "Give me your number. I'll contact you when I have an idea of my schedule."

I wonder why healing has become such a weak proficiency. And how did spatial magic all but disappear? Shouldn't all magics be encouraged, developed, and made to be the best they can be? I need to talk to Mom about this.

It was late when they left the hospital. They were all hungry and decided to head to a restaurant for dinner. Aunt Monte's favorite spot was a bit upscale, but they decided to splurge.

When they arrived, the place was full. Ember sighed. "I'll go put our name in. Aunt Monte, you can rest." Ember knew this would probably be out of Vatra's wheelhouse.

They weaved their way through the crowd to the hostess stand. There were a few people in front of them, a couple who looked to be on a date, and a family of four. Listening to the time, Ember's body drooped thinking about how long everything would take.

"How many?"

The pert voice caught Ember off guard. They'd been lost in thought and missed when the other people had moved off. "Oh, yeah, sorry. Table for three, please."

The blond woman looked up from her pad. "That'll be—" Her jaw dropped. "Gods above, you're the person from the video, or *videos*, right? You did that thing with fire. You made words, right? You're Ember ... Ember Savita. Hold on."

Before Ember could say another word, the woman dashed off. There was a ruckus, and then a man returned, tall and round, with a thick mustache and beard. "Well, Ms. Savita—can I call you that?"

"Um ... sure?" Part of Ember wanted to gather Aunt Monte and Vatra and run. They were completely lost with everything that was going on. "It's my name. Unless you'd rather just call me Ember."

A wide smile spread across the man's face. "Why, yes. I'd like that."

A hand landed on Ember's shoulder, and they quickly looked back to see that Vatra and Aunt Monte had joined them.

It took another few seconds, but the man, who had been searching the reservation book, finally looked back up. "Did you mention if you'd prefer a table by the window?"

"No." Ember couldn't imagine how much longer specifying where they wanted to sit would take. "Just the first available, please. We've had a long day."

"Right, right, of course you have. Follow me. We'll put you in the best seat we can. Next time, call first and we'll do better."

Confused, but unwilling to argue with immediate seating, the three followed the man to a table near the center of the restaurant.

At the table, Ember leaned in. "What just happened?"

Vatra chuckled. "You're a celebrity. Didn't you know? Everyone knows you. Especially in the right crowds."

Scrunching up their face, Ember resisted growling. "I can't believe how much fuss those videos have caused."

He gave them a warm smile. "Well, at least you're getting something good from all of it., right?"

"That's true."

After reading over the menus, they ordered. As they waited for their food, a shadow darkened the table. Ember looked up and saw Ambrose's dad and Mr. Shade.

All the happy goodwill fled from Ember, replaced with a burning hate. They hadn't seen their jailers since they'd left Ember in Cress's care after days of trying to figure out creative ways to harm them. If anyone personified evil, it was these two.

Across from them, they saw Vatra's eyes narrow, as if he were classifying who the two men were.

Ember's voice dropped to a growl. "What do you want?"

Mr. Shade scoffed. "Better question, what are the likes of *you* doing here? Shouldn't you be slumming it somewhere?"

Aunt Monte laughed. "Really? We're sitting at a restaurant, and you want to know what we're doing? Are you dumber than I thought? Because, if I were to be honest, I thought you were pretty limited to begin with."

Vatra nodded, then shook his head. Ember figured he'd identified the two bullies.

Both men's lips twitched. Mr. Shade's voice lowered as he ignored Aunt Monte and continued to stare at Ember. "Are these your family members? More phoenixes?" He said the last as if the word left a bad taste in his mouth.

"Look, Tad," Aunt Monte narrowed her eyes. Apparently, she didn't think he deserved any sort of respect ... her being older and a ton wiser, Ember didn't blame her. "I just got done healing people you and your goons put into the hospital. I'm tired, I'm hungry, and frankly, I don't need to or want to spend time speaking with you and any of your 'entourage.' Would you please leave? I assume you have your own table somewhere in this establishment."

Mr. Wells scoffed. "Just because you claim to have used magic doesn't mean you aren't a firebird." He waved his hand toward Ember. "This one is both witch and phoenix." His face crumpled in disgust. "How many of you half-breeds are there, anyway?"

Vatra scoffed. "You two should leave. This is a restaurant, not a schoolyard. And frankly, none of us are intimidated by you."

"Sure you are," Mr. Shade snapped back. "Because none of you have answered if you're phoenixes or not. What, are you ashamed?"

"No," Ember said, sighing heavily. "We're tired and hungry. She," Ember pointed to Aunt Monte, "already explained she's been healing all day. I had school, and he," they pointed at Vatra, "just arrived in town. All we want to do is eat in peace. But you wouldn't know about peace, would you?"

Mr. Shade opened his mouth to respond, but one of the servers came over. "Please, sirs, if you could please return to your seats. You're disturbing the other customers, and your meal is ready."

Mr. Shade turned on the server. "Do you know you're serving known human-lovers? Do you support the humans in this establishment? Do you serve them? Do you treat humans and shifters as equals to witches?" His voice rose with each question. He rotated on the spot, throwing his arms in the air. "I refuse to give my hard-earned money to an establishment that treats humans as equals to magic users. A place that serves *them!*" He pointed at Ember.

As the two men left, the other diners paused to watch them go. None of them applauded or followed, they just gazed, then returned to their meal. Impressively, no one seemed to give Ember or their table any extra attention, either.

At the door, Mr. Shade huffed in annoyance, before walking out.

Aunt Monte leaned in. "The owner is part of our group. I'm surprised those idiots even came here."

A smile spread on Ember's face as they leaned back and relaxed, ready to enjoy the rest of the night.

Chapter 24 - A Very Long Day

Ember

On Tuesday morning, Ember watched as everyone worked on their air magic. Everyone seemed to be focused and doing well. There was over a half-hour left of class, and Ember didn't think anyone needed their help.

When they passed the teacher during the circling of the students, they caught her attention. "Mrs. Vintl?"

"Yes?" They both watched as one of the tenth-years got their notebook to lift an inch before it crashed down. It was the best Sonny had done yet. "Good job, Sonny, keep it up!"

"Everyone is doing great. Do you think I could go to the practice room alone and do some independent study? Mom has given me some lessons to work on." Ember raised both their eyebrows and smiled wide.

Mrs. Vintl rotated in a full circle, checking over where each student was in their lesson. Then she nodded. "I think that will work. But remember, Ember: you're here to help, not for independent study."

"I know. I won't make this a habit. Thank you!"

Ember opened the door and gave the class one last look. Daisy gave them a questioning gaze. Simon glared. They waved at Daisy and mouthed 'later.' Simon, they ignored.

Sitting crossed-legged in the center of the room, Ember began their spatial lesson. This morning they'd left an energy bar in the back seat of their parents' car, just in case. This would help expand their ability by shifting their target. It would also give them the calories they needed if they succeeded.

It took four attempts to fully get the car formed in their mind and the magic portal created. It had been the same with their desk, but they'd hoped it wouldn't take so much of their energy. Once they had the bar in their hand,

Ember slumped and quickly ate it. Their body trembled but a feeling of triumph surged through them. *I did it!*

When they looked at their watch, there was only a few minutes left of class. They left the room and found a student to help.

In their third period math class, Ember dropped into their seat with a grunt. They liked this class. No expectation beyond sit, take notes, and be a nameless student in the crowd.

Felix sat down next to them. "You act like you've been mauled by a bear, you know that right? Last period wasn't bad."

"Cress returned and he was in fine form. I forgot how nice it was to not have him in any of my classes." Ember sighed. "Did you see how many slights he slid into his answers about both humans and phoenixes? He stayed just under the line of appropriateness." They blew out a breath. "Mr. Elias appeared just as annoyed as us. Do you think Cress has been trained?"

"Probably." Felix laughed. "He's not clever enough to be able to do that on his own. And, if you think about the last week, Ambrose hasn't been as snide lately. And Josie, she's been downright silent."

"Ember, we need to talk." Zahra, Xander's sister, slid into the desk in front of Ember's. It was still empty, and there wasn't a seating chart. That said, students rarely changed where they sat.

So much for my relaxing class. Yesterday, Xander yelled at me. What? Did he tell Zahra so she could tag-team with him today?

"Yeah, sure." Ember's voice was flat. "What? We only have a couple of minutes, you know."

Next to them, Felix looked interested. Ember hadn't told him about their encounter with Xander. There hadn't been a good time up until now.

"Right, I wanted to talk to you about Ring of Fire." Her face stayed tight with challenge.

Ember raised their eyebrows. Ring of Fire was the name of an elite fire magic club only accessible to the twelfth-year students. The best of the best were invited in and given lessons on high-level magic by teachers and members of the community. These were the students who were given scholarships to the best colleges and who ended up being leaders in magical society ... without having to pay their way in.

The other proficiencies had their own clubs, but historically, fire was the top of the top. There was no way the group would be opening its doors to an eleventh-year.

That would never happen, though a spark of hope kindled within Ember. *What would the rest of the school think if I got into such an elite club?* They had to bite back a snort. "Sure, what?"

"I need you to teach me something so I can get in with them."

The feeling of ice-cold water extinguished that spark of hope, bringing Ember back down to reality. "What? Why?"

She huffed. "Because you—" Zahra bit her bottom lip. "Look, you helped me before. You know how my magic works. I just thought ... maybe. Can you help me?"

Ember slumped. "But don't you want to avoid being seen with a phoenix? Someone who respects humans?"

Zahra barked out a laugh. "Xander?" Ember nodded but tried not to sneer. Zahra continued, "He's an idiot. He told me what he did yesterday, and I gave him a piece of my mind about *that*. One day he'll grow up, and if I'm lucky, that day will be really soon." She looked between Ember and Felix and shook her head. "This whole Infinite WISDOM thing is crap. Anyone who follows them is a mindless imbecile. I have no idea how it's grown so fast."

The teacher stood at his desk, and Zahra's eyes grew, gazing between the front of the room and Ember. She mouthed, 'Please?'

Ember nodded. "Yeah, okay, fine. After school."

At lunch, Ember sat with Daisy, Tansy, and Olivia. When Felix arrived, he leaned in and said, "Okay, spill. What did Xander do in Air Magic class yesterday? And why didn't you tell us?"

Ember turned to Tansy. "Did Olivia tell you about my fire tutorial?"

Tansy's brow furrowed. "When you helped Zahra?"

Olivia's eyes widened. "You said the time before there had been an issue with a fireball. Xander was so happy he'd done something ... but it wasn't him, was it? And wait, hold on, you didn't even need me there, did you?"

Ember sighed. "Xander already yelled at me about this." They went on to tell them about Monday's class.

"Gods above and below, what arrogance!" Daisy snapped. "You help him and his sister. He thinks he manages something for the first time. My guess is, instead of taking the lesson slow, he jumped into something big. Then he got burned. Feeling embarrassed, he blamed you, like an infantile brat."

"Exactly!" Tansy agreed. "What a jerk."

"Did you tell him where to stuff it?" Olivia asked.

Felix just wrapped his arm around Ember's waist.

Muscles Ember didn't realize were tense relaxed. This was why they had the best friends in the school.

"Despite that, you're going to help Zahra after school?" Felix asked.

"What?" Daisy asked, face contorted in disgust. "Is she in the Shady camp as well?"

"No," Ember laughed sardonically, "I don't think so." They described what happened in math class.

Olivia perked up. "Can I come? I'd love to see some advanced fire magic. What we're learning in class is interesting, but class is always slow. Ambrose tries to act like she's the only one who can do anything and takes over. It's obnoxious."

"I guess," Ember nodded, understanding how Ambrose could be ... Ambrose. "But I don't think all of us showing up would be good. Zahra may get overwhelmed."

Olivia and Daisy joined Ember to the courtyard. Daisy argued that having someone with water magic couldn't be all bad when playing with fire, though Ember couldn't imagine what the others could do with fire that they couldn't undo.

Zahra showed up with her brother. Ember's face hardened upon seeing Xander.

Isn't it enough that I have to see him tomorrow?

Xander stopped halfway between Ember and their friends, and the door. He screwed his face up into a scowl and crossed his arms over his chest.

Zahra closed the distance. "I had to bring Xander; I'm his ride home. I told him to stay in the library or my car, but he refused, saying he didn't trust me with you."

"Whatever," Ember mumbled. "Okay, do you have any idea of what you want to do?"

The courtyard got quiet. Then Xander barked out a laugh. "You're a hack, Ember. You can't help my sister. Zahra, we should go. This is a waste of time."

"Xander, I told you if you said anything you'd have to leave. Last chance. One more word and you're walking home." Zahra glared at him.

"But that's over a mile!" he complained.

She just looked at him, face tight, eyebrows high.

Xander didn't respond.

Finally, Zahra turned back to Ember. "Can you teach me to create something besides a fireball?"

Ember turned to the center of the courtyard and debated as images flitted through their mind. Then a rose, a tree, a cat, and the word 'hi', each appeared. "What do you think you'd like to try to create?"

Zahra's eyes widened. "What's easiest?"

Olivia stepped up. "Fire likes to be in a circle or rectangle. The rose and word would be hard." She squinted, then waved her hand and a distorted cupcake appeared.

A smile spread on Ember's face. "Rotate your hand about halfway and close your fingers ... slowly."

When her fingers were halfway closed, the cupcake became clear, and Olivia laughed in glee.

Zahra nodded. "Okay, I think I see what she did." She pushed out her own magic and a small sideways rectangle appeared.

"That's great." Daisy said. "But what is it?"

"A cake." Zahra said. "At least that's what I thought I was making."

"Good, good." Ember could see where Zahra had been going with it. "Okay, let's try something. With your other hand imagine a number one—thin and small. Then in a reverse karate chop, move the hand upwards."

Zahra took a calming breath, then followed Ember's directions. A small fiery line grew from the top of the rectangular fire. It was a bit crooked. Ember and Zahra discussed a few alterations of hand position and speed, and after a few minutes, the small bit of fire on top took the shape of a candle, making it look like a cake.

They all dissipated their fire and Zahra hugged Ember. "Thank you. That was ... hard, but great. I know I need to practice, but I see what you did with softening the corners and stiffening the sides. I don't think anyone in the school but the three of us can do this now. Again, thank you."

"I can't believe you hugged a human-loving phoenix," Xander mumbled.

With a sigh, Zahra rolled her eyes. "You get to walk."

Ember clamped their jaw shut, breathing slowly to avoid showing any reaction. Part of them was thrilled Xander was getting a consequence for his remarks, but there was no reason for him to know that. Shooting Olivia and Daisy quick glances, they saw similar blank expressions.

"What? Why?" Xander whined.

"I did warn you. Not to mention, I don't really want to spend any more time with such hate. It's not my idea of time well spent."

Chapter 25 - Here And ... Still Here

Ember

Wednesday slid by without incident. In Air Magic, Xander ignored Ember, successfully performing his skills as usual. Cress was absent from Magical History, and no one seemed to miss him. In math, Zahra told Ember and Felix she arranged an interview for Ring of Fire on Friday. She could have two witnesses.

"Can you invite Olivia for me? Both of you helped, and I think she'll probably be in the club next year," Zahra got out before the class began.

Olivia had to cover her excitement during Magical Creations, where they both created four glass spheres. Ember made two air balls and two fireballs; Olivia's balls were all fire. Her other proficiencies were mind and void—not really ones that were easily stuffed into a container of glass.

Once they were at lunch she exploded. "Oh, my gods. I can't believe I'm going to be going to one of those meetings. They are so ... I don't know, exclusive. Ambrose always brags that she'll be the next leader, never considering anyone else is good enough." Olivia smirked. "I mean, I know my fire magic is good, and the group uses class scores not popularity, but I'm quiet. I just ... my mind is blown."

Gym, English, and Spanish slipped by, and then Ember was ready to head home. They invited Daisy to join them. There was a project they were assigned in Spanish, and if they worked quickly, they could get it done in an hour and have one less assignment hanging over their head.

In the kitchen, Daisy unpacked her bag while Ember collected sustenance: chips, bananas, and sodas.

The two got to work, and by the time Dad came in to shoo them out, they'd finished Spanish and had moved on to math, each working on their own homework.

"I need to get dinner started and you're taking up part of my prep space. Don't you have a bedroom or living room or dining room you can do all of that stuff in?" He waved his hand at their collective clutter.

Ember stood and kissed his cheek. "Sorry, Dad. We'll get out of your way. We were just finishing up, anyway."

"Maybe I should go. I don't want to get in the way." Daisy slung her bag over one shoulder.

Ember looked over to ask Dad if Daisy could stay, but he was already lost in his cooking.

Mom walked in and looked at the two of them. "You could go, or you could watch Ember's next lesson ... that is, if you don't mind, love."

Daisy's eyes widened and a huge smile spread across her face. "Can I?"

Absently, Ember nodded at Daisy but spoke to Mom. "Am I doing more of the same? I've been practicing, and it *is* getting a bit easier."

"No." Mom jerked her head towards the backyard. "I want you to know and understand all the intricacies of this proficiency. Even if you can't do everything I teach right away, with practice, it'll come."

Ember spun on their heel and headed back to the fridge to grab the remainder of the tray of brownies. There were only a few left. Then they headed out back.

"So, you want to fill my head with complicated magic. Have me practice. And expect me to fail?" They asked slowly with a bit of humor in their tone. Ember placed the tray down and selected a brownie.

"Not exactly. I'm hoping you'll be successful. I just don't want to set either of our expectations too high."

Daisy took one of the brownies and sat in a lawn chair. "What exactly will Ember be able to do ... you know, if they don't fail?"

Mom smiled. "I want Ember to create a bend in space, touching two locations together—"

"Like a taco," Ember said in a droll tone.

"Like a taco," Mom agreed. "At a high enough level, this can create a portal that moves a person ... or two, over a distance."

"Who am I moving and where?"

"Well, ideally, you move yourself. As I stated before, this can take time and may be dangerous," Mom said. "The magic recognizes the practitioner and protects them. Anyone traveling with the witch ... they can get hurt. So, until you have this down and can do it well, you will only do this with yourself."

Ember gulped. "Okay, never with a passenger. Check."

Daisy laughed.

Mom launched into the theory behind the magic and what Ember needed to do. The process was similar to what they'd been doing to grab items through small portals ... but so much more. Their head spun a bit with all the new information. Once the lesson was over, Ember closed their eyes and took a moment to breathe. Then they began.

The focus and drain in power caused their body to tremble. Their head pounded. This wasn't a single release but a continual pouring of everything the witch had into the spell.

After what felt like a lifetime, Ember sagged and opened their eyes. The air wavered in front of them, but when they waved their hand in the distortion, they knew it hadn't worked.

"It's okay, love. No one gets it on the first try." Mom handed them a mug of steaming hot coffee. When Ember took a sip, it was sweeter than normal, but right then, they didn't care. They just needed the energy boost and something to help with the dizziness.

"Can you try again?" Daisy asked. "I know your mom said you had to keep a constant flow of magic pouring out, but did you drain yourself dry?"

Ember slowly nodded. "Not dry, but close to. I don't think that's something you do more than once a day ... or maybe once a week. I'm exhausted."

Mom scoffed. "Nonsense. You'll be able to try again tomorrow. Every night until you figure it out."

Ember gaped, and Daisy laughed.

Chapter 26 - Hitting A Wall

Ember

Despite a good night's sleep, Ember woke up Thursday morning with a headache. The new schedule of magic lessons was taking a toll on their reserves, and their body felt beaten up.

Trembling, they pushed themself from bed and found their favorite outfit: a soft sweatshirt that read, '*My favorite thing about people is their pets*', and a well-worn pair of jeans.

In the kitchen they found everyone: Mom, Dad, and cousin Vatra. A full breakfast was set out. Ember moaned with as much joy as they could muster at seeing the food as they filled a plate with scrambled eggs, bacon, and toast. Dad poured them some coffee.

He narrowed his eyes. "You don't look very good. Are you sick?"

"No, just drained."

Mom sat down next to them. "It'll get better, love. I promise." She rubbed Ember's back. "That was your first attempt at such a big spatial magic spell, and you did a great job."

Ember made a noncommittal sound as they dug into their food. "It isn't about if I'll get used to it, but how long it'll take."

Mom just smiled as she sipped her coffee.

Vatra put down his mug. "Have you heard about the protests? I want to go and check them out, see how bad they are. Maybe we can help the businesses that are being targeted."

Dad grunted. "Idiots. The damn mindless followers of that man. They're disrupting everything."

"Wait, what's happening?" Ember perked up a bit, pulled from their own thoughts, and searched all the faces at the table.

Vatra sighed. "The Infinite WISDOM followers ... they're picketing any business that allows humans to shop in their establishment. In some cases, they just march if they think a human is in the building. They really haven't done any due diligence."

"The idiots are popping up like cockroaches," Dad mumbled.

"Are the cops doing anything to stop this?" Ember finished their breakfast and stood to clear their dishes and make lunch for school. Food and coffee really helped to make them feel human. Given the conversation, the thought made them smile. *Why can't everyone see we're all just human in the end?*

Mom followed them and pointed to a bag she'd already prepared. "There are too many locations being protested. They need to make sure they're available for real crimes."

"Like the people ending up in the hospital?" Ember asked, giving their mom a quick hug in thanks for making them lunch.

"Like exactly that," Dad agreed.

Ember put their shoes on. "Is it safe? I mean, no offense, but Vatra, you're pretty new to all of this."

Dad grunted. "I'm going with him. We all need to know what's going on. Nuri may join us as well."

Ember looked forward to seeing Daisy this morning. She knew about the previous night's lesson and how tired they would be. Ember hoped the class was as independent as Tuesday and no one needed their help. After everything they'd done, Ember was pretty sure they couldn't do any complicated air magic. Right now they only felt confident with their fire.

Ironic—the only thing I feel good about doing is the one thing I don't ever do in school.

Sitting in the Air Magic classroom, they sagged against the wall and bent up their knees. They rested their forehead on their legs. It was fifteen minutes before class and probably five minutes until the class started filling in.

Footsteps approached. They looked up, expecting to see Daisy. Mrs. Vintl stood staring down at them. "Ember, are you okay?"

"You are not the first to ask me that, but yeah, I'm fine. I'm just tired. What are we doing today?" They pushed up to standing.

"I'm tempted to tell you to go into the private study room and nap." Ember's eyes widened in hope. "But, unfortunately, I can't. The class is continuing to work on the same lesson. As you know, they're all doing well."

"I'm confused. If the class is doing well, what will I be doing? Are there some students you want me to help move ahead in some way?" It felt like a hammer was beating on the left side of their head. They'd do almost anything for more coffee.

"Well, not in this class. Mr. Tine in Fire Magic class asked if you could come down to the east field and help him today. We were discussing lessons, and he mentioned he'd love a second person to help with his demonstration. I hope you don't mind that I offered you."

A tsunami of emotions slammed into Ember. Though everyone knew they were a phoenix, they still hadn't done any fire magic for a crowd. They had done a bit on camera, but that felt different; that was just Felix and Daisy. This was a group of other people ... live and in person—not to mention the people were students in their grade.

They huffed out a breath and smiled. Considering how tired they were, fire was probably a better proficiency for them to use. "Yeah, it's fine. I'll head out now. I'm glad you have confidence in me." Ember collected their bag. "I'll see you on Monday."

Daisy was on the stairs heading up as Ember walked down. "What are you doing? Class is that way, teach!"

"I'm being sent on a mission, and after yesterday, I'm less 'teach' and more 'sleepy friend dragging.'" Ember sagged for a moment against the stairway wall before smiling at Daisy.

"I feared you'd be hurting today. You pushed yourself hard last night." Daisy held up a travel mug. "I brought you a gift."

"Gods above, you're the best."

"I know I am." She winked. "But for reals, where are you headed?"

"Mr. Tine wants me on the east field to help with fire. I don't know why, but off I go."

Daisy's jaw dropped. "Isn't Ambrose in that class?"

Ember stiffened, then perked up. "So is Olivia." They smiled wide. "Okay, enough procrastinating. I have to put on my big girl panties and do the thing."

Daisy laughed as she headed up the stairs. "That you do, my friend. That you do."

By the time Ember reached the field, class was about to start. As they approached the teacher, one of the students yelled, "Are you joining our class, Ember? Is the school still trying to figure out where you belong?"

"In a different school," another student laughed. Ember couldn't help a quick glance. Jared, Cress's friend ... of course.

Deciding they'd try to ignore the hecklers, Ember found the teacher by looking for the person taking attendance. "Hi. Mr. Tine?"

"Hi, Ember, I hope you don't mind helping me out today." He didn't look at Ember as he searched the faces of all the students milling about the field and marked things off on his clipboard.

"No, but shouldn't you know my abilities before you sign me on?" It bugged Ember that they were being asked to help with no prior knowledge or testing. For all Mr. Tine knew, Ember had no control or didn't know how to work fire magic with a partner.

He chuckled. "I think you'll work out fine. I need someone who can make a lot of fireballs quickly. Zahra told me how you helped her. I think you should be able to do this much. Though, class often shifts from my original plan; I may change the direction of what I ask you to do. If you feel it's beyond your ability or are uncomfortable, just let me know."

Ember nodded. They could do that—fire was always at their beck and call—but they weren't sure Mr. Tine understood the kind of fire they made. Ember would have to explain the power behind their fire if it became important.

"Okay class," Mr. Tine said, stepping away from Ember. "In today's lesson, we're going to learn how fire can be used for defense. Our proficiency is often thought of as an offensive power, but we can do some things with fire to protect ourselves."

A few ideas flitted through Ember's mind. They wondered what direction the class would take.

"Are we learning this to protect ourselves from the phoenixes? Is that why *she's* here?"

Ember was so focused on thinking about the lesson, they missed who spoke. They only heard the high-five at the end of the comment. Looking up, they wondered if it was Jared again.

Mr. Tine's face hardened. "You are in Ember's grade. You know they use 'they.' If you want to be disrespectful, you're welcome to miss this lesson and take the failing grade. You know where the library is. It's your grade. As always, every lesson in this class is optional; you are all old enough to determine what grades you want in school, what type of fire-user you want to be, and the caliber of witch you want to be in society."

Jared glared at Ember. "But Ember's not—"

"If I were you," Mr. Tine snapped, "I wouldn't finish that statement. Do *not* forget, this is my class. I give you some freedom, but at the end of the day, there are options available in this school for students to only learn two proficiencies."

The class got quiet. Looking at the faces, Ember noted some looked grim, but many, like Olivia, looked satisfied with how quickly Mr. Tine shut down the heckling. Interestingly enough, Ambrose looked bored.

Ember caught Olivia's gaze, and they smiled at each other. It was nice to have a friend in the class.

Mr. Tine waited several seconds. "Good. Now, can we move on to our lesson?" No one said anything. "Perfect. You'll get into groups of three. One person is going to create a wall of fire. That will be your defense. The second person will throw fireballs, trying to breach the wall. The third person is there in case any balls do penetrate the wall."

There were murmurs among the students as they discussed how weird it all sounded. Ember tried not to smile at how normal everything felt.

Mr. Tine let everyone take a moment to let the assignment settle. "When you create your wall, make sure it's a good meter away from you. It should be large enough to protect your body. For now, this is a static drill. In future lessons, we may move to creating active blocks after the fireball is in flight to 'eat them up.'"

Ambrose raised her hand. She waited to be called on. "As fire practitioners, why wouldn't we create our fireballs on the other side of the wall? I understand why we aren't for this drill, but in a battle, the wall seems ... useless."

Mr. Tine nodded. "Great question. We can create our fireballs at any point, but the closer to us, the more control we have. But also, if we create the wall, that can be a visual block to our opponent." He turned to Ember. "Can you create a wall and hide?"

Ember backed up, then did as he asked. Once the wall was up, they slowly moved from behind the wall so they could watch the continuation of the lesson.

"As you can see." Mr. Tine waved his hand at the block of fire about a foot taller than Ember and double their width. "We don't know exactly where Ember is. If I throw a fireball," he did, "they can absorb it into their wall. If one gets through..." He threw a bigger one, harder. It didn't get through. Ember wasn't sure he could create one that would ever penetrate what they'd made. "Um, Ember. Did either of my balls penetrate?"

They stepped up to stand next to him. "No. I don't think so." They worried what the class would think if they explained how strong the wall was.

Mr. Tine jumped. "Oh, you're here. Is the wall still stable?"

"Umm, yeah." Ember said, wondering if they'd done something beyond what the teacher could do. "I just wanted to hear everything you were doing and it's easier from this side."

He nodded. "Okay, good." He smiled at the class. "Well, that's pretty much what you'll be doing. Ember and I will walk around and answer any questions you may have." His eyes shifted from the wall to them. "Um, if you don't mind."

Ember dissipated the wall and thought about why they'd never been in a Fire Magic class before. They just didn't know how to dumb the proficiency down.

For the remainder of class, they walked around helping students with their walls and fireballs. There were a lot of students who struggled with the basics. Some of their classmates refused Ember's help, others were open to receiving advice. Of those latter students, Ember got their walls and fireballs tighter and stronger.

When Ember got to Olivia, she didn't need much help, but they spent a few minutes working together, just for a moment of downtime.

Near the end of class, Ember saw that Ambrose excelled, but she could do better. They debated. Then, with a sigh of resignation, Ember approached someone they decidedly didn't like. "You're good at this."

"Of course I am. I'm the best in this class."

Ember snorted. "Almost. But we can go with that."

"Why are you here, Ember?" Her tone dripped with derision.

"I can help you get better, if you want. Or I can walk away. It's all up to you." *Please choose walk away, please choose walk away.* Ember didn't cross their fingers, but it was close.

"I don't believe you. Your 'I can help everyone' act is grating at best, obnoxiously annoying at worst. But go for it. Fix me, phoenix girl."

It took Ember a second to unclench their jaw. "Okay, create a quarter-wall."

Ambrose did.

"You used both your hands. Some of your magic is being wasted. Focus your spell on one hand, the right, and only use your middle finger to make the circle."

Ambrose scoffed, rolling her eyes.

Ember sighed. "Look, you're doing too much. The motions you're currently doing are hampering the magic from flowing to the full potential."

After tightening her jaw, Ambrose shook her head. "You know you're full of it, right? I'm going to do what you said, only to show everyone who's watching us how much malarky you spread."

Ember shrugged. "Up to you."

After a small mocking laugh, Ambrose adjusted her gestures. Her wall doubled in size and the heat it gave off intensified. She snapped her hands back as if burnt and made fists. "Whatever." She spun, picked up her bag, and headed to the school.

Before anyone else could say anything or Ember could move to the next student, the bell rang.

Ember sighed in relief. It was finally time to be a student again.

Chapter 27 - Looking To The Future

Ambrose

"I hear the phoenix helped you with your fire magic today, Ambrose." Cress leaned back in his seat, eyebrow raised, smug look on his face.

Ambrose used her years of training to hold her face blank, but under the table she wrung her napkin, wishing it could be Cress's neck ... or Mr. Shade's. It took every ounce of her control to act civil.

She sat still at the dinner table with everyone important from the household. Today, Cress's father, Mr. Walsh, had joined them. He mirrored his son in how he looked at her. His smirk and hungry expression made her shiver.

He was one more man to remind Ambrose and her mother that women were meant to be seen and not heard. At least, since they'd returned to Feniks, they had staff to do the cooking for them ... magical staff. No more humans working for the Wells family.

I wonder if that's because humans refuse to work for us or if Mr. Shade dictated that no humans were allowed near Infinite WISDOM. Not that anyone would tell me. Not a mere female.

A couple months ago, Ambrose would've laughed at Cress's statement and had a full discussion with Father about school, classes, and her thoughts about what happened. She may have even demonstrated the spell with and without Ember's modifications to get his take on the difference.

But this wasn't a couple months ago, and she no longer trusted or respected the men sitting around the table with her.

Cress hadn't actually asked her a question. She could speak, but it wasn't required. With slow deliberation, Ambrose released her hand from the napkin she throttled, gently clasped her fork, and took a bite of the chicken masala the hotel chef had prepared for the entree portion of their dinner.

The meal tasted okay, but she missed their old chef, the one who knew exactly what everyone liked—like more seasoning and flavor to their meals. The family had specific culinary desires, but with Mr. Shade directing the order to the kitchen, and his love of everything bland, most of the food wasn't as good as it could be.

Father sipped his white wine. "Well, Ambrose, is it true? I didn't think that human-loving phoenix was in your Fire Magic class." He looked back and forth between Ambrose and Cress.

"The phoenix isn't." Cress smirked. "Jared is." Cress's smile widened, as if that explained everything. "He said that the wannabe witch came down from wherever they perched during first period and invaded their class."

Ambrose sighed. "Mr. Tine asked Ember to help out in class for a demonstration, that's it. It isn't as nefarious as you're making it sound." As much as Ambrose disliked Ember, she didn't feel the story needed any embellishments.

"So ... did that ... person help you or not?" Mr. Shade leaned back in his seat. His voice, low and gentle, set off warning bells in Ambrose's head.

Gods above, I hate him. He's oily and mean. I want him out of our house and my life. If I say the wrong answer, am I in danger? The sweat trickling down her back made her shiver. It took every muscle tensing to hide the reaction with all eyes on her. She could hear her elevated heart rate from the blood pounding in her ears.

"They gave me a suggestion, as they did to everyone in class." It hadn't been everyone, but that wasn't a detail anyone needed. Ambrose took another bite, the food turning sour in her stomach. *I've spent my life playing the part of the leader. This man will not take me down a peg, no matter if he's turned my family against me or not.*

"But was it helpful?" Cress asked, unwilling to let the subject drop.

On the other side of the table, Mother just observed, being the perfect woman, seen but not heard. She probably would've answered the question. She probably wouldn't have taken Ember's advice in the fire lesson.

Ambrose turned to Father, pointedly ignoring the boy. "When will our house be ready for us to move home? It's been weeks. Shouldn't the roof be fixed by now?"

"Actually, yes. We're moving home on Saturday. I wanted to bring that up during this meal." He smiled.

"I see what you mean, Cress. She's very impertinent, isn't she?" Mr. Walsh said.

I will not respond.

The last time Ambrose had spent time at Cress's house—before Infinite WISDOM, before Mr. Shade, before ... just *before*—Mr. Walsh had seemed to like her. Their interaction had only been when Ambrose's driver took her to his house to pick Cress up, and Mr. Walsh came out to greet her.

Cress's mother had left his father before she and Cress had started grade nine. Ambrose never knew why, but Ambrose's interactions with the family had been limited. This dinner was probably the most time she'd spent with the man, and she wasn't impressed. She was starting to piece together a possible reason Mrs. Walsh had left ... though Ambrose had always felt bad for Cress. Now she just wanted to rid herself of all the men in this room ... even Father, unless he found his mind and spine again.

Mr. Shade chuckled. "She's only insolent to a man unworthy of her. Ambrose is smart, strong of will, and beautiful. That's why, as Infinite WISDOM grows, she will become my queen." He turned to Father as Ambrose dug fingers into her leg to keep from sneering ... or gaging. "I think we should make that transition sooner than later. I know we planned on that happening over the summer between grades, but I don't think we should wait." He narrowed his eyes and looked Ambrose up and down. "Maybe during one of the next couple of events. She and I can present together rather than her and Cress. I believe the two of us would be striking together."

His gaze made her want to take a shower. It took a lifetime of training to not visibly react, though a shiver of disgust raced through her body. *I will not partner with this slimeball of a monster.*

There was a moment of silence. Ambrose could hope the others were as disgusted as she was, but she doubted it.

Father nodded as a smile stretched across his face. Ambrose realized he only saw this as a means to more power. She'd hoped he would want more for her, his daughter, but in the end she was a pawn, nothing more than something he could use like any other currency to better his station.

She locked her jaw as he said, "That's always been the plan, the two of you ending up together. If you want to move up the timetable, we can work with you. Cress," he turned, "are you going to argue against this? Do you think it will cause an issue at school?"

Cress smiled. "I don't think so, sir. I think there's another girl who's a better match for me anyway. Much more ... malleable." His lower lip curled into his mouth and his eyes narrowed as he all but glared at Ambrose. *Gods, he's not even trying to hide his duplicity with Josie.* Then his grin returned. "I'm sure we can make it work. Maybe start having her do some of the presentations with me during the events? Have the two of us be seen together."

Bile rose at how easily these men planned their lives, as if their opinions didn't matter. Ambrose entertained thoughts of getting up and walking away ... just leaving and never coming back. She couldn't. Running would be a sign of weakness, but to be away from all of them would be a relief.

Well, they'll learn that when they mess with me, they're playing with fire ... I'll get them back eventually. I know I'm smarter than anyone in this room. Her mind drifted to Josie and what would happen with her friend ... or someone as close to being a friend as Ambrose allowed.

I would warn Josie, but she's just going to be over the moon about this. Another mindless drone in this gods-awful machine.

Mr. Shade clapped. "Excellent. That's solved. Now, next issue. We need more teens involved in the leadership roles of Infinite **WISDOM**. We are not a big enough force within the school. And Cress, I don't mean idiots like that Brett boy. He didn't even think to try to run when the authorities showed up. Good work with his memories, by the way."

"Thanks." Cress lifted his glass as if to toast.

Ambrose hadn't heard Cress had messed with Brett's mind on the run. Of course she hadn't. Why would they tell her, a mere female, anything? The fact that she could probably help with planning went way above all their heads. She only hoped Brett could feed himself with that kind of brute invasion.

"Do you have a thought?" Mr. Shade continued, only focusing on Cress, as if he had two brain cells to rub together. "Any people who would work? This shouldn't be someone for the stage ... just for the extracurricular activities you've been doing. I don't want to risk your face. A leader for the security side, so to speak."

Cress rolled his eyes. "None of those wusses are going to lay a finger on me, but I get it. I think my friend Jared would be perfect."

Jared was marginally smarter than Brett, but not by much. He was also a bully ... so just what Mr. Shade wanted. A cold shiver ran down Ambrose's back. This was not the organization she thought it was and every day it got dirtier and more despicable. For the past few weeks, she'd felt more and more dirty, but she wasn't sure what she could do to stop this train-wreck beyond the one email she'd sent out to that website.

Mr. Walsh clapped his hands. "So, what's the plan? Do we just invite this kid to join us?"

Ambrose shut her eyes and clamped her jaw tight. This guy was an utter imbecile. *Does he have no idea how Infinite WISDOM works?*

"I was thinking Saturday." Cress ignored his father. "That alley downtown under your apartment, Mr. Shade. Jared and I can lure someone there. It's fairly private. It's close to the coffee shop and the bakery—both hot-spots for human-loving sympathizers. You can watch and see his commitment. Observe how he works. Then you'll know he's good to act as another leader in the school."

A smile slithered onto Mr. Shade's face. He reminded Ambrose of a snake.

Ambrose stood. She waited for Father to nod his head, fury burning within her. Despite being part of the family, she was treated barely better than the help. "May I be excused? I have some schoolwork that needs to be completed before tomorrow. I'd like to have the weekend free."

Again, her father nodded, barely taking more notice of her than the servers bringing small individual cakes for dessert. The offerings looked dry and nothing like the lavish plates their old chef made. *Definitely not worth eating.*

She slowly turned and walked away. *This is not a retreat. I am preparing for a later battle.*

In her bedroom, Ambrose sat on the bed. There wasn't really any other option. Last Friday she'd sent a note to that FB website telling them where to find Mr. Shade and Cress. Either the site wasn't monitored, or they hadn't shown up. For all Ambrose knew, the authorities happened on the spot of their own accord. Needless to say, Mr. Shade was still a thorn in her side.

Frustrated, she hadn't returned to the site or checked if they'd replied to her inside information.

When she'd sent the message, Ambrose had used a school computer because Father had taken her phone for talking back. After the conversation at dinner, she decided to see if the group had replied to her. Something had to be done, and she wasn't sure where else to turn.

It took a few minutes to log into the dummy email account she'd used when she'd messaged the FB coalition. There was only one email on that account. She read it quickly. Whoever monitored the site explained they hadn't received her message until Saturday morning ... too late to be of real use. They thanked her and would appreciate any other information she was willing to share.

That was the question; would Ambrose give them more? On the one hand, this was her family, her potential future, and a whole lot of power. If anyone in this hotel suite knew what she was considering, at best, she would end up in the hospital. At worst ... Ambrose shivered. She knew Mr. Shade still had his moonstone box, and it wasn't empty.

Last weekend, she'd headed to her room to study in peace and quiet. There were too many people always blabbing on about something in the suite, and the hotel was too small and not soundproofed. From her room, she heard Father, Cress, and Mr. Shade speaking in the living room.

"But do you still have that stone box? The one with the phoenix fire?" Father asked. "I just want to know if I should be worried. That stuff was terrifying and we're living in much smaller quarters. There isn't a cell that can contain it here."

A bark of laughter. "We ran for our safety after that phoenix made fools of all of us. Other phoenixes were burning the house down around us. Do you think moonstone was anywhere near the top of my priorities?" Mr. Shade sounded condescending.

"Of course not!" Father agreed. He sighed, sounding relieved. "Very good. That fire is dangerous."

Since 'that fire' and 'that stone' had been Mr. Shade's life work, Ambrose was shocked Father had dismissed it so quickly.

She hadn't really cared, she just wanted to study. To avoid their talking, she decided to head out to the patio where it would be quiet.

The patio was large, wrapping around two sides of the suite. Ambrose liked to sit in a seat hidden from view, surrounded by trees and bushes. She could study, read, play on her phone, or just relax for hours, and no one would find her ... or maybe they just didn't think about her. Either way, she could unwind.

As she studied, she heard someone come out and shut and lock the patio door. Mr. Shade's voice slithered over her, making her shiver. "Did you get the box where I left it in the garage?" A break while he listened. "And was there an issue getting more fire from the cave?" A snarl. "Okay, tomorrow we'll go together. I guess you have to have my level of void magic to move it. I'm sorry I sent you alone to get it." His apology sounded more like a sarcastic dismissal. Ambrose wouldn't have wanted to be on the receiving end of it.

As Ambrose left dinner and headed to her room, she noticed Mr. Shade's door cracked open. He usually kept his door shut and locked. She knew it was locked because she heard him locking it every time he went in, but for some reason she could see into his room, and there, atop his dresser, sat the box. Which meant, they had Everfire in their hotel suite.

The memory of the box and what she'd seen him do with it in her basement before winter break began playing on repeat in her mind, as it did often ... a horror show she couldn't rid herself of.

A shiver of fear ran down her back. *I have to do something.*

Ambrose tapped on reply. The only reason he would want Everfire was to kill his enemies.

As annoyed as she was with the FB coalition, she was disgusted with every male in the hotel, especially Mr. Shade. She was neutral on her mother, so perfect at being seen and not heard. *Why has she never grown a backbone?*

In as few words as she could, Ambrose explained where Cress and Jared would be on Saturday and what they would be doing. She tried to emphasize they had to be there early if they wanted to catch Mr. Shade. He'd probably only be there at the start.

She debated adding something about the Everfire, but thought she'd talk to Father about it first. She knew he didn't like it any more than she did. Maybe she could use it to turn the tides and bring back the man he used to be. It may take time, but she hoped to get him back.

Chapter 28 - A Very Different Evening

Ember

Thursday ended so much better than it began. When Ember woke up that morning, head pounding and weak as a newborn, they weren't sure they could stand. Strangely, their energy improved throughout the day instead of worsening. It was almost like they could *perceive* their magic filling them. Every time Daisy or Felix texted to ask how they were, Ember could give a better report of their condition.

By the end of the day, the trembling stopped, and they felt like a new person.

At home, Ember dropped their bag by the front door, grabbed a banana and a soda, and dashed through the house to the back.

They sat in one of the chairs and ate the banana. After they were done, they shut their eyes and thought about the steps Mom had told them the night before. Though it still seemed complicated, Ember thought it may be manageable now.

First they centered themself, then they imagined their room in as much detail as they could. They tried to visualize it to the point that they could take a step from the backyard to a spot next to their bed.

As they weaved the image of their room they pushed out their magic in a slow trickle. The more detail they formed in their mind, the more magic spilled out into the spell.

Ember's breathing got choppier and faster.

There was a point when there was almost a buzzing in Ember's ear, a click in their soul, and a knowledge that they'd done all they could do.

With a grunt, they slowed the release of their power and opened their eyes. The air ahead of them shimmered as if someone smudged the view right in front of them.

Elation filled Ember as they slowly stood. Hand shaking, they stepped towards the splotch in the air ... and nothing. The magic hadn't fully connected. It was another failure.

Ember flopped back down onto the chair. They checked their watch. It had taken an hour of constant focus, and it hadn't worked. All the energy they'd felt built within them by the end of the school day was once again gone. Their muscles felt like sludge as they trembled in the cool afternoon weather. They knew it wouldn't take long to be at least able to sit up, if not stand.

After a few minutes, Vatra joined them with a bowl of nuts. "Why are you out here alone? Were you practicing? Want something to eat? Do you want privacy? I could head back in."

"No, you can stay." Ember shook their head and reached for the bowl. "I just wanted to practice what Mom taught me again."

"Really? You looked wiped this morning. I know I asked, but it was partly a joke. I didn't think you'd try anything for like a month. To be honest, you don't look any better now." He shrugged and scooped out a couple of cashews. "Do you need anything else?"

Ember wanted to say no—he was a guest—but that would be a lie. "If you're really offering, I'd take more food? Maybe something to drink? I brought out a banana, but it wasn't enough." They held up the bowl. "This is better, but still not enough."

"Sure, stay right there." He held out both his hands as if Ember would leap up and run off, then he chuckled to himself.

It only took a few minutes, then he returned with a plate piled with cheese, crackers, and an apple muffin.

Behind him, Mom followed with a tea tray. "I hear you zapped your magic again, love."

Ember pushed themself up to a sitting position and snagged the muffin and a mug of peppermint tea. "I felt great on the way home from school. It only took time for me to stop feeling like the walking dead."

"And?"

"Pretty much the same as last night, though I'm not feeling quite as headachy."

Dad came out. "Dinner will be done in ten minutes. Are we eating out here?"

Mom shook her head. "No, these are appetizers. We'll join you in a few minutes."

Each bite soothed Ember, and their body healed, rebuilding its strength.

By the time they got into the kitchen, Dad had set out lasagna, garlic bread, and a salad. It all smelled delicious, and Ember's stomach growled at the aroma. Even after all they'd eaten, they were still hungry.

Everyone filled a plate. "Did you go to the protests? Were there that many of the mindless followers out and about?"

Dad grumbled low, and Vatra scoffed.

Vatra sipped his glass of soda. "It was much what you'd predict. We ended up checking out four spots. In each place, there was a crowd with signs. Some were for Infinite WISDOM. Some were anti-human. The rest ran the spectrum of the rants you'd expect. There was only violence at one, and the authorities got there in time to break it up. No one ended up at the hospital, and five people got arrested."

Ember massaged their temples. "That sounds awful. Is this only happening here in Feniks, or has it grown?"

Mom made a face of disgust. "We're the hot-spot, but with the internet, the news, and social media, it's growing. It isn't as bad in other places as it is here, but the movement is like the tide, pushing its way across the county."

"Will Aunts Nuri and Monte move the FB coalition to a new location if Mr. Shade moves? They said they came here because of him. Would we move? What happens if this grows more?" Ember didn't want to imagine this getting that big, but things like this often took on a life of their own. It could grow like a cancer, destroying the good around it.

"We won't be following it. You have school and we want to keep you safe," Mom said, then looked at Dad. "There's a chance we'll send you to Serafina Landing next year."

"No! I want to finish school with my friends." Ember hated this idea.

Dad's face tightened. "But the school isn't teaching you enough new material. When it was about you meeting new people, making connections, and your safety wasn't an issue, that was one thing. But everything has changed. Now that my banishment is lifted, your phoenix education is top priority. There's a lot you need to learn that traditional school can't teach you."

"But—" Ember wanted to debate more.

"No." Dad's voice brooked no argument. "Your friends aren't going anywhere. If you leave for this very important schooling, they'll still be here when you graduate, I promise."

"Not to mention," Mom added with a small smile, "you can visit them. It's not like you'll be banished to a place with no hope of return." Her look turned mischievous. "And this really gives you a reason to master your spatial magic, no?"

Ember slumped. If their parents agreed, there was little they could do to change their minds.

Dad's phone rang. Normally he'd ignored it, but his brow furrowed as he checked the display. "It's Monte. I'm not sure why she'd be calling, but I'm going to get this." He got up and headed into the living room.

When he returned he had a wan smile on his face. "Apparently our new mole in Infinite WISDOM is at it again. We have another message and may be able to catch Tad after all."

Chapter 29 - Welcome To The Club

Ember

Ember texted both Felix and Daisy about Cress's plan for Saturday morning as soon as they got to their room that night. Part of the reason was to convince them to stay home. Downtown would not be safe, and they knew Daisy liked reading at the café on mornings there wasn't school. The other part was they didn't want other students to overhear. The fewer people who knew about a mole, the safer the information was.

Daisy called right away.

"I know that alley. It's where Cress cornered me after my meeting with Simon. Gods above! He's so predictable." Her voice quavered.

"Are you okay? We've talked about that some, but not enough." Ember wished they were in the same room as their friend so they could give her a hug. *If only I could make a stupid portal!*

"Yes, well, no. To be beaten up by a school-mate sucks." Daisy laughed weakly.

Ember pulled a mug of tea up from the kitchen with a small push of magic. They needed something soothing. *Too bad I can't send Daisy a cup of tea.* They had to bite back a chuckle at the thought of Daisy leaping into the air as a mug appeared in front of her. "Have you thought about going to counseling? You got your body healed, but I want you to feel better everywhere."

Daisy sighed. "Yeah. As soon as Mom and Dad understood what happened, they signed me up. I haven't really talked to you and Felix about it, but it's been good."

"I'm glad." Ember relaxed. "If there's anything I can do, just let me know." *Like setting Cress on fire?* They shook their head. Ember knew that wasn't an option, but some days they had to remind themself why it was wrong.

"Of course. I always do."

Friday morning, Ember woke up feeling better than Thursday … but not by much. Their head didn't pound as hard, and standing was easier. Once again, breakfast and lunch were prepared before they'd made it to the kitchen—a fact they were very grateful for. They weren't sure who was doing all the cooking and preparing, but they weren't going to complain.

Fridays were always the easiest day of the week. They started with a study hall and after that all the teachers seemed to want as easy a day as the students. Everyone was ready for the weekend and classes slipped by without much incident.

During lunch, one of the students Ember didn't know well handed them a sealed envelope. When Ember tried to ask, the student walked away, ignoring them.

With a sigh, Ember opened it up and saw it was an invitation to attend the Ring Of Fire Initiation after school. There was one for Olivia as well.

Olivia squealed in delight when she saw it, and said, "Yes!"

The others at the table smiled at her exuberance.

Felix grinned. "That's fantastic. I've heard those initiations are *hot*."

Daisy's eyes danced. "Yeah, like, everyone's ignited to go."

Tansy groaned and threw fries at them. "Daisy, that was weak. You're both fired!"

"Apparently you got her steamed," Ember said, eyebrows raised.

Everyone laughed.

Between bad puns and other speculations about what would happen that afternoon at the Ring of Fire event, Ember debated telling everyone about the mole in Infinite WISDOM. In the end, they decided to only tell Felix and Daisy. The fewer people who knew, the safer the information was. They'd have to wait until they got home to be able to text them both.

Olivia and Ember headed out to the east field together after school. When they arrived, Mr. Tine waved them to the side to join a few other spectators on his left. A group of ten twelfth-year students wearing robes gathered on his right. The robes were mostly deep red, almost wine in color with gold embellishments along the bottom and arms in a fire motif. There was one student in a dark purple robe. *I wonder if that one is a leader of some sort.*

In front of the 'stage' sat a couple dozen spectators.

Olivia leaned over. "The audience is former members. Everyone has worn a robe, either here or at whatever school they attended. Across from us are the current members. There are initiations at the start of the year and after winter break."

Ember nodded. "Why not just at the start of the year?"

"Fire magic is volatile and hard to master. It takes time. Some students come into their control later in the year. Because of that, they allow for two trials. It's more prestigious to get into the club earlier, but any student who can earn a robe is pretty much a rockstar."

"Got it." Ember checked out the four other people sitting with them. "Why are we over here and not with the main spectators?"

Olivia looked at everyone. As she did, Ember re-examined who all attended this event. The current members across from them, the mass of people to their left, and the three people between the other two groups looking worried. Zahra was in that last group.

Olivia's face lit up. "I think we're in—"

Mr. Tine walked to the center of the group. "Welcome, everyone, to the Ring of Fire initiation." He waited for the applause to quiet down. "I want to give a special welcome to the potential initiates for next year, let's give them a *warm*—" he smiled at the inference while some in the crowd snickered and guffawed, "—welcome." Then he waved his hand towards the group where Ember sat.

"These six students have shown great progress in their fire control and manipulation this year and I believe they will be strong contenders for the Ring of Fire next year."

Ember whispered to Olivia. "Where's Ambrose? Isn't she top of the class? Could she already have a robe?" The idea sickened Ember. They knew these clubs were only for twelfth-year students, but with how things were going, and Ambrose's family's money, they didn't trust anything anymore.

Olivia rolled her eyes. "She isn't a member. Trust me. Everyone would know if she were. She probably came to the last initiation. She's been privately tutored her whole life."

Mr. Tine continued. "Today we have three twelfth-year students who are auditioning for a spot in the Ring of Fire: Zahra Bear, Ferris Gill, and Curren Moore. They have prepared a fire skill beyond what is taught in class to present today. If they impress the audience, the current members—" he paused, "—and me, I, along with the president of the current club, and the chosen leader from those of you attending today, will consider them for the honor of the ring."

A wave of anticipation rolled through the crowd. Several people leaned forward. The excitement dug deep into Ember, and they smiled, bumping shoulders with Olivia. "This is fun."

"It is! I really want to be part of this next year." Her eyes practically glowed.

"If I can help you in any way, let me know. Maybe we can work on something in our spare time."

Olivia's jaw dropped open. "You'd do that for me?"

"Of course! We're friends."

"First up, Zahra Bear." Mr. Tine waved his hand in a wide arc. Who knew a teacher could be such a showman?

Zahra stood and wiped her hands on her thighs. Then she made fists before walking to where Mr. Tine stood. As she gazed over the audience, she shook out her hands and smiled. "Hi, everyone. I'm Zahra. Many of you already know me. Thank you for your consideration."

Then she made tight fists, took a breath, and slowly let it out relaxing her hands. With her right hand, she created a fiery rectangle. That alone got several people in the crowd to clap. There were murmurs about her control and nods of approval.

Ember nodded and tried to will Zahra to do more. *Come on! Finish the cake. Give it a candle. I know you can do it.*

Zahra stood still, gazing at her creation for a full minute. Then she lifted her left hand. It took a bit of maneuvering, but a thin line rose from the center of the top.

Pride burst in Ember's chest, and they wanted to leap up and cheer. Not only had Zahra done it, she'd performed in front of an audience in a high-pressure situation.

Someone in the audience laughed. "It's a cake. A cake with a candle—and that's the only thing not lit. That's hilarious!"

Everyone started to laugh and applaud. Ember watched Zahra. She slumped as she released the magic, and her creation dissipated.

Next up was Curren. He created three fireballs and had them mimic juggling from afar. It was fun to watch, but Ember wasn't sure if that was beyond what students could do in class. They thought the task Zahra originally came to Ember to help her with was harder. Though, they'd never paid much attention to what students learned so it was all new to them. The audience watched and as the balls interwove, they applauded politely.

Last up was Ferris. He took his spot and did his own introduction, speaking to the audience and Mr. Tine.

Then he turned to Ember and sneered. "I just have one question. Can you really play with fire, human-lover? Catch, phoenix!"

He threw a fireball at least two feet across directly at Ember.

Ember leapt up and dissipated the fire, annoyed at his audacity. It wasn't just Ember he would harm with his stunt. Then Ember grabbed any fire the boy had in him, taking his magic away temporarily. Ember wasn't sure what else he had planned, but if he couldn't use fire magic, he couldn't get into any more trouble.

Face tight, Ember watched to see what would happen next. They noticed Mr. Tine's hands up, ready to intervene, his face hard, but Ember had dealt with the situation before the teacher could. Everything had happened so fast, they hadn't given the teacher time to respond.

Ferris lifted his hands, but nothing happened. He tried again, but still, nothing. He turned to Mr. Tine. "What did you do to me?!"

"What do you mean?" Mr. Tine sounded confused.

"My magic! Did you take away my fire?" Ferris's voice rose. "Where is it? I don't have my fire anymore. It isn't inside me! I can't do fire magic. Did you take it away? Can teachers do that?"

Mr. Tine gazed at Ember as if something they'd heard suddenly made sense. "No. Only very high-level fire practitioners have that ability. You'll probably get it back later today, but after that stunt you did, I'm not sad it's gone. You will not be invited into Ring of Fire, but you probably already knew that. I'm going to speak to the principal about a suspension."

"Why would I want to be in your stupid club? You allow human-loving witches in. I wouldn't want to be part of it anyway." He waved his hand, and ice covered the ground all around the field. "Go ahead and suspend me;

it isn't like this school teaches us anything important." He turned and headed back towards the school.

The group sat, stunned.

Ember slowly made their way back to their seat and focused on melting the ice. It didn't take much power.

Mr. Tine shook his head as the field turned from frozen ice to soggy turf and then to steam rising from the lawn. Ember made sure to use a low enough heat to not harm the grass. The teacher didn't look toward Ember, just waited until it was done. "We'd like to thank Zahra and Curren for their excellent displays of magic. The selection committee will inform each of them on Monday whether they have been selected for a robe. If they are, there will be a robing ceremony on Monday afternoon. As for the rest of you, I encourage you to mingle. There are refreshments."

Olivia clasped Ember's arm. "Did you really take away that jerk's magic? And the ice. It had to be you, right? Who else has that kind of finesse?"

Ember looked around to make sure it was only the two of them, then nodded slightly. "But don't spread it around. I get harassed about being a phoenix around here enough already."

She chuckled. "Did you do that to Ambrose during the field trip last semester? She was freaking out about it in class the following Monday. She demanded to know who had done it."

As they both wandered over to the table to get food, Ember snorted and said, "What do you think?"

Chapter 30 - Taking Down An Enemy

Ember

Late Saturday morning, Ember sat at home waiting to hear the news about what had happened at the rally and with the attack in the alley. Felix and Daisy had come over to wait, but none of them spoke; it was all too tense.

Felix finally broke. "How many times have you tried your new spell, Ember?"

"The one that knocks me out?"

"No, the one to fireproof your socks." He gazed at them deadpan, then one of his brows rose. "Yeah, that one." He smiled.

"Twice, Wednesday and Thursday nights. After the Ring of Fire debacle, I decided I'd had enough fun with magic Friday. Why?" Ember took a bite of the breakfast casserole Dad had made. Layers of potatoes, eggs, sausage, and cheese made their belly happy. He didn't make the dish often, but Ember always enjoyed it when he did.

"I just thought, it takes a bit of time, why not try now?"

Ember considered. "It's really boring to watch. I just sit, not moving. Then the air distorts, marking my failure. But if you want to observe me not doing anything, sure. But I need to finish my breakfast and coffee first."

Daisy laughed. "It's not as boring as all that. It's slow, but you do see the shimmer build."

It was cold enough outside that they'd need coats, and since the adults were all gone, they decided to sit in the living room. Ember closed their eyes and began weaving their spell. They continued to use their bedroom as the place they wanted to portal. Despite their prediction of failure, deep down they hoped for success. They wanted to show their friends something spectacular.

When they felt the spell click, they opened their eyes to see the distortion in the air in front of them.

"Whoa," Felix said. "That looks exactly like what your mom created.

Ember snorted. They stood and pushed their hand into the shimmering air. Nothing.

The disappointment from everyone was palpable.

"How long did that take me?"

Daisy checked her watch. "Just under an hour."

"Okay, my head doesn't hurt too much, and I'm not a pile of goo, but let's go have more food and coffee all the same. I'm worried about my energy for the rest of the day, and I'm hoping for a big announcement once everyone returns. Wouldn't it be amazing if one of them— Mr. Shade, Mr. Wells, Cress, one of the other goons, any of them really—got caught and arrested?"

Felix smiled. "I'll put on a fresh pot for coffee."

When Vatra got home, he poured himself some coffee and joined them. "Your parents are monitoring the scene."

"What happened?" Ember asked, eating an apple muffin.

"The mole's information was spot on. We had the police on hand. They saw everything going down just as predicted. The only thing that was off was Mr. Shade wasn't there; it was Mr. Wells. Cress has been arrested, as has Jared and Mr. Wells."

"What about Cress's ability to change memories? He's played that trick several times." Felix stood and paced, his face hard. The two had been in mind magic classes their whole lives together. Ember knew how offended Felix was that Cress was changing memories willy-nilly; it was a big deal in their world.

Vatra turned to Felix, hands up in peace. "Not an issue. Thanks for the warning about his mental magic and tomfoolery. The police all had mental walls in place before the operation. Because they felt the attack, his power will be stripped." He narrowed his eyes and gazed up at the ceiling before nodding and looking back down at them. "That's the word right? Sadie was explaining it to me. A circle of five witches will first take away the power, then put in a block so that proficiency can't be used again. It's a longish process?"

Daisy shivered. "Yeah, it's something that's used as a threat, but rarely needed for follow through."

Felix's face was hard as stone. "Well, you can't have him playing with the minds of his counselors or jailers. Wouldn't want him creating a gang by manipulating other kids in the detention center. Personally, I'm glad they made sure his mind control days are well and truly gone."

A tiny thrill infused Ember. During the field trip, Cress had done a mental attack on them. Ember had thought Daisy was in trouble and they'd run through the woods at top speed. The terror-filled sprint had ended with a sprained ankle and bruised pride. Cress had no compunction about messing in other people's minds. He shouldn't be left free to continue doing so.

"But what about Mr. Shade?" Daisy said. "He's the mastermind behind all this. He's the worst. If he's still out there, nothing's going to stop."

Vatra nodded. "We know. Taking down two of the leaders will help, but we still have more to do. We can only hope we get more insight on where to find the head of the snake."

Chapter 31 - A Needed Break

Ember

Once everyone was home, Dad slumped in his chair. "I need to fly. Is it time yet? Is everyone ready to head up to the woods?"

Ember cheered. "Is Aunt Nuri joining us? Vatra?"

"I'm definitely in," Vatra said.

"I'll contact Nuri. I'm sure she'll join us." Dad pulled out his phone and started typing out a text.

Felix smiled. "Do you want me to head out and take Daisy home, or are you inviting spectators?"

Daisy sat quiet for a whole two seconds. "I'd really like to join you. I've barely seen Ember as a phoenix and it would be so amazing and ... well, can I? I'll be quiet, you won't even know I'm there."

Vatra barked out a laugh. "She's so much like my Fotia. The idea that you'll stay quiet, child, is a hoot. Can you go anywhere unnoticed?"

Mom smiled warmly. "I don't mind having the extra company, but it isn't up to me. It's up to all of you."

"You know my opinion," Ember said, throwing their arm around Daisy.

Dad grunted and continued to type. After a few nods he looked up. "Nuri doesn't care one way or another. She just wants us to pack enough food for the army we're apparently bringing."

Both Felix and Daisy texted their parents that they'd be gone for the rest of the day, and everyone piled into cars.

As they drove, Felix explained the 'look away' magic to Daisy. "To keep this place safe, Ember's family has a mental spell worked into the property so that anyone not welcomed in actively doesn't want to acknowledge the space."

Daisy shivered. "I hear your words and understand what each means. I'll even be really impressed, eventually.

But Felix, not right now, please." Her voice sounded strained and she looked pained while the car drove parallel to the woods. At least that part of the drive wasn't long. Once the group made it past the fences and she was introduced to the wards, she visibly relaxed.

"These woods are fantastic. How do you keep them so pristine?" Daisy leaned against the window, looking up towards the tops of the trees. "Oh, wait, the spell, right? It's just, it's amazing out here. We should camp some weekend. We could have a fantastic time and not have to worry about any pranks."

Ember snorted. "You know, people camp in a lot of places and don't worry about pranks."

"True," Felix agreed. "Pranks are a specialty of the night plants field trip."

When they arrived at the clearing, Aunt Nuri and Ember slid behind one car, Dad and Vatra another. Ember was slower at shifting than any of the adults. By the time they were done, Ember looked up to see the iridescent blue bellies and red-orange wings of Dad and Aunt Nuri and Vatra's night blue body with fiery orange shoulders.

With the help of a bit of air magic—though Ember didn't expect much after their failed attempt at magic this morning—they pushed up into the air. As they launched and cleared the cars, they heard a gasp, and assumed it was Daisy. Ember was also surprised at the momentum the magic gave them. *Did Mom help out? I had more magical air assistance than I expected.*

In the sky, they circled the other three, stretching their wings.

Then Dad led the way towards the ocean.

The beach was empty ... thankfully, and Ember flew low, letting their tail feathers drag in the water. The icy cold waves splashed up to cool them.

They shot up, seeing an obstacle course made in the currents of the air. It was different than normal. *Did Vatra make it?* Ember always loved a challenge to test their wits and hone their flying skills. With a cry of joy, they flew faster.

It took two tries to get through the twists and turns correctly, and then they did a loop of celebration.

'Good work, dear. You're getting stronger.'

'Thanks, Dad.'

They continued to fly and play for a while longer, then Ember's stomach growled.

Spinning fast, they flew straight up towards the sun. A signal they'd created with Dad over the years to say, 'time's up for me.' Then they headed back to the clearing.

With four of them flying instead of two, Ember wasn't sure the others would follow or continue to play.

Ember slowly dropped down in the camp site where their friends could really see them.

Felix and Daisy both shot up, but then approached slowly.

Felix shot a glance at Mom. "Can we … is it okay …"

Mom laughed, but before she could answer, Ember made the words in fire a bit off in the distance to not harm anyone. *'It's fine. I just thought you'd like to see me up close.'*

"You're amazing Ember." Daisy knelt and gently brushed a hand down their head. "Oh! And your feathers are soft."

Felix did the same.

Ember slowly extended their wings, and both Daisy and Felix started before they smiled wide. Another grumble of their belly and Mom said, "Okay, time for food. Shift, dear."

They moved behind the car with their clothes, shifted, and dressed. Once their clothes were on, they saw the other phoenixes descending.

"Oh, my gods, Ember, that was … wow!" Daisy leapt up and gave them a hug. "I wish I could fly. It was amazing to watch. Did you know fire words appeared in front of your mom saying back in five? Did you do that? But you also made words. It's mind boggling, all of you."

Ember laughed. "Not this time."

The two of them sat and Ember selected two sandwiches and a soda. They spent the remainder of the afternoon eating and relaxing. It surprised them how good they felt. "Dad, does shifting fill my magic? I can't remember the last time I felt so strong and healthy."

Dad grunted. "How would I know? I'm not a witch."

Mom considered them. "That would make sense. We should add that to your lessons when you feel drained. See if we can increase your practice."

Groaning, Ember slumped and grabbed another sandwich.

Chapter 32 - The Truth Comes Out

Ambrose

Ambrose sat in her room at the vanity, staring in the mirror. Earlier, Father and Cress had been taken away. It was a win of sorts, but also a big loss. It was supposed to be Mr. Shade.

The big move from the hotel to their home happened today. She no longer had to be in close proximity to Mr. Shade, but he still lived in her house. Without Father there as a shield, as small of a protection as he was,

Ambrose shuddered to think what Mr. Shade may try. Cress was gone as well, leaving no buffer between her and the horrifying man. At least her room was on the other side of the house; she had some distance, unlike in the hotel, but as far as she was concerned, he was still too close for her liking.

As the movers transported all their belongings, Mr. Shade said he had some private and delicate personal items he didn't trust to the random strangers and wanted to transport most of his possessions himself. Annoyed, she figured it was the stone box. Because of that dangerous fire, Mr. Shade had asked at breakfast early Saturday morning that Father oversee the initiation of Jared.

No one had anticipated this would lead to losing two high-ranking members of the organization and a new recruit.

Mr. Shade had railed all afternoon, stomping around the house and snapping at the help. When he saw Ambrose, he snarled. "Cress better have cleared out all of their memories before he was taken. Jared's, the police, maybe even your father's. We'd spoken about the worst case scenario, I just didn't imagine it coming to fruition." Stomp. Stomp. Stomp. "What are the chances the police would be walking by the alley right then?" A banging of a cupboard door, a crash of ... something. Ambrose tried not to pay attention.

As soon as she could, she slipped off to her room and shut the door. She went to lock it, but realized the lock had been removed. Anger ignited within her and she paced to keep her fire from escaping her control. Once she knew she wouldn't burn down this wing of the mansion, she sat at her vanity and assessed the weapons at her disposal.

Before Father turned against me, back when I had my tutors, we'd discussed the best ways to use my fire to protect myself. Ambrose felt the fire spread through her veins. *A fireball the size of a golf ball will do if that man decides to come into my room. I may end up in a cell next to Father, but I refuse to let him near me.*

A knock came to Ambrose's door. Before she could say anything, the door opened. Ambrose's hands lifted, but when she saw Mother come in, she clenched them into fists as she lowered them. Her nails bit into her palms.

"What are you doing here?" The door shut with barely a sound as Mother stared at her with a tight face. "You can't just barge in there. I almost incinerated you. I could've killed you, Mother. This is my room." Ambrose didn't want to spend time with her meek mother. Right now, when she felt she needed to prepare for battle, her mother's perfect little woman act rubbed her wrong.

Ignoring Ambrose, Mother came over, selected a hairbrush, and began brushing her daughter's hair. She hadn't done this in years. "You don't need to worry about that, dear. Believe it or not, I've survived this long for a reason."

"Mother!"

"Hush now." She clicked her tongue. "We don't want anyone to hear us. If someone comes in, I have to have a reason for being in here."

"Isn't being my mother enough? And why *are* you here?" Ambrose insisted.

Mother's face hardened. It was more emotion than Ambrose was used to seeing in her. "Of course not. I know you don't respect me and since your father was arrested, there are very few reasons for me to be in here. Some are good, some look bad on both of us. One is I'm consoling you. To men, that will take the form of grooming."

Ambrose was grudgingly impressed by Mother's understanding of the situation. "Okay. Fine. But that still doesn't explain why you're here."

"I thought you were a daddy's girl." Mother started to style Ambrose's hair. She wasn't sure what Mother did or how as her hands moved quickly over her head. With a shrug, she figured whatever it was could be undone easily enough.

"Are you changing the subject?" She watched her mother through the mirror. Though her face was calm, there was fire in her eyes.

"Did you get him arrested?"

"Mother! You know I'm completely in step with ... well, everything."

"Are you?" She scoffed. "I see you, even when those ... well, when the men ignore us. You may think you have a great poker face, but I see your sneers and when you roll your eyes. You may have tried to hide out on the patio, but you're not always completely hidden. And for goodness sakes, matched up with *him*?" She paused in what she was doing with Ambrose's hair as she shivered, a sneer on her face. "That man is too old for *me*, not to mention you. There is no way he's getting his clutches on my daughter."

Though what Mother said was scandalous in this house, Ambrose secretly cheered. She wouldn't agree out loud with her mother—it wasn't safe.

After a few moments, Ambrose asked, "Do you support Infinite WISDOM?"

Mom chuckled. "No, of course not. I liked the message of magic users supporting each other, but that's it. But we both know that isn't what Infinite WISDOM is about, don't we? It's about power and culling anyone who gets in the way of the *men* of this organization. The group is dangerous. The men are morons. I've been working to bring all of it down from the start. Who do you think told them where to find that kid from your school held in the cells beneath this house? Unlike you, who are fairly obvious in your disgust, I know how to be subtle ... how to play along. "

Ambrose's jaw dropped. "You're a mole?"

"Hush." Mother swatted her shoulder. "You need to learn to modulate your volume. Do you want me to be taken away as well? Then who would you be left with?"

A shiver ran down Ambrose's back and bile filled her mouth. The only non-servant adult left in the house would be Mr. Shade. Where would she go then?

Mother shook her head. "Start using that brain of yours. You got your intelligence from me, you know. Now, either be smarter than the nitwits around you or we're both going to end up in places we don't want to be."

"Do you think we're in danger?" Real fear started sinking into Ambrose. It hadn't occurred to her that anything could happen to them.

"I know we are."

Chapter 33 - Rumors and Hearsay

Ember

Monday morning, Ember sat and watched as Ms. Vintl tested the Air Magic students on their latest skill set. It would take both classes this week to get through everyone. Those who hadn't tested practiced. Those who had were given a challenge project. In groups of three—assigned by Ms. Vintl—students created an air ball and tried to play catch. The challenge was to pass the control of the spell at the apex of the throw.

As Ember circled the room, some students asked them questions, but most worked on their own, knowing what to do and what they needed to study.

Ember took out their homework for Magical History to look over. It wasn't due until Wednesday, but it was almost complete and they had the time. As Ember worked, they heard the students around them talking as they practiced, not loud enough to disturb the teacher as she tested others, but Ember had stellar hearing and heard more than most knew.

"Did you read the news? Ambrose's dad was arrested. He and Cress were caught beating some guy up in an alleyway."

"No, it was Cress and Jared."

"I thought it was all three of them."

"No, you're wrong. Mr. Wells was just supervising them."

"Why were they beating someone up in the first place?"

A scoff of disbelief that Ember agreed with. "The person was bad mouthing Infinite WISDOM, idiot. Why do you think the hospitals are so full? Where have you been? Is your head in the sand?"

"That's all lies. Infinite WISDOM isn't harming people."

"Are you that dumb?"

Ember shook their head. Why were people so blind to the truth?

Someone knocked at the door. Mrs. Vintl finished with the student they were working with. "Yes? Can I help you?"

The same student who'd given Ember a letter at lunch last week stood just outside the room, looking bored. "I have a note for Ember. Can I give it to them?"

Mrs. Vintl waved them in, then got back to the testing.

The student handed Ember an envelope then turned to walk away.

Ember stared at the delivery, confused. From across the room, Xander scoffed. "Why'd you get one of those? You aren't a fire magic student."

Ignoring him, Ember tucked the envelope into their bag.

He marched across the room and stood over Ember. "Open it up," he demanded.

"No." Ember slowly looked up at him. "Why do you even care? It isn't even for you. Worry about your test, not my things."

"Zahra should be getting that letter, not you. Did you help my sister out so that you could take her spot? You're a weasel, aren't you?" He sneered.

Mrs. Vintl walked up next to him. "Xander! Step away from Ember. Their business is just that: theirs, not yours. You have your own things to worry about. Now, unless you want to head to the principal's office for misbehaving, walk away."

Xander's face contorted and he glared, but he whipped around and stomped back to the other side of the room.

Mrs. Vintl squatted. "Sorry about that. Everyone is on edge with everything going on. I have no idea what's in that letter, but there's twenty minutes of class left, and I don't see anyone asking you any questions. Do you want to use the private practice room or go to the library? I saw you studying; the tables downstairs may be better for that."

A weight lifted from Ember's shoulders. "The library, if you don't mind."

"Go ahead."

Once alone in the library, Ember pulled the letter out.

To: Ember Savita

From: The Committee of Fire and Mr. Tine, leader of the committee, and mentor for the Ring of Fire

Re: Your show of fire magic – tamping out Ferris Gill's fire and drying a field of ice without burning any grass.

Congratulations! We would like to offer you a robe and a spot in our club. It is rare, though not unheard of, that an eleventh-year student be offered a spot in the Ring of Fire.

Though you weren't officially at the testing as an initiate, your display of control over the fire magic proficiency elevated you from potential in the eyes of everyone there.

Never in the history of our club have we seen the clarity of mind and calm control you displayed under distress in dissipating a fireball greater than half a meter in diameter. Your ability to follow that up by the above stated skills lets us know we are more than correct in our decision.

Please join us for a welcome and robe ceremony after school on Monday, January 24th.

~Ring of Fire

After reading the letter twice, Ember took a picture of it, then slipped it back in the envelope. They squeezed their eyes shut as a huge smile spread across their face. *I can't believe it. This is fantastic! Gods above, I hope Zahra made it, too!*

They texted it to their parents so they knew Ember would be late.

Dad texted back: *That's not a lot of warning time.*

Ember laughed in agreement. *Most people trying to get in probably knew and left the afternoon open in hopes they got in.*

True. Well, have fun, dear.

Ember put their phone away and thought about Olivia. *I hope she isn't upset that I got in. I don't want to lose a friend over a club. I guess if she's mad, I could always refuse the invitation ... friendship is more important.*

As Ember walked to second period, they heard more students talking in the halls about Mr. Wells and Cress getting caught on Saturday. Everyone's story was a bit different, but it seemed everyone had something to share.

A few spoke about Jared as well, but he wasn't as interesting as Cress, the spokesman of Infinite WISDOM, and Mr. Wells, a leader both for the movement and in the community as well as a rich icon in their community.

There weren't many people in Magical History when Ember arrived. They sat and watched as other students filed in. There were some murmurs in the back corner that abruptly stopped as Ambrose sauntered in and took her seat.

She sat tall and proud, as she did every day. *Always the image with her. I wonder if she's happy or sad about Cress? Her dad getting caught, on the other hand, probably sucks for her. Though he was pretty awful when I was a prisoner. Did she know her dad's thoughts back then?*

Felix, Daisy, and Josie followed shortly after from Earth Magic class. *Are Josie's eyes puffy? Has she been crying?* Despite her clenched jaws and forlorn look, Josie sat just as tall and proud as Ambrose.

Felix came and sat behind Ember. Daisy's assigned spot was on the other side of the room so Ember would have to wait until later to tell her their news.

"How was your morning?" Felix asked, pulling out his notebook.

Ember handed him their phone with the image of the letter on the screen. His brows rose as he read, then he laughed softly. "So, boring as always, I see."

"Exactly."

Before they could discuss further, Mr. Elias started class. "I know that this weekend was exciting. That said, we are in school to learn. We study history in this class. We won't be talking about anything that happened in current events. I expect all of you are here for class and not to gossip." He slowly eyed everyone in the room to make sure his message was clear.

It ended up being one of the only classes during the day in which Ember didn't hear crazier and more obnoxious stories about Mr. Wells, Cress, and Jared.

The other class that focused on class material and not current events was fourth period, Magical Creations. Ms. Hewett started off class much the same as Mr. Elias. Then she launched into a complicated lesson on making their glass ball opaque. "If people know what's inside the balls," she said, "they'll lose their shock value."

It took half the class to explain the theory and show a demonstration of how to do the magic. Combining creating colored glass with the glass that evaporated when broken was harder than it sounded. By the end of class, no one had created one.

While they worked, Ember spoke softly to Olivia. "I want to tell you something. But ..." They stopped, uncertain how to continue. Olivia was so excited about everything Ring of Fire, Ember didn't want her hurt that they'd gotten in and Olivia hadn't.

Olivia smiled, eyes twinkling. "Don't tell me, you got asked to join the Ring of Fire." There was a level of snark in Olivia's voice, but also a level of expectation. She waggled her eyebrows in challenge.

Ember's jaw dropped and their eyes widened. A moment later, Olivia mirrored their look. "No way! Really? I was half kidding, but you did?" During their conversation, they both kept their voices soft so the students at the adjacent tables wouldn't be able to hear them.

Smiling sheepishly, Ember pulled out their phone and showed Olivia the image of the letter. They didn't want to pull out the actual letter, it would be too telling to other people in the class.

"Whoa! I never thought I'd see that letter, in person, as an image, or in any form. They're legendary. My gods, Ember! Above, below, besides, in a tornado, like, everywhere. Yes! A thousand times, yes. I'm friends with a unicorn." Despite her enthusiasm, she kept her voice low.

That last did Ember in, and they covered their face with a laugh. "Technically, a phoenix. Unicorns aren't real."

"Gods, don't remind me."

After class, at lunch, Ember finally got to tell Daisy. It was probably good their friend found out at lunch because Daisy whooped loud enough students at adjacent tables stared. Ember blushed, but inside they bubbled with happiness.

After school, Ember walked out to the east field. In two and a half years, they'd never been to the Fire Magic class domain, and now, within two weeks, this was their third visit.

The members of the Ring of Fire were well known in the school and community at large. They were the leaders. The club never had more than fifteen members, and often fewer.

All the proficiencies had their creme de la creme group, but somehow fire magic was the most distinguished of the lot ... this one and mind magic. Anyone asked into either of those two groups were set for college and probably an important job afterwards.

As Ember walked out, the field looked similar to last Friday. An audience, the ten robed members on the 'stage' with their dark red robes and one dark purple robe, and Mr. Tine. Zahra stood where Ember and Olivia had sat watching … alone. Curran wasn't anywhere to be seen.

Mr. Tine saw Ember and pointed to Zahra. They went to stand next to her.

Ember would've told Zahra in math class about the letter, but they didn't sit next to each other and there hadn't been time. They also didn't want to ask Zahra about it if Zahra hadn't gotten in. Xander had made a big enough scene in Air Magic class.

"What are you doing here?" Zahra hissed.

"I got a letter this morning. I have no idea." Ember shrugged as they made a confused face.

Zahra smiled wide. "Good. That means this group really knows their business and they don't put their arrogance and age restrictions ahead of what makes sense."

Ember gave Zahra a quick side-hug as they waited for the initiation to begin.

Mr. Tine stood in front of the audience—adults from the community ranging in age from barely out of school, to some probably in their sixties or seventies. Many wore business attire, though some came in jeans looking ready to relax for the rest of the evening. "Welcome again, former members of the Ring of Fire. I am thrilled you all took the time to join us today. Some of you were here Friday, others could only make it for the formal robe initiation. I know a few of you are confused, but for those of you in attendance last week, I'd like to explain what you may or may not have seen or understood. Last Friday, we had three initiates. Zahra Bear, Ferris Gill, and Curren Moore. One of our hopefuls, Ferris Gill, took it upon himself to attack an observer in the future potential candidates' stand, Ember Savita."

One of the audience members raised a hand, a middle-aged man in a suit. "Isn't Ember a phoenix? Doesn't that give them an advantage with fire? To my knowledge, we've never invited their kind into our fellowship."

"It may be true that Ember is a phoenix and has a leg up over magic users with a proficiency in magic, but I—and others of the former and current members—have searched the charter of this club to determine whether their status as a phoenix matters and found nothing. Long story short, it doesn't."

Chatter erupted in the audience and several people pulled out their phones to look things up.

Mr. Tine waited. After a respectful amount of time, he continued. "What the Ring of Fire focuses on is whether or not the practitioner can control fire. Ember first stopped a fireball thrown with no warning, extinguishing it in a flash. The ball was over half a meter in diameter. It wasn't thrown just at them, but at a group of six students. If they hadn't stopped it, we'd have had to send those students to the hospital for major burns. Then Ember dampened the fire of their attacker, a skill many in this group don't possess. This ensured no more attacks against them or any of the other attendees. Then, the attacker used ice to freeze the field."

The members of the audience began to talk. People were explaining what they saw to the attendees who hadn't been there. Ember could hear them answering small questions, verifying, and filling in.

Finally, Mr. Tine nodded. "Okay, now that everyone has a scope of the field of ice. Ember Savita used fire magic, but not fire itself, to melt and dry the field. It was a level of magic sophistication I don't think any of us could replicate. The control and intensity was beyond amazing to watch. I, for one, will be requesting lessons be taught, as of old, on some of the skills the Savita family can do. I would love to learn this drying technique."

Someone in the back, an older woman, stood. "I want to see proof of this 'drying technique' as you call it. It sounds too good to be true."

Mr. Tine looked at Ember.

They stood for a moment and considered. Every day there seemed to be a new obstacle they needed to prove themselves against. Finally, they stepped forward with a shrug. "There are two ways to do this. The simplest is if you'd be willing to allow someone with water magic to wet part of your outfit, and then I'll dry you off."

"You'll burn me. Why not just dry the grass?" she snapped.

"I won't, that's the point. And as for the grass, I did that already, and obviously you don't believe that skill was enough." Ember tried not to sound waspish ... or to let their face betray their annoyance.

"I'll do it," Zahra volunteered.

The woman laughed bitterly. "You're her friend, I saw you two hug. You'll support the phoenix whatever happens. That's not a real test."

Again, Ember worked at keeping a blank face. They worried about getting a headache from how tight they kept their muscles.

A man in the middle stood. He looked to be about Mr. Tine's age. He wore jeans and a long-sleeved shirt that stated, *If you say Gullible slowly enough, it sounds like Oranges.* "I'll do it. I have water magic and if I feel like I'm about to be burned, I'll splash both of us. If someone can bring two buckets of water?"

Once the water was brought, the man made it dance around him, then splashed it over both of them, soaking Ember to the skin. He smirked at Ember, then winked at the crowd, all laughing uproariously.

With an annoyed huff, Ember raised an eyebrow and warmed their outfits. As the water steamed off them, Ember waved both their hands out to the side, gazing between the man and the audience until they were dry. They could've done it faster, but today was apparently about a show.

When they both stood dry, the man smiled at Ember. "Nicely done. Warm and dry. Do you fold the clothes, as well?"

"With you in them?" Ember asked.

He threw his head back and laughed. "I like this one. An excellent addition for a robe!" He made his way back to his seat.

Mr. Tine placed a hand on Ember's back. "Nice work. You can head back over to Zahra."

There were no more disagreements, and the formalities began. Ember was shocked that it took over an hour of pomp and ceremony, but in the end they stood in a champagne robe with gold and royal blue embellishments. Pride, relief, and disbelief all played within Ember.

As the hour came to an end, Ember realized they were bubbling with happiness at being part of a group, being accepted, and being able to work with fire with other people her age. *I can finally do some of what I love.*

Zahra stood next to them, her face alight with joy.

Chapter 34 - Is Everyone Guilty?

Felix

Monday morning, Felix walked to Earth Magic class alone. Daisy usually headed to class early. He missed having Ember in this class. They weren't good at this proficiency, but they could talk, and the teacher never minded.

"Can you believe the story?" Kit, a girl from class walking ahead of him, whispered to Cera. The two had been friends for as long as Felix knew them. They were nice enough, though they tended to avoid confrontation.

Cera shook her head. "No way. There is absolutely no way Cress has been out beating up people on the weekends. It's all sensationalism."

"But it wasn't on one of the social media sites, it was on the news. Dad told me he saw it on the local ten o'clock," Kit insisted. "And that Cress will be out of school for a while."

"Really? And when he shows up for class today?"

Kit made a show of looking around. "I don't see him now, and he's usually early with Josie. She's over there ... and is she crying?"

"No way."

Felix searched and saw Josie glaring at everyone in the class. He knew she was a big part of the terrible three, their enforcer, but why would she cry for Cress?

Daisy came over to Felix and smirked. "It's about time she got a bit of her own."

"Are you really happy to see her upset?"

"Yep. Did you know she and Cress were discussing how and when he'd break up with Ambrose? That's why she's crying." Daisy rolled her eyes.

"He didn't do it!" Josie's eyes flashed as she yelled at a group of students, her fists tight at her sides. "He was framed. He's nice and gentle and a good person. Don't talk about Cress that way!"

Felix watched, wondering how she'd been kept so oblivious of everything that had happened around her. *Was it mind magic? Did Cress mess with her? She has been quieter lately.*

After school, Felix gave Ember a hug and a quick kiss on their cheek. "Good luck at your super-secret fire cult meeting."

Ember laughed. "Thanks. I'll call tonight and tell you all about it. I'm sure it'll be boring."

"Absolutely."

Daisy walked up. "Have fun, Ember. Don't burn down the school."

"What? You're taking away all my fun!" Ember headed down the hall to the wing that led to the east field. *I love how confident they are now that they don't have to keep as many secrets. Ember is amazing. All the things they can do ... I can't even imagine it.*

Felix and Daisy walked towards the front of the school.

Daisy hitched up her bag. "Doing anything interesting tonight?"

"Mainly homework. I'm hoping for boring. You?" Dozens of students milled around the stairs, lawn, and sidewalk. They had to sidestep and swerve to escape the building.

"Same. I have a few water magic spells I want to work on. I've been trying to combine proficiencies. It's getting better."

"Whoa!" Felix couldn't imagine. "That sounds amazing. With everything else, how do you find the time?"

"Magic!" She waved her fingers in the air and laughed.

"Leave me alone," Ambrose's voice snapped out.

Ambrose stood off to the side, arms crossed, glaring at a group of six students. Felix didn't recognize them ... they looked like freshmen. *They're probably only willing to approach her in a group, too afraid to talk to her individually.* "I told you, it was all a misunderstanding. My father will be released soon."

"What about Cress?" one of her tormentors asked. His face scrunched up into a sneer and his arms bent, as if he were ready to swing one of his fists.

Gazing at the other five, Felix realized they all stood with hands clenched, muscles tight, and narrowed eyes. *This group is ready to fight.*

"What about him? Why don't you go visit Cress and ask if you want to know? I am not now, nor have I ever been, his keeper." Her face hardened.

A second person laughed nastily, the sound carrying across the yard. "If your dad and boyfriend were out beating up people, doesn't it follow that you're doing this stuff too? Are the authorities coming for you?"

Daisy narrowed her eyes. "I don't like her, but this is insane. Why is that group attacking her?"

"This morning you were okay with Josie crying. Why is that okay, but not this?"

Daisy harrumphed. "Josie was crying because she's trying to take Cress from Ambrose—something I don't think Ambrose should try to stop, by the way. This is a witch hunt ... literally. And it's ugly. I want to go slap some people. Just because someone's a bully, doesn't mean they deserve to be bullied. I mean, maybe a one-on-one confrontation, but there are six of them."

Felix agreed with Daisy. The two started walking towards the group with the unspoken agreement to help.

"How many people have *you* put in the hospital, Ambrose?" a third student asked. Felix wished he recognized these kids so he could report them, but he didn't even remember seeing them in the halls or lunchroom.

Ambrose's eyes practically glowed with suppressed fire. *Do these kids understand the trouble they're in if they push her too far?*

Before they reached the mess or Ambrose could respond, a dark sedan with tinted windows pulled up and she got in. Though it was a retreat, Ambrose made her escape look regal, as if the students should bow down to her and thank her for her time.

Instead of appreciating her time, the group laughed at her running from them.

A rock of disgust filled Felix's gut. With tension growing on both sides, it wouldn't be long before a real fight broke out on school grounds.

Chapter 35 - Pain Au Chocolat

Ember

Tuesday after school, Ember and Felix said their goodbyes and were about to walk their separate ways when Vatra drove up. "Busy?"

They both stopped. Ember tilted their head. "What's up, cuz?"

"Your parents and I are heading to the bakery. There's a protest happening because they put up a sign stating 'all are welcome.' The FB coalition is launching a counter-protest. We thought you two may like to join. Felix, your parents are already down there."

"Nice, I'm in," Felix said, opening the back door of the car and getting in.

Smiling, Ember slid into the front.

It didn't take them long to arrive at a quiet side street. When they moved to get out, Vatra stopped them. "From the few times I've observed these protests, if we stay across the street, we'll be fine. That said, I don't think that's exactly the plan. Also, there's never a guarantee. Stay safe and listen to me and your parents."

"Of course," Ember agreed. After their time in the basement of the Wells's house, Ember knew how dangerous these people could be. Both they and Felix knew to listen to the adults in these situations.

Felix nodded. "Understood."

They walked a couple blocks to the downtown center. A group of a dozen people milled around on the sidewalk, blocking the door to the bakery. They all held signs. Some just had the infinity symbol with the cauldron in one of two circles and a "not equal" sign in the other. *Infinite WISDOM* was written along the curve of the bottom of the right side.

Other signs said: *Witches Above Humans. Purify Our People. They Won't Enslave Us. Witches > Humans. Down With Humans. Go Home Phoenixes! I support Tad Shade.*

Ember stopped reading, disgust bubbling up in their gut, their upper lip twitching into a sneer. They'd seen and read it all. There wasn't anything new. On the other side of the street, their parents stood near Felix's mom and dad.

Searching the faces, they found Aunt Nuri and Aunt Monte surrounded by a bunch of adults. It looked like they were organizing something.

As they approached, Aunt Monte spoke. "Okay, here's the plan. We'll need five people, linked arm in arm, and one person to walk behind them—someone who wants to buy something in the bakery. We'll walk down the sidewalk chanting, 'Rights For All.' Our line should be wide enough to sweep the protesters away and clear the door for our 'shopper.'"

She looked around the group to make sure everyone understood. As soon as everyone nodded, she continued. "Once we pass the door, pushing the protesters back, the person in the back will go into the store. They can't claim we're trying to break up their protest. We're just trying to safely get someone into the shop."

One of the volunteers raised his hand. Someone Ember didn't know. "What if they fight back?"

"Well, we all have magic. We'll start with peaceful means and hope that's enough to keep them at bay."

Ember raised their hand. "What happens next?"

"Good question. We do it again. When the line passes, the first person comes out with a bag of goodies. If they don't buy something, the opposition can call foul on us. Then the next person goes in and comes out with their purchase, and so on. The point is, give the bakery business and break up the backbone of their protest."

Dad grunted. "Who makes up the line and who are the shoppers?"

Aunt Nuri smiled at him. "I was thinking Ember and Felix could be our first shoppers. The line would be made up of the stronger adults. If we make it to a third or fourth round, we should only have strong magic practitioners; the protesters will be mad and ready to either fight or leave."

Looking over the faces, Ember saw everyone was in agreement, including their parents and Felix's.

Ember raised their hand. "I'll go first." Felix gazed at them, brow furrowed, then shrugged. "If we're wrong and they decide to be violent, I have the most active proficiencies. Not to mention, they know I'm a phoenix; no one's going to touch me."

Dad grunted and Aunt Nuri nodded. Beyond their family, none of the others seemed to care one way or the other.

Ember stood behind Aunt Monte, Vatra, Mom, Felix's mom, and someone they didn't know. The five strong magic users linked arms and walked forward, chanting. Ember followed as the adults plowed the protesters from the front of the shop. When a clear path to the front door opened up, Ember quickly slipped inside.

The scent of warm caramelized sugar and warm chocolate made Ember's belly grumble. They usually had an after-school treat, and the place smelled divine.

The proprietor looked up, her eyes wide and hair frizzing out from her ponytail. "How did you get past all the madness?"

Ember's heart raced in their chest. A wild smile spread across their face as they looked over the options. "The FB coalition is trying to remove them. I'm in the first wave. I'll have a chocolate croissant ... um." Ember read the small sign. "Pain au chocolat." While the woman wrapped it up, Ember checked over the rest of the options. "I'll probably be back later. This all looks amazing. Tell the next guy who comes in I drooled over the fruit tart. Anyway, what do I owe you?"

The woman shook her head. "On the house. I just appreciate what your group is doing."

"No, really. Part of our plan is to ensure you get business. How much?"

With a grateful smile, she gave a price, and Ember paid.

The woman pointed to the window with her chin. "Now go. It looks like your ride is here."

Ember saw Aunt Nuri walking past the window. They trotted over to the door in time for Felix to open it. He walked in as Ember exited, each smiling goofily at each other. The path to the right was clear, so they darted to the rest of the FB group.

One of the Infinite WISDOM protesters yelled, "It's one of the phoenixes! They have the phoenixes with them! They're the reason our people are getting arrested! Get 'em!"

Where did they get that idea?

Ember made it back to the group and turned. Several of the adults around them ran towards the bakery. They heard rumblings about how to extract Felix.

Hands wrapped around Ember's shoulders, stopping them from darting back to the bakery. "Stay here," Vatra said.

Ember wanted to argue, to help their boyfriend.

Dad opened the bakery door and a moment later he fought his way back with Felix, who also held a white bag. Ember wasn't sure why Felix worried about getting something from the bakery, it seemed so useless in the middle of all the fighting. Then again, he'd been in the store and may not have realized what had happened on the street. He was just continuing on with the plan.

And he would insist on supporting the baker. Just as I did.

Behind Dad, fireballs and ice darts filled the air, as well as small ice twisters and arrows that had a distinct look of water. Each spell was countered, but the fray was getting ugly. People on both sides yelled and grunted, claiming who they'd go after.

Ember narrowed their eyes, debating if they could take one of the idiots out. *Can I? Am I ready to fight with my fire?*

Dad got to them and leaned down to be heard. "Go home, both of you."

Felix's dad jogged over and handed Felix keys. "Take our car. It's over there, two blocks away on Seventh Street." He pointed.

Dad nodded. "Perfect. We'll get you home."

They ran towards the fighting and Felix and Ember retreated. As much as Ember wanted to help, and they assumed Felix did as well, they were young and not yet strong enough or trained enough to fight.

The path to the car was clear. As relieved as Ember was for their and Felix's safety, they worried over the rest of the people trying to break up the protest.

In the car, Ember sighed. "Should we have fought against leaving? I could've stripped fire from some of the protesters."

Next to them, Felix navigated, avoiding the streets with the fighting. "I don't know. There are things I could've done as well from a distance. Earth can be used to knock people down or make a shield. Calming people down isn't a forbidden mind skill. I just ... I don't know."

The two got lost in their thoughts, driving the rest of the way in silence.

At Ember's place, they waited in the living room, watching the clock and listening to the news. Ember handed Felix the pain au chocolat they'd gotten and with a small smile, he handed them his bag with the fruit tart. As they ate, they watched their phones, both placed on the table. Neither buzzed with a message.

"Those desserts were really good," Felix said, smiling. "We should go there again."

"I agree." Ember watched their phone. "Do you want coffee, some real food?"

"Sure."

Ember went into the kitchen and made coffee, pulling out the leftover mac and cheese bake from the night before.

While they worked, Felix asked, "Did you see those spells? Like, in class, they challenge us, but it's nothing like what we saw."

They each took a portion and, unable to tamp their frustration, Ember warmed the meal with their fire. "I know, some of what they did on both sides ... like, is that taught in college? Community center classes for self-defense?"

Felix snorted. "No idea."

Ember continued to text with Daisy as they discussed the different spells they had seen.

While they ate, everyone returned. Aunt Monte, Mom, Dad, Felix's mom, Aunt Nuri, and Felix's dad, all filed into the living room. The mac and cheese sat like a boulder in Ember's gut. Numb, Ember followed them, then re-counted the adults. No matter how many times they looked over all the faces, Vatra didn't appear.

They tried to swallow, but their mouth had gone dry. "Where's Vatra?"

Mom slowly shook her head. "The fighting got ... confusing. There were people everywhere."

"But where is Vatra?"

She continued as if Ember hadn't spoken. "Five of theirs ended up being arrested."

"But Mom." Ember said, tiny dread spikes attacking their body. "Where is Vatra?"

Dad slumped. "We think someone from Infinite WISDOM took him."

Chapter 36 - I See You

Ambrose

Saturday night, Mr. Shade swaggered into the dining room. Mother and Mr. Walsh were already at the table, though Ambrose had no idea why Cress's dad was eating dinner with them.

"What did the chef prepare for our meal?" Mr. Shade bellowed as he crossed to the head of the table.

A server ran over and poured white wine into his glass. "Tonight the chef has prepared a five-course menu. For the first course, he's prepared Korean barbecue bao buns. The second course is hot and sour soup. For the third course, he has rolled perfect rainbow sushi. The entree will be Mongolian Beef, extra spicy. And finally, for dessert, there will be a selection of ice creams: mango, red bean, and lime."

Extra spice? Since when do we have flavor in our food? I thought good food had disappeared with all our long term staff. Despite herself, Ambrose was interested.

Mr. Shade leaned back with a serpentine smile. His eyes shifted to her with a leer that made Ambrose feel dirty, as if he wanted her to know she better appreciate everything he was doing for her. "That is acceptable. Have the chef create his menus for the week and have it on my desk by noon tomorrow."

"Your ... desk? Sir?" The server hovered with the wine bottle held slightly askew over Mother's glass.

"Yes, *my* desk. I'm using the main office as no one else is around to occupy that room. Is there any reason why I *shouldn't* claim it as my own?"

The bottle began to clatter against the buttons of his top as the server clutched the bottle to his chest and trembled. "No, sir." He retreated as quickly as he could.

Mr. Shade took a long sip of his wine. "Does anyone else have an issue with my new office?"

Ambrose clenched her jaw but otherwise didn't respond. She hadn't been responding too much over the last month, so he shouldn't take this as anything new.

Mother smiled. "Sounds delightful." Ambrose wondered if anyone else heard the tightness in her voice. She wouldn't have noticed it herself before, but she now paid attention. Her mother had gone from black and white to technicolor in one small conversation.

A smile slithered over Mr. Shade's face. "I'm considering painting the room. The feng shui is all wrong."

Before anyone could respond, four servers came out and placed the bao buns in front of them. The food smelled great. Ambrose picked up a fork and knife and sliced off a quarter to try. Both men picked up their offering. Mr. Shade took a healthy bite, and Mr. Welsh popped the full thing in his mouth.

I wonder if I could put some slow-acting poison in their food. Who would know?

Ambrose shut her eyes to banish the thought. She had to get control of herself. She forced herself to ignore them as she finished the buns.

The first two courses were delicious, if blander than she preferred. 'Spicy' wasn't what it used to be. Mr. Shade didn't really enjoy things with that much flavor. Mr. Shade and Mr. Walsh discussed the day.

"Were you here during the full move?" Mr. Shade asked the other man. There was no chance he'd ask

Ambrose or Mother. He knew that answer anyway. "I was busy setting up my room and office, so I haven't been monitoring anyone else's actions."

Mr. Walsh lifted his bowl to drink the last dredges of his soup. A slurp signaled when he'd drained the last bit. Everyone at the table watched him. *Does he not know how to behave in civilized company?* Ambrose looked down at her soup bowl to hide the disgust she felt.

"Nah," Mr. Walsh said. She looked up in time to see him wipe his mouth on the sleeve of his shirt. "I was sitting at home watching a movie and realized I was lonely. Usually I have Cress around, but of course, he's gone. I thought about visiting him, but I wasn't sure if that was allowed. So, I came here to ask. Before I could tell the door person my reason for coming, I was being ushered to a chair in here." He smiled at everyone at the table. "Well, now, who am I to say 'no' to a fine free meal with good company?"

"Very good! You're welcome any time." Mr. Shade smiled. "And of course you can visit your son any time you want."

Ambrose's whole body tightened in fury. This wasn't his house. These weren't his servants. He wasn't paying for any of it. What right did he have to dictate anything? She shot a glance at Mother, but she just shook her head as if to say, 'later.' Her motion morphed as she smiled. "Of course he is. We always welcome guests."

Ambrose was amazed at how subtle her mother could be. All these years and she'd never known.

"Great. You are such good people, Mr. Shade," Mr. Walsh said, smiling wide.

"Call me Tad."

"Only if you'll call me Brian."

They tapped their wine glasses.

The sushi roll was served next. As with the first two courses, it was well made. Ambrose wasn't sure who the chef was, but their culinary skills were top-notch.

After two bites, Mr. Shade turned to Mother. "So, did you know there have been protesters popping up all over town?"

Mother's eyes widened and she gave the impression of a lost doe. "I didn't, sir. Where have they been picketing?" She blinked, twice. Ambrose could almost hear the action. She could swear she felt the vapid response grate against her soul. It was at that moment she realized the skill Mother had developed to spy, to gather information, and to survive in this patriarchal world.

I don't know that I want to follow in Mother's footsteps, but I can admire her subtlety and acting ability. And even if I don't follow, I can learn.

Knowing they couldn't change their situation, Ambrose clenched her jaw then relaxed and went back to eating.

"Well, first it was our supporters telling businesses that let humans pass through their doors that they won't support them. But then counter-protests have sprung up."

Mother's eyes grew even wider, and her eyebrows rose. "Really? How did they find the rallies?"

"Oh, honey. That isn't hard. They're all over the place, and they aren't quiet. You know, that's the point of protesting." His voice dripped with condescension. "The interesting part is, one of our leaders brought me a gift. He knocked out one of their people and dragged him here. I had circulated images from some probable creatures I ran into at a restaurant. Now, I don't know for sure that this man is a phoenix, but I know the best way to find out." He chuckled. "I'm taking care of that tonight, if you care to join me."

Ambrose coughed, choking on the last bite of food she ate. She grabbed her glass of water and drank deeply, trying to clear her airways. *Did he so cavalierly claim he'd kill someone? He doesn't know they're a phoenix; for all he knows, it would just be murder.*

Mr. Walsh's blanched and he pushed his plate a bit away from himself.

Mother shrank back as if slapped. "Oh."

Mr. Shade smiled, then looked between Ambrose and her mother, ending on Mother. "I expect the fact that I have a phoenix to remain amongst the four of us. I know I have a leak; how else was your husband and Cress caught? My guess is the mole, the tender heart that's telling all our darkest secrets, is your daughter, Julia. I hope I'm wrong. I wouldn't want to have to punish her."

He narrowed his eyes and pinned Ambrose with his gaze. "If I learn that someone in this family has been working for the other side, I won't be happy. You, Ambrose, know what happens when I'm not happy."

Ambrose trembled under his glare, too tongue-tied to get words out. She remembered her mom's words and, trying to look cowed, forced a nod, then looked down at her plate. *I can't let him see the hate boiling within me. If he stares much longer, my fire will be clear as day.*

Mother's voice cracked out, "Why would you think Ambrose is behind this? She is such a daddy's girl. She has always supported this cause. She is the last person ..."

Mother, no! You're saying too much. There are only two of us.

Mr. Shade's hungry gaze shifted to her. "Why are you speaking? I don't remember asking for your opinion. I didn't say it *was* Ambrose, just that it was my best guess. I could always be wrong. I'm just reminding everyone that anyone in this household found working against us would end up in one of the cells in the basement."

Mother stared back, not saying anything else. A tension in her body belied her normal ignorant posturing.

"Julia, is there something you want to tell me?" Mr. Shade's voice came out soft and smooth and very dangerous.

"No," Mother said, her doe-like expression returning with a soft smile.

Terror surged through Ambrose. She wasn't sure what to do next. Was she in danger? What would Mr. Shade do to her mom? And who was in the basement?

The rest of dinner was consumed in a tense silence. Once Ambrose had tasted each of the ice creams, she stood. She'd gotten into that habit with Father, and didn't even think about changing it with Mr. Shade.

Why do I have to ask this interloper permission to leave my table? He shouldn't even be here.

Mr. Shade smiled. "You may be excused, Ambrose. I'll see you at seven tomorrow morning for breakfast."

Though she wanted to run, she walked slowly and kept her back stiff. She had a last thought for her mom, but there was nothing she could do for her. There never had been, not with that man who was willing to lock them up and do so much worse.

Sunday morning, Ambrose arrived in the dining room at six fifty-eight for breakfast. There was no way she would be late and tempt the irrational ire of the man who'd somehow taken over her home.

After she sat, a nervous server set a plate with a poached egg and toast in front of her. Then he brought her a glass of freshly squeezed orange juice and a mug of coffee. A moment later, Mr. Shade joined her and was given the same meal.

They ate in silence. Ambrose kept expecting her mother to arrive; she was usually more punctual than this, but there was no sign of her. It wasn't like her to miss a meal or do anything that would rock the boat.

When Ambrose finished, she stood.

"You may be excused, Ambrose."

She tempted fate. "May I ask a question?"

"Sure, ask away."

"Do you know where my mother is?"

"Yes, of course. I know everything that happens around me. I offered her a choice last night. Join me in my bed or admit she was the mole and sleep in a cage in the basement. She chose the latter. I'm afraid it may be some time before you see your mother again, not that there was much love lost between the two of you."

Ambrose nodded in understanding and walked to her room, icicles of terror shooting through her as Mr. Shade laughed.

Chapter 37 - An Unlikely Alliance

Ember

Sunday was a long day. Ember and their parents had spoken and decided the most likely place Vatra had been taken was the cells underneath the Wells's home where Ember had been held. They knew the cells and the monotony they held. It hurt them to their soul to imagine anyone, especially Vatra down there.

Their lessons on folding space using spatial magic had gone from theory and practice to something much more important. Ember was the one who knew the area well enough to portal there. They had to figure the spell out. The need pulsated through them, making them feel like a kite string, taught and ready to snap.

During the day, Ember had attempted to connect themself to the underground cells three times. They hadn't been so attuned to that place, even while trapped there. The only thing that they'd achieved was to confirm the shift to phoenix did heal their body, soul, and drained magic.

Ember trembled with the effort. They knew they should eat but worry gnawed at them and their stomach cramped. It got to the point that they ate small bits of high calorie foods to keep their energy up since the idea of a big meal made them feel like falling from the sky out of control.

Dad shopped to stock more and more of the foods Ember loved to keep up with the amount of magical and transformational needs that everyone predicted in Ember's future. Despite the stress eating at them now, everyone knew food was a key ingredient for this to work.

As excited as the prospect of chips, muffins, fruits, cheese, and crackers made them, they'd prefer to just have Vatra home.

After their third failure, Mom sat next to Ember. "I know this is hard, Ember, but I really do believe in you.

No spatial magic practitioner figures this out quickly. Don't beat yourself up. It'll happen. You're doing great."

Ember nodded. Nothing felt great about the situation, but they hung on to the complement.

Ember woke up early on Monday morning to try one more time. They didn't think it would work, but the more times they practiced, the easier the process felt. It got to the point that they really understood what they were doing, but for some reason, just couldn't get all the pieces aligned to work. Something was missing.

Sitting at breakfast, Ember drank their coffee and ate a bagel. Dad sat next to them with his own breakfast. He looked haggard, as if he too, weren't sleeping well.

After they finished their food, Ember got up to make lunch. "Do you think he's testing Vatra like he tested me?"

"To what end?" Dad asked.

"The same I guess." Ember shrugged. "When Mr. Shade ran into us at dinner the other day, you know, at that restaurant, he kept asking who of us were phoenixes. He's obsessed."

Dad clenched his jaw, eyes narrowing. "Put me in a room with that man for a minute." He shook his head. "Sorry, Ember, I shouldn't talk, or even think like that, but he's a roach ... a disease that needs to be stopped. The idea that he has the arrogance to try to play with phoenixes—" Dad just shook his head, unable to finish his statement.

"And what happens if he does harm Vatra?" Ember's words came out soft, but Dad flinched, mouth tightening before he responded.

"Do you have any ideas?" He watched Ember move around, collecting food into a small reusable canvas lunch bag, then he sipped his coffee.

"He collects Everfire. He had some in that moonstone box. Maybe he's trying to get more? Ambrose dissipated the stuff he had when I was imprisoned."

The look Dad gave told Ember everything they needed to know about that plan. He shook his head. "Well, when we left Serafina Landing and the Phoenix Forest, we all had moonstone on us. I believe Vatra has his in his pocket. He should be fine. It'll hurt, but that's about it. He's an old enough phoenix to suck it up and he knew what could happen when he followed us home to help."

Ember bit their lower lip. "What if Mr. Shade *uses* Everfire. Could he have secured more?"

Dad laughed humorlessly. "That presumptuous little—" He shook his head. "Our fire doesn't bring final death, dear. It would be awful, but Vatra can't be taken away from us without deciding he's ready to leave this world. It's the one thing you need to understand about our kind. And if he is in phoenix form, it wouldn't even harm a feather on his body. It's how we transport the stuff."

It felt like a weight was lifted from their shoulders. They knew this was true in the back of their mind, but hearing it again was comforting.

"This is why you need to attend phoenix school, Ember. These aren't the things you should be worrying about."

Ember wrinkled their nose and snorted. "Speaking of school, I was wondering, should I stay home and continue to try to get to Vatra?"

Mom came into the kitchen and poured herself coffee. "No, dear. I don't want you to burn yourself out. It's good to practice, but you need breaks. Give your mind and body time to adjust to the trials and what you've learned. Once a day is great. You're up to three times a day. More than that won't make the necessary connections in your mind."

"Yeah, whatever, fine." Ember sighed. "Anyway, I'm off to school. Don't forget, I have my first meeting of the Ring of Fire thingy after school today."

Dad's smile seemed a bit sad and distracted. "Have fun."

The morning was slow and uneventful, exactly how Ember had hoped it would go. They kept thinking about their cousin Vatra and what he was going through. They'd been in the cell and could picture the day in and day out boredom he experienced. Not to mention the testing.

Ember wished they could figure out their stupid magic and make the connection.

Why is this so hard?

At lunch, Olivia was the first to join them. "Your meeting with the Ring of Fire is tonight. I'm so excited."

"You'd think you were the one who got in, not me." Ember smiled, taking a bite of their ham and cheese sandwich.

"I mean, I know it was you, but someone I know and like made it in. It makes it seem so much more real. And you did it before Ambrose. First person in our grade. It means something, you know."

"It wasn't real before?" Ember laughed at Olivia's exuberance, glad for something to distract them from their thoughts of Vatra.

"No. I mean, yes, but before everyone involved was so ... I don't know, like a movie star. Someone you never spoke with." Olivia shook her head. "I don't know. I'm explaining this poorly."

Ember shook their head.

Daisy sat down. "Any word on Vatra?"

"No. And before you ask ... no." They didn't want Daisy accidentally asking about their magic attempts. Explaining without bringing up spatial magic would be difficult. They were still keeping spatial magic on the down low. Even though Olivia was becoming a closer friend, Ember wasn't ready to let her know about this.

Daisy made a sour face. "That's rough. I'm sorry, Ember. I wish I could help you figure it out."

Olivia watched them. "What are you trying to figure out? We've done some good brainstorming together in Magical Creations. Maybe I can help."

Ember bit their bottom lip and shook their head. "I ... I'd love to get your input, but this is different. Mom is helping me and it's her specialty. She's been studying this for ... well, a really long time."

Olivia's face fell and she gave a slight shrug before digging into her lunch. Ember felt bad, but knew this was the right decision.

Felix and Tansy made it to the table, and they all spent a few minutes eating.

Felix rubbed Ember's arm. "So, what's the news on—"

"Ember, we need to talk." Ambrose stood above them, arms crossed, face set in a scowl.

Ember glared back. "Do we?"

It felt like they'd had this conversation before. Why was she always approaching them?

"Yes. This is important. Either we talk here, in front of all of … them." The last word dripped with disgust. "Or we talk in private. I think you'd rather this be private."

Searching the faces of their friends, Ember was pretty sure it was Ambrose that would prefer the conversation be secret, but at the end of the day, it didn't matter. Ember just wanted the conversation over with. "Fine, let's go."

Ambrose gazed at their lunch. "Take that, this may take some time."

Ember grunted, sounding a lot like Dad. They followed Ambrose and they ended up in a stairway that was rarely used.

The two sat as far away as possible to have a quiet conversation. Ambrose visibly clamped her jaw for a moment while Ember pulled out the remains of their sandwich and continued to eat.

I don't know why I'm here, but I'm not going to lose out on potential energy because of her.

Finally, Ambrose said, "Do you know where your … protest person is?" She waved her hand as if uncertain how to describe whoever she was talking about. "Are they a phoenix, by the way? Mr. Shade seems to think so."

"You mean my cousin? He's in the cells beneath your house. If that's what this is about, we figured that out already."

Ambrose scoffed. "Right. Well, you need to get him out. Mr. Shade isn't sane. He's going to hurt him."

Ember barked out a laugh then covered their mouth as Ambrose glared. They tensed their muscles at the knowledge as remembered pain flared in their body, but the information didn't shock Ember. "Sorry, was that supposed to be news? He's been spouting asinine stuff since the beginning. Wait ... *you've* been speaking his ridiculous words from the start. Moreover, my mom taught him when he went to university. He's been off his rocker since back then."

"Of course he has," Ambrose mumbled, rubbing her forehead with her thumb and finger. "Has he always been sexist, too?"

"No idea, but probably." Ember had to tamp down any sympathy they may have felt for Ambrose. They weren't sure where that comment came from and weren't going to ask. They had to focus on Vatra.

"Well, you still need to get your person ... your cousin out. You think he's going to be okay, but you need to clear him and the other prisoners out. Even if your guy will survive, what about the others? Have you thought about that? Of them? You know what it's like down there."

Ember rubbed their eyes with one hand. "Ambrose, it isn't that easy. You live there; why don't *you* let them out?"

"Ember, please. Get the people to safety. Can you, I don't know, mobilize your side? Those people? They came to save you. What will it take?"

"What's wrong, Ambrose? Why are you so hell-bent on the prisoners being saved? You weren't this concerned last time." What was Ember missing?

"This." Ambrose showed Ember a video of Mr. Shade using Everfire against a prisoner. It made Ember's stomach turn and they stuffed the rest of their lunch back in their backpack.

"How did you get this? Where did it come from?" There was a tremor in Ember's voice.

"The security footage from before your people came to save you. I had more freedom of movement back then. I made copies of a few of the 'test' subjects."

Ember's heart beat a fast staccato in their chest. "Any videos of me?"

"No. Only of the humans. I destroyed the ones of you. I think all of it is despicable, but when it crossed over to magic users, that was the last straw. My hard line."

Ambrose has some weird theories of right and wrong. Ember wasn't about to question her. Everything she said made their head hurt. *Gods, I don't want to care. It's Ambrose; she's been in this from the beginning. I can't care.*

After taking a breath, Ember decided they were a better person than that. "Are you safe at home?"

Ambrose sighed. "Probably not, but I'm not leaving while that monster has Mother locked up."

"Right." Ember thought, then paused, the feeling of utter dread washing through them. "Wait, he has your *mom* in one of those cells?"

"Focus, Savita. We have to save the prisoners." Ambrose blushed, but her voice was stern.

"Right, prisoners. Can you send me the videos?" Ember asked. "That could help."

Ambrose shook her head. "Not until my mother is safe."

Chapter 38 - Blending Into The Crowd

Ember

After school on Monday, Felix met Ember at their locker. "Okay, we haven't had time to talk. What did Ambrose want at lunch?"

Ember stacked most of their school things in the locker. They didn't have anything they needed to work on before Tuesday. "It's a long story. I have to get to that Ring of Fire thing. My first official meeting is today. Maybe we can talk afterwards?"

"Sure. Can I come over tonight? Maybe after dinner? Say seven?" Once Ember's locker was shut, Felix pulled them in for a quick hug.

"Gods above! We're in school. Can't you two behave?" Daisy's voice was full of mirth as she opened her own locker and started rummaging through it. "So, what were you two discussing, or do I not want to know?"

Ember winked at Daisy. "Felix is coming over at seven to discuss what happened at lunch. I have to run to that meeting." Ember was feeling less and less excited about Ring of Fire. They knew it was a great opportunity, but they weren't sure it was a good fit for their life in the long run. Would they even be around next year? Would they be attending a university with witches? Did any of it really matter?

"Oh, yeah, that's today." Bookbag set for home, Daisy shut her locker and spun to face them. "You're one of the elite of the elite, top of the top, coolest of the—"

"Stop!" Ember said as their friend teased them, putting up both hands. "I have never been any of those things, and you know it. Maybe next year when Felix gets invited into the Mystic Mind Masters he can be all of them. I'm just me."

Daisy laughed as Felix rolled his eyes. She said, "Well, you're not wrong about that. Now, about this evening. Is this a private hang-out with the boyfriend, or can I crash?"

They both turned to Felix, who shrugged. "I can swing by and pick you up. I have no problem with that."

That figured out, they each left and headed in their own direction.

Ember slowly walked through the halls towards the east field. They had to text their parents about Ambrose. There hadn't been time during classes. Teachers frowned on students using their phones. They explained most of the situation and that they were heading to the Ring of Fire event and would be home to discuss afterwards.

At the door out of the school, they stopped and texted more. *Should I come home and skip this meeting? It seems so trivial compared to everything happening.*

Mom replied first. *No, love. Go. We need to get plans in place. We can't just rush in without a plan. We don't know if he's set up any traps or fail-safes to automatically harm his prisoners.*

Slumping against the wall, Ember clenched their jaw to stop themself from tearing up. It was just so much. *Okay, but let me know if you change your mind.*

Dad replied with a thumbs up, including that he'd speak with Monte and Aunt Nuri about everything as well.

That done, Ember quickened their step to get out to the east field. Part of them was excited to get to the Ring of Fire meeting and see what all the mystery was about, but they were also worried.

Will anyone act like those people in the audience? Will people think that because I'm a phoenix I don't belong? Will I get weird looks because I'm not a twelfth-year? How uptight will these people be? Do I have to act ... snobbish? Can I even act that way? Gah! Maybe I should've talked to Zahra, gotten her advice before math class. Or maybe Ambrose at lunch.

That thought cheered them. The image of Ambrose's expression of horror and disgust put a lightness in Ember's step.

As they approached the location of the Fire Magic class where the Ring of Fire met, Ember saw everyone milling about in small groups talking. The members all wore their robes, except Mr. Tine who sat off to the side as an observer. Where the 'stage' had been, chairs were set up in a circle. No one stood near them, as if that were another part of the meeting they weren't ready to face yet.

Once Ember reached the other students, they dropped their bag, found the robe from the initiation ceremony in their bag, and slipped it on.

A female student broke away from one of the smaller groups. "Okay, everyone, we're all here. Please take a seat so we can meet the new members."

Ember looked at the eleven people in the field and found Zahra. Not knowing anyone else, they walked up to her and said, "Can we sit together?"

Zahra nodded. "Absolutely. I know most of the people, but not everyone ... at least not well."

They found seats across from the speaker, who continued. "We're going to play one of those games we all hate. We have a couple of new faces in the crowd, and they need to know our names. And, for the first time in over fifteen years, or so I've been informed, we have an eleventh-year." She leaned in. "That makes us special. We get to be put in some history books, or something. So, everyone!" She clapped. "Name, rank, and serial number."

Another female laughed, shaking her head. "Tara, not helpful. What information do you really want?"

The first speaker—Tara?—wore the dark purple robe. Everyone else wore the same deep red robe as Ember and Zahra. *So, does that make Tara the leader?* Tara smiled at the second speaker. "How about your name and one boring fact about yourself?"

There was grumbling as everyone made unhappy faces.

Ember whispered to Zahra, "Boring?"

Zahra shrugged. "No idea, but it sounds way less stressful than a fun fact or what we did over winter break."

Ember thought about it and decided they agreed. *Over winter break I got thrown in a cell, poisoned, rescued, learned about a community of over a hundred phoenixes, and had my fire magic tested ... much more intensely than anything this group could imagine.* Nope, that wouldn't go over well at all.

The leader spoke again. "Okay, I'll go first. My name is Tara, and I own three horses that I love to ride on the weekends."

A boy snorted. "Since you talk nonstop about your horses, you're right about that being boring."

Tara smirked. "And that's how you do it. Okay, Christina, you're next."

The second person who'd spoken smiled. "Hi, new fire friends. I'm Christina, and a boring thing about me? I always put my socks on before my pants."

Everyone in the group laughed, and the boy commented, "Not boring enough!"

Ember relaxed as one by one people gave boring facts: I love cereal for breakfast; I put my left shoe on before my right; I've lived in the same house my whole life ... it went on and on.

When it was Ember's turn, they said, "My name is Ember, and I was home-schooled before coming here."

To them, home schooling had been dull in comparison to public school. Different teachers, so many students, and bullies. It had taken them over a month until they no longer got lost roaming the school. Daisy had been their lifeline.

"Nope, that's definitely interesting. Try again." Ember tilted their head. Who was the speaker, Jonathan? Jason? Josiah? Julian!

Ember laughed. "Fine, I like chocolate ice cream better than vanilla."

The heckler slapped his hand on his chest. "Say it isn't so." Then he winked.

"Hi, most of you know me, and those who don't will appreciate this," Zahra said. "I'm Zahra, and I have the most annoying brother in this school."

Everyone laughed. It seemed Ember wasn't the only one who knew Xander to be a bit obnoxious.

When everyone was finished, Ember smiled, feeling less nervous and almost like they belonged.

Tara stood. "This week's meeting will be short. We wanted to have an opportunity to meet the two of you," she waved at Ember and Zahra, "and let you know about what we do. Normally we meet once each week, as you know. There are a few ways the meetings run. Some weeks, we have a community leader come to speak on what they do for the city, county, or state. It's nice to have the opportunity to network as well as learn about possible occupations."

Tara started walking around the group as if playing a slow game of duck-duck-goose. "A second way we run these club meetings, is to have a demonstration of a way fire magic can be used that maybe none of us thought of before. Then, there is a lesson on how it is done. To be honest, this is the most common thing we do. We are great because we can do more. As a group, we like to dream, challenge ourselves with 'what could be possible with our fire?' It's a goal to take those questions and push ourselves. Can we make the impossible possible? We all love knowing more than the student next to us in class."

Tara stopped behind Ember's seat and placed her hands on their shoulders. "We're hoping next week that you, Ember, would maybe show us how you dry things, like you did with the lawn during the audition, or maybe start smaller with clothes. We are all excited about the prospect."

There were enthusiastic comments and big smiles from all round the circle.

Ember searched all the faces then shrugged. "Yeah, sure, I'd love to try to show you."

"Excellent. I'm predicting Mr. Tine will join us in that lesson. Maybe some other people, too. You do know that some of your everyday teachers have a proficiency in fire magic, right?" Tara smirked towards Ember and Zahra. "Some of the former members of Ring of Fire may attend as well. We have a website and always post what our challenges are and what future lessons will be. Our large network of expert fire practitioners provides us with the greatest opportunities to learn and teach fire magic."

Ember tensed at the thought of teaching so many people, especially a teacher … maybe multiple teachers and adults. They'd been helping out in Air Magic class, but that was students, not adults.

Tara continued on her path. "Sometimes we go on field trips or discuss what we need to do to be successful either here in secondary school or later on, at university. There are a lot of things we do, and we're thrilled to have more members."

Christina raised her hand.

Tara nodded. "Christina."

"Can we go back to challenge ideas and make a new list of insane things we want to do with fire, but aren't sure are even possible? That way we have research topics if we want them."

"That sounds like a great way to end this meeting. Do you have an offering?"

"Yeah, I want to create fire that doesn't burn."

Julian laughed. "What's the point of fire that doesn't burn?"

She shook her head at him, as if he weren't seeing the bigger picture. "We could create something that could warm us up without burning. Maybe share that heat with others."

His eyebrow rose. "Oh! Then we could make the fire different colors. People could carry the colored fireballs to keep warm and support sports teams or celebrate holidays like Christmas."

"Or Valentine's day," one of the girls on the other side of the circle said.

"What about words? Ember, that thing you did on the video, was that real?" Tara asked.

"How about objects? Zahra, that cake was so cool. What else can you do?"

Zahra shot a glance at Ember and smiled sheepishly.

"Can fire be used to cool?" Everyone gaped at the person asking. "You know, if we can pull fire *out* of the thing, wouldn't it be *less* hot?"

By the end of the meeting, Ember felt giddy as they realized they had more things to think about than they'd ever expected.

Chapter 39 - If At First You Don't Succeed ...

Felix

Felix sat in the backyard with Ember and Daisy. Every day, he was amazed at the skills Ember had. Watching as they learned and grew thrilled him. It also made him happy that Daisy could join in. It was good for Ember to have their village of friends and supporters around.

On the table between them all sat a tray with crackers and cheese, a few cookies, and hummus. There was a second tray with tea.

"Okay." Ember took a long breath. "I guess there's nothing to do but try to create the portal, shift, and try again. It's pretty much been my days and nights for like … ever."

Daisy shook her head. "Before you jump in, let's talk. You've been beating yourself up. Doing the same thing over and over, right?"

Ember spread their hands and shrugged. "Well, yeah. That's how we learn new magical skills, right? Practice, practice, practice. The same thing, over and over. Eventually, everything falls into place, and we succeed. It's been getting easier and faster. I figure I can't fail forever. Right?"

Amusement surged through Felix at their assessment of the situation. "You aren't all wrong, but that's also the definition of insanity." He smiled at them both. "In reality, I believe you can do this, Ember. Just like your mom said. It's within your abilities … your amazing abilities."

For a moment, Daisy just stared at Ember, face blank, then she sighed. "Let's take this from the top. Do you think you *can* do this?"

"Well, yeah, right? Eventually. Like, at some point? In the future. You know, when my magic is better, stronger, more … I don't know, mature." Ember bit their lower lip and sagged. "I mean, one day. Mom's a master. She can do anything, and it isn't easy for her. I'm just an eleventh-year student in secondary school. A teen who's only half a witch."

A small growl erupted from Daisy and Felix shut his eyes. *Why didn't I see this? Ember's confidence is shot.*

He opened his mouth to respond, but Daisy got there first.

She leaned forward, clasping one of Ember's hands in both of hers. "You won't be able to do this if you don't *think* you can. Every time I've been around, you start with saying you're going to fail. Or you just want to get the next attempt over with. Or something pretty negative. If you plan on failing, is it any wonder you haven't put all the pieces together?"

The side of Felix's mouth lifted, and he huffed out a laugh. "I don't know why I hadn't seen this. Self-sabotage. You can't let anyone down if no one expects success. Clever, Miss Autumn, very clever." Daisy was so bubbly and upbeat that people often missed how smart she was.

Felix reached out to rub Ember's back, so they didn't think the two of them were ganging up on them.

"Thank you. I've been thinking about this a lot. But that isn't it. I have more. Just wait for my brilliance." Daisy winked at Felix, who chuckled. *What does she have up her sleeves?* "Ember isn't wrong that they are a phoenix."

"Really?" Ember laughed. "I am? I hadn't noticed. What part gave it away? It was when I started flying around in the sky, wasn't it?"

"Stop." Daisy smiled back. "What I mean is, you do things differently. The rules don't always work the same way with you. It's like how you can help people with their magic—something I've been meaning to talk to you about." She shook her head. "But not tonight."

"What are you talking about, Daisy? You're rambling." Ember rolled their free hand in a 'get to the point' motion.

Daisy released her breath and sat back. "True but hear me out. What if you combined your spatial magic with fire? Do you think you could give what you're doing a magical boost?"

"Combine? Is that possible?" Ember's brow furrowed as they made a cheese and cracker sandwich.

Felix thought about magic and combining proficiencies. It wasn't anything he'd ever heard or thought about before. He'd have to speak with his parents and ask if it was something taught at university.

Daisy got up and grabbed a garden bucket. She filled it with water. "Okay, trust me on this ... combining proficiencies is what I've been doing in my free time for a month or so."

She lifted a hand, and a perfect sphere of water lifted from the bucket. It was just over a foot across. Both Felix and Ember made small gasping sounds of approval. Neither of them had water magic proficiency. Felix didn't have a frame of reference to gauge Daisy's skill level, but what she was doing looked impressive.

"That's not the interesting thing," Daisy said, sounding distracted. "That wasn't that hard. Just ... hold on." Daisy lifted her left and wiggled her pointer finger. A small disruption formed in the center of the water ball.

Felix leaned closer, watching the blues, purples, and greens play across the surface of the sphere. It was mesmerizing.

"Is that a twister? Like did you ... are you doing two proficiencies? Together?" Ember sounded as fascinated as Felix felt.

"Yes. Now, unless you want a shower, let me focus." The colors stopped swirling and then the water poured back into the bucket. "You see," Daisy said, once all the magic had dissipated, "I've been playing with combining things. I think I have that one down, though beyond being beautiful, or watering a field in a single blast, I'm not sure of the applications. I'm still playing around. I figure, once I've done some research, I can ask my parents or some teachers at school." She gave a sheepish smile. "I was kind of wondering if you could combine your fire with the spatial magic to help with the portal."

Felix bit back a laugh. *Of course she wanted to do research before speaking with anyone about it. She needs to become as much of an expert as she can.*

Ember's face hardened. "You want me to create a fire passage? Burn my way to Vatra?"

"No, you're thinking too literally."

Felix leaned back in his chair, both hands wrapped around his cup of tea. *A fire tunnel? Fire. What is fire? Fire burns. Fire destroys. Fire is power.* He looked up. "Fire is energy."

Daisy smiled at him, as if he'd finally figured out what she'd been hinting out. "Yes, but ... can one magical proficiency boost another? Can phoenix fire strengthen what you're trying to do?"

They both turned to Ember.

The color drained from their face. "I ... whoa. I don't know. I mean, you're right, fire has historically and traditionally been used as an energy source ... but for magic. That's ... I don't know if that is the worst idea I've ever heard, the most bizarre, or the beginning of utter genius." They turned to Daisy. "Considering the source, I guess I'll go with 'yes.'"

Daisy laughed. Ember stared off into space, breathing slowly. "Okay, use my fire to fuel my spatial magic. Then, bam! I have a portal. Give me a few seconds to work this out. If it works ..." Ember's eyes widened. "Gods above and below! If this actually works, I may have something that I can sustain on this side."

Ember settled back in their chair and closed their eyes.

Felix knew the process could take a lot of time. They ate some crackers and hummus, then pointed at the sliding doors. Daisy nodded, staying behind so Ember wasn't alone.

He found Ember's parents, along with Vi and Monte, in the living room with blueprints of Ambrose's house. He explained Daisy's theory.

Mr. Savita tilted his head. "This whole phoenix-witch thing. If I knew what a hassle it would be having a child who was both—"

"What, dear?" Mrs. Savita asked, one eyebrow raising.

"I'd have tried sooner?" he ended, leaning over to give her a quick kiss.

She laughed. "Good save." She turned to Felix. "Okay, Ember is trying to fuel their witch magic with phoenix fire. If this works, they'll have almost an unlimited supply of *oomph*." She shook her head. "I wish you'd come in and told us before starting this madness. I think we should all go out back. I, for one, don't want to miss the outcome of this experiment."

As they stood, Vi turned to Felix. "This was Daisy's idea? She always seems so ... I don't know ... flighty."

Felix smiled. "She's one of the top students at school. She hides her intelligence behind an energetic personality, but don't be fooled. She's also been practicing combining her magics. She did a demonstration ... it was amazing."

Mrs. Savita laughed. "In secondary school, our proficiencies are challenging enough that we need to use both concentration and hand motions. Even the theory of combining isn't usually brought up until university. Students trying it can lead to bigger issues. Historically, students have burned themselves—or buildings—down. You say she had control?"

"She did."

"Amazing."

Once they'd reached the backyard, Felix saw that the air to the left of Ember was already starting to ripple. He hadn't been gone that long. The phoenix fire really was helping.

Everyone watched as the distortion started to coalesce into a shimmering oval. Breathing hard, Ember opened their eyes. They glowed an amber, like the heart of a fire, and Ember looked a bit wild ... but excited.

Their arm trembled as they slowly lifted it towards the affected air. A tension filled the backyard as everyone held their breath. And then a cheer went up as Ember's hand disappeared.

Voice soft and wavering, as if they were with them, but also on the other side of the portal, Ember said, "Okay, I am ... really good. I think I can hold this a while. The fire helps. Why doesn't someone head over and get Vatra?"

Felix stepped up. "I'll go. I have mind magic and have protection from anyone messing with me. I also can encourage whoever is there to forget I came."

Monte also volunteered. "What about any electronic evidence? I'm needed for that. Ember, can two go and three return?"

"Four, maybe more. Mr. Shade locked up Ambrose's mom; you need to save her, too. Possibly others. And yes. I don't think it's the number of passages, it's the time. I'd say ... ten minutes?"

Vi swore. "Mrs. Wells is our mole. I wonder how she was caught?"

Ember shook their head. "Save now, question later."

Felix grabbed Monte's arm. "Wait." He shut his eyes, found her mind, and imagined an impermeable wall around it. "Okay, your mind should be safe for at least an hour."

She blinked. "Thanks."

Felix walked through first, and then immediately stepped to the side. He found himself in a cool, dimly lit corridor surrounded by large picture windows. Looking through one he saw an empty room with a bed.

Monte appeared behind him. They followed the corridor until they found a door labeled, 'Security.'

Inside, there weren't any guards, but eight monitors displayed the inside of six empty and two occupied rooms. Felix noted the locations and grabbed the keys under the monitors. "Should we be suspicious at how obvious these keys are?" he asked.

Monte snorted. "No. Who would be down here but Tad and the guards, who are all idiots? They need this area to be easy access."

Amused, Felix headed out as Monte started typing on the keyboard.

In the first room, Felix found Vatra. He had on a white robe and looked different ... softer maybe? He flinched, but when he saw Felix, he relaxed. "Felix, is that really you?"

"Yeah, come on. Let's get you out of here."

Vatra tightened the robe and followed Felix out. They slunk through the hall. A pressure on Felix's mind let him know there was someone else nearby. He held up a hand. Turning he whispered, "Hold on."

A guard turned the corner and, seeing them, his eyes widened.

A waterfall of thoughts streamed through Felix's mind as he captured the other man's mind and froze his thoughts. *Can I really change his memories? I made a promise, to Daisy, to myself, to my integrity ... but this is so much bigger. If I don't do this, everything is lost.* His body began to tremble as the internal debate heated up.

Am I any better than Cress?

As a tear streamed down his cheek. He knew it didn't matter. Too many lives were at stake, and if he didn't act fast, they'd all be stuck here. Ember had a limited source of power to keep the portal open.

You decided you need to use the toilet. The one that's on the next floor up is so much better. There's no danger on this floor and nothing to see. It turned Felix's stomach how easy it was to implant the suggestion in the man's thoughts.

After the guard turned, Felix's body shook more. Vatra rubbed his shoulders, bringing peace. "I don't know what you did, but I'm proud of you. It took speed, skill, fast thinking, and determination. But I'm guessing we don't have a lot of time."

Finally able to take a full breath, Felix nodded, and they started looking in windows, trying to find Ambrose's mom. It took three more rooms to find her.

Felix opened the door, and she sat up. Unlike Vatra, she still wore normal clothes: a nice ankle-length blue skirt, a white button-down shirt, and black flats. "Do I know you? Oh, wait, Felix? Is that you? I haven't seen you in years! What are you doing here?"

"I'm here to get you out, Mrs. Wells. Come on."

She trembled. "Where are you taking me?"

"To safety ... away from here. We don't have a lot of time."

She nodded and followed. "What about Ambrose?"

He shook his head. "She isn't down here. We'll worry about her once you're safe."

"He told me ... Gah! Doesn't matter. Promise we'll save my daughter." Her voice quivered with anger or fear. Her eyes burned with determination and unleashed rage.

I don't think I've ever seen so much emotion from her. Where has she hidden it in the past? And how much danger is Ambrose in? If Mr. Shade has locked up Mrs. Wells, what will he do next? Now wasn't the time or place to get these answers. "We'll do our best, ma'am."

When they got to the security room, Monte stood outside waiting. "Come on, let's get out of here."

At the portal, Monte sent Felix back first. In the backyard, Felix watched as Mrs. Wells tumbled through, eyes wide in shock. Vi caught her and took the woman aside to speak quietly with her.

Next was Monte and last Vatra, looking ragged in his white robe.

Mr. Savita swore. "What was it? You had the moonstone on you."

Vatra nodded. "I did, but after he attacked with the Everfire and my clothes burned up, he took the stone away. After that, all bets were off."

Felix shook his head. "What am I missing?"

Vatra sighed. "After years of Fotia having two dads, she's back to having a dad and a mom."

Ember flinched. "Oh, no! What does Mr. Shade know about phoenixes and our secrets? How are we going to fix it?" They dissipated their portal, and their eyes widened. Felix's heart sped up and they stepped forward as they began to shake.

Ember's dad shot forward as their face drained of color and they crumpled. He caught them before their head hit the ground.

Lifting Ember, Mr. Savita whispered, "Damn, child, you'll be the death of me, yet."

Chapter 40 - Caught On Video

Ember

Ember woke. The living room spun for a moment. Despite the full band playing in their head, they pushed up to sitting position and waited for everything to settle. The room seemed full of people. A quick search revealed family, but Ember really didn't look very close.

A moment later, Mom and Aunt Nuri sat down next to them, as if they worried Ember would topple back down. Thinking about it, Ember thought they might be right.

"Hey sweets," Mom said. "Do you need anything?"

"A new head?" Ember massaged their temples and top of their head where everything beat ... hard. "Maybe something to drink?"

She smiled. "How about some hot chocolate and your Aunt Monte?"

Ember perked up at that, then noticed the mug Mom held. After taking a sip they saw Aunt Monte among the friends and family in the room. She came over and placed her hands on Ember's head. A few moments later a coolness washed through Ember and the pain was gone.

Ember sighed with the cessation of pain. "That was fantastic. You're a great person to have around for when one pushes their magic too far, you know that?"

"Or, you could just not push yourself to the point of passing out. Has that happened before?" Aunt Monte raised her eyebrows.

Ember rubbed their eyes. Although their headache had gone, they still felt weak. "No, that was a first. And I don't plan on doing it again."

As Monte got up, Felix slipped in next to them. "Unless you perform another amazing feat of magic well beyond anyone's imagination."

Heat flooded Ember's face. "I mean ... I just did what needed doing, right?" They ducked their head.

Felix bumped shoulders with them as the others in the room all reacted.

"That's exactly what you did." Daisy said, voice flat.

"It was amazing." Mom chimed in.

"I'm getting more snacks." Dad harrumphed. "Ember is obviously still addled."

Laughter bubbled up, and Ember finally gazed into the faces of all the people they loved. "Okay, fine. It was more than nothing, but I don't plan on doing it again for a few days, training or no." Ember found Mom who'd returned to a seat across from them. "And I do want to figure it out without my fire."

Mom hummed. "I don't disagree, but the combination that Daisy suggested accelerated your skill, love. I think we need to continue that, but maybe with less time and fewer people. Build up to what you did to save Vatra."

Memories started to surface. "Wait, Vatra." They looked around. "Where is he? Wait, no ... she, right?"

Because most phoenixes, especially the older ones, tended to learn how to avoid dying for many years, they tended to adopt the pronouns of whichever sex their body currently had. It was why Ember felt so drawn towards being nonbinary. They truly weren't male or female.

Once, before they started in public school, they'd asked Dad about what would happen if a phoenix were pregnant and died. He chuckled, telling them that the baby waited until the next death. He had a friend when he and Nuri were young who'd been pregnant for just over three years.

Shaking themselves from the memory, Ember watched as Aunt Monte got up and headed towards the kitchen. "I'm going to go start dinner."

Vatra came in and sat next to Ember. She didn't look much different than her old self ... just like Dad when he changed. Vatra wore jeans and a loose shirt, just like before. She slipped an arm around Ember's waist. "Thanks." She kissed Ember's head.

Aunt Nuri said. "That jerk, Tad, is playing with things he doesn't understand. Everfire? We really need to figure out a way to stop him."

"At least it isn't *your* house he's taken over." Another woman said as she walked in. Her hair was damp, and she wore some of Mom's clothes.

Ember watched as she headed over to sit next to Aunt Nuri in the love seat. The woman looked a bit like Ambrose. *Is this her mom? Was that part of the rescue successful, too?* The woman's voice dropped to a snarl. "He's claimed every space that isn't tied down and has been spending like we're made of money. I'm worried about checking the finances, though I did find a way to hide some accounts."

Ember shivered at the thought, then sipped their hot chocolate. "That sounds awful. You're Ambrose's mom, right? Is she still there? How long was I out?"

Mom filled a plate with some cheese and crackers. "Only a few minutes. Not long. And yes, this is Ambrose's mom, Julia. You helped save her."

"And Ambrose? Is she still there?" Ember felt scattered, like they needed to get all their ducks in a row, but their ducks were at a rave, and they were in a different state. *Didn't Ambrose imply she also wasn't safe with Mr. Shade?*

"We haven't gotten ahold of her. I need a phone. I didn't have one while locked in the basement."

Ember handed her their phone. "You can use mine."

She smiled and dialed. After a minute she sighed. "Ambrose, this is your Mother. I'm using someone else's phone. Please call me back."

Most people Ember's age didn't like to use their phone for calls. "Why don't you text her as well. It may be faster."

Mrs. Wells nodded. "Fair point." It took a few moments, but then she put the phone down.

They all sat in an awkward silence. Ember debated heading up to their room, but they didn't want to demand their phone back. Just as they finished their hot chocolate, their phone rang. Mrs. Wells checked the display and smiled. "Hello, Ambrose." She paused. "Yes, I got out.

I'm at Ember's place." She leaned back. "Yes, if you can, that would be great. I'll text you the address."

She hung up the phone and handed it to Ember. "If you don't mind."

They nodded and found the last text. They quickly sent Ambrose, one of the last people they'd want at their house, their address.

Looking up, Ember asked, "How will she get here? Will Mr. Shade let her leave the house? Does she have a car? Will she walk?"

"She'll probably sneak out and walk. I don't think she trusts anyone at the house. I know I wouldn't." Mrs. Wells's face tightened. "That jerk has been firing and hiring people so fast, we don't have any staff loyalty anymore. Three months ago, everyone working at the house had been there for years. We knew them all by name. Now they're all cronies to the charlatan my husband invited in."

The hurt and bitterness oozed from her. Ember didn't envy her or Ambrose the situation, it sounded awful. They never thought they'd feel bad for Ambrose and her position, it was strange.

"Okay, why doesn't Felix go pick her up? It'll be safer and faster. He can drop Daisy off on the way since Ambrose will need a minute to escape ... or so I assume."

Before anyone could protest, Felix said, "Sounds good to me."

Ember sent off the text to Ambrose letting her know the plan.

Chapter 41 - Hide And Go Seek

Ambrose

Ambrose wondered if Chef remembered to season the enchiladas. Every evening, the meals tasted more and more bland.

"I really appreciate the invite again, Tad. The food here always impresses." Mr. Walsh smiled, a piece of food stuck in his teeth.

I need time away from this place and these sexist men. I feel like the walls are closing in on me. Maybe tomorrow

I can go home with Josie ... or— It occurred to her she didn't have many friends.

"I'm glad you're enjoying the food. I had to work with the cook to get the recipes just right. He kept messing them up." Mr. Shade sneered. "He's done a wonderful job at fixing his mistakes, don't you agree, Ambrose?"

A shiver ran down her back at his use of her name. She was beginning to feel nauseous being near him. "He's very good at adjusting things, yes." She smiled. "But I'm pretty full. Could I go take an after dinner walk?"

Mr. Shade's face tightened. "You know my feelings about women being off on their own, Ambrose. If you are full, you can go to your room. You know your options."

This isn't even your house. My options? What about the living room? Library? Despite the anger she felt and the questions whirling through her mind, Ambrose just nodded, stood, and turned to walk out.

"And Ambrose, I expect you back at seven sharp for breakfast. We will be civil and eat before you head off to school. I know we can't marry until you're of age, but we will start our routine now."

She'd paused when he started to speak and continued to walk as soon as he stopped. All the muscles in her body were held tight until she shut her bedroom door and began to tremble. Her lock had been removed, but with the door shut she felt a bit of safety from the monsters roaming within the wall of her home.

On the far side of her room was a table and chairs. The only thing left to do was wallow in depression or do her homework. She may as well get her work done. Being smart was one of the hallmarks of who she was. She could at least continue to be smarter than the men around her.

Mr. Shade walked in. "Studying? Again? I've told you. You don't need to do that anymore. You'll be my queen. Thinking won't be necessary, Ambrose. You should be working on your looks and beauty. That will be your use, not," he waved his hand, "that."

"Of course. I just don't want the teachers questioning my lack of work. They may become suspicious." She tried to emulate her mother as she blinked up at him.

It looked as if her words confused him as he squinted and tilted his head. Finally he nodded. "Very good. But soon you'll need to focus more on being a beauty ... well, more of one." His leer was acidic and made bile fill the back of her throat.

When he finally left, she opened the nearest book and began to work.

While she was lost in math, her phone rang. The display showed a number she didn't recognize, and she huffed out a laugh and rolled her eyes. "Who makes phone calls? And they expect me to answer? As if."

A few moments later the thing vibrated. With a sigh, she looked. *Ambrose. It's your mother. Please call.*

Her heart beat faster and she realized her nails bit into her palms as she made fists while gazing at the display. "There's no way," she whispered. "Is this a trap?"

Ambrose swung her head around the room, trying to figure out what was going on. She saw her gym duffle peeking out from under her bed. She'd packed it the day she'd returned. If they had to escape again, she wanted to be prepared.

I can't see Mr. Shade getting a new phone to test me, and if I call this number and hear any other voice ... With a final breath, she decided to make the call.

The line only rang once before ... "Hello, Ambrose."

A lump formed in Ambrose's throat. She couldn't believe it. Her mom's voice came from the other end. How was this possible? "Is it really you? Did you escape?"

There was a quiver in her mom's voice. "Yes, I got out. I'm at the Savita's place."

Ambrose should have been expecting to hear that. She'd gone to Ember to ask for help, but that was the last name she'd wanted to hear. Her upper lip twitched. "If I can get out of the house, do you want me to try to get over there?"

The response came fast. "Yes, if you can, that would be great. I'll text you the address."

After hanging up, Ambrose didn't waste time. She had the overnight bag set. All she needed now was to stuff her school papers back in her bag and escape this hellhole.

That's all I needed, somewhere else to hide. Mr. Shade has finally done it, run us all from our home.

It disgusted her that she was leaving and not him, but as a teen, in theory, she didn't have as much power ... for now.

As kids, she and Felix had learned how to escape from her room through the window without alerting anyone. It was easier when her window wasn't locked, but a bit of fire and water fixed that problem. Her room was on the second floor, but a tree with sturdy branches allowed for a quick descent.

Once at the bottom of the tree, her phone vibrated, and she heard the door of her room open. *Damn it, I forgot to turn off the light. Idiot!*

"Ambrose? Are you in the bathroom? Where did you go?"

She backed into a shadow as she saw Mr. Walsh gaze out the window. At least it was him, probably the stupidest of all the people in the house. But what was he even doing in her room?

"Guards! She's gone! Search the house! Search the grounds. Find her!"

Ambrose ran.

Escape! I have to get away before I'm caught.

She knew the fastest way out, and the shadows hid her path. When she reached the gate, there was an opening most people didn't know about large enough for her to slip through. She continued to run. It wouldn't take the guards long to realize she wasn't in the house. Once the dogs found her scent, they'd know they'd need a vehicle to find her.

She pulled out the phone. *Where the hell am I going, anyway?*

A car stopped in front of her, and she bit back a scream, her heart nearly stopping. "Ambrose, it's me."

The light from the car illuminated Felix. "What are you doing here?" she snapped.

"We just thought a ride may be easier than running all the way. But it's up to you." He slipped back into his car.

Ambrose quickly followed. "You're taking me to my mom?"

"Yes."

"Is she ... is she okay?"

"Yes." They drove for a few blocks. "Are you okay?"

Ambrose just watched the road ahead. She wasn't ready to talk to anyone about what she'd been living through for the last few days ... or weeks, or maybe months.

Chapter 42 – Reunion

Ember

It didn't take long for both Felix and Ambrose to arrive. Ambrose walked in and sneered. "Wow, Ember, your house is ... quaint. So ... lovely." The disdain dripped from her words.

Dad walked up behind Ember. "Welcome to our home," his voice was hard and not at all welcoming. "I'm glad we could offer you a safe haven, even for one night.

Your mom is in the living room. Can we offer you something to eat or drink?"

She lifted an eyebrow and shook her head. "No, thank you, Mr. Savita." She sounded much more respectful. "I'll be fine." Turning, she walked away.

"In my time, we knew about manners," Dad mumbled as he followed behind. "Kids today."

Felix took Ember's hand and led them towards the kitchen. "Wow, you'd think she'd be less ... you know, her. You *did* just save her mom and all."

"Nope, not at all," Ember said. "I expected nothing but pure Ambrose. Always and forever. Anything less may make my head explode."

Felix laughed. "Well, she was quiet the whole ride over. Didn't say a word. I guess she was saving it all for you."

Aunt Monte sat at the kitchen table sipping wine. Ember shook their head as they remembered. "Aunt Monte, Ambrose has some videos on her phone. Make sure you or Aunt Nuri get them. She promised."

Their aunt nodded and stood. "Sounds good, dear. I'll see what I can do."

Ember and Felix sat. Too tired to stand, Ember used their spatial magic to pull a couple of sodas for them.

He sighed. "Do you think she'll really spend the night? A slumber party? Maybe the two of you can do each other's makeup and share your deepest secrets."

"Watch out, buster, I still can use fire magic. That never goes away."

He threw his head back and laughed. "Fine. Do you need something to eat?"

"Chips, and there's salsa in the fridge."

They started eating, trying to ignore the talking and movement of all the other people around them. A knock echoed through the house, sharp and distinct.

Dad grunted from the living room. "Who's knocking at this hour? I got it." He stomped to the door.

Ember checked their watch. It was almost ten. "Do you need to get home?"

Felix shrugged. "Yeah, probably. I just wanted to make sure you were okay after all the excitement."

"Than—"

Dad's voice came out low. "What do you want?"

"Sir. We're looking for Mrs. Wells and her daughter. We were told they were both here." There was a pause and Ember noticed Felix leaned forward like they did as if hanging on an answer to a question that wasn't asked.

Finally, Dad grunted. "I'm waiting for a question. You didn't ask me anything."

Ember heard a snort from the living room but wasn't sure who held back a laugh.

"Mr. Savita, are you holding Mrs. Julia and Miss Ambrose Wells against their wills?"

"No," Dad's voice snapped back. His respect for authority had probably died several hundred years ago.

Ember got up to check out who Dad was speaking with. A couple of men in police uniforms stood just outside the door, badges showing.

"We've received an anonymous tip that the Wells have been kidnapped from their home by the phoenixes living in this house. We ask that you let us search the premises. Do we have your permission, sir?"

"Do you have a warrant?" His voice was stern, but respectful.

"Sir, we ask for your cooperation."

Dad barked out a laugh. "So, you don't have a warrant. Why would I let you enter my home?"

Ambrose's mom dashed toward the front door. "Who the hell said I was kidnapped? I'm here visiting my friends. The call you received was a bunch of hogwash. If I were to guess, you were called by the man squatting in my home. He was the one who had *me* locked up in the basement of my own home for days. I feared for my life. I escaped. This is the first time I've felt safe in weeks."

Ember and Felix had drifted to the opening between the kitchen and the hall to watch the drama. The officer who spoke to Dad wore black slacks and a dark gray button-down shirt. Behind him were two uniformed officers.

The officer's face hardened. "Which is it, ma'am? Were you locked up, or are you visiting of your own accord?"

"Did you not hear me? I said I escaped. Are you deaf or are you working for that monster?" She reached back to grasp Ambrose's hand. "I worried about what he could've done to my daughter." Tears ran down her cheek and Aunt Nuri handed her a handkerchief.

Dad held up a hand. "It's okay, Julia, let me take care of this. You're safe now."

The second officer watched the drama unfold while writing in a small notebook. Ember was impressed at his ability to do both things.

Aunt Monte pushed forward. "Maybe I can clear a bit of this up. I have some videos from the basement of the Wells's home. I think you'll be interested in this."

The first officer tried to keep a blank face, but his mouth tightened, then he sighed. "I'm just trying to get to the bottom of *this* incident, not start a new one. Is this video important?"

"Yes, I believe it is." She held out her phone. "There are a total of five videos. I've muted them, but if you want sound, that can be arranged."

The man grunted and tapped the screen and began watching. As the videos played his eyes widened and the color drained from his face. By the end, his mouth hung slightly open.

The officer snapped his mouth shut and handed the phone back. "Can you get copies of those videos to the precinct? Ma'am, Miss Wells, I believe I will leave you here. I'm going to your home to collect Mr. Shade. I would appreciate it if you *didn't* let him know. I'll be calling for more back-up. Do you know his magical proficiencies?"

Mom stepped forward. "His main skill lies in void magic. If you try to throw anything at him, he'll knock it down. His secondary and tertiary magic proficiencies are air and earth magic. He's never been very good at either of them."

Mrs. Wells shook her head. "He may not have much, but he's surrounded himself with others who have mind, air, and fire. Be careful."

The man nodded. "I would recommend staying away for the remainder of tonight. You can return home tomorrow. We'll try to keep this on the down-low; we know he's made quite a name for himself, and we don't need picketing at the precinct."

Everyone agreed and the officers left.

Once he was gone, Mrs. Wells leaned against the wall looking exhausted. "Ambrose, are you okay with staying here tonight?"

Ambrose shrugged. "I managed to grab a bag with my school stuff and an outfit for tomorrow. You know me: always prepared, Mother."

Aunt Nuri gazed at Mrs. Wells. "We're close to the same size. I'm certain we can find more clothes for you in my wardrobe. I know there's room here, but Monte and I have a guest suite with two bedrooms, a sitting room, and a bathroom. We tend to house dignitaries visiting for a few days. Would you want to stay with us? I'd love to really meet the woman who has been helping us from within since the beginning."

Ember was shocked to learn that Ambrose's mom had been the informant. They couldn't imagine the woman's strength.

Ambrose shifted her eyes to Ember and sniffed. "I'm good with staying somewhere else ... anywhere else. Why can't we go to a hotel?"

Her mom sighed. "I don't have my purse. We don't have money, and if we're trying to stay under the radar, then checking into a hotel using your credit card is pretty much the exact opposite."

Ambrose looked frustrated, but they left with Aunt Nuri and Aunt Monte. Though it was only four people, it felt like a much larger group as everyone in the house relaxed.

Felix gave Ember a hug. "See you tomorrow."

"Sounds good. At least they're keeping the arrest under wraps. Maybe it'll take a day or two before the insanity of it all reaches our hallowed halls."

Felix smirked. "Yeah, maybe."

Chapter 43 - Learning To Fly

Daisy

Tuesday morning, Daisy was at the lockers with two large travel mugs of coffee. She buzzed with everything that had happened the night before. *I still can't believe I helped figure out spatial magic. That there is spatial magic.* Chills ran down her back.

Ever since she'd met Ember, her life had been better, but in the last few weeks, she felt her mind would explode every other day.

She gazed up at the ceiling towards Air Magic class. *I wonder how they're doing up there. When Felix dropped me off last night, he was heading to pick up Queen Snootie Pants. I can't imagine any of them getting much sleep. I mean, Ember did text that they'd arrived safely, but that was it, radio silence.*

"Is one of those for me?" Daisy nearly leapt out of her skin at Ember's question. She hadn't heard her friend approach.

"Gods above! Where did you come from? Why aren't you up in class? Don't you usually arrive super early to TA?" Shaking her head, Daisy handed one of the coffees to Ember, who looked like the walking dead. "How are you doing? It was such a long night. How was ... you know."

"You think I was the most entertaining thing last night, but in reality, I wasn't." The side of their mouth twitched as they worked on getting their bag set for their morning classes.

Daisy's mouth dropped open. "Wait, more happened after," she waved her hand, "they arrived?"

Ember explained about Ambrose, her mom, and the police as they finished up at the locker and headed up the stairs for class.

By the end, the pep was back in Daisy's step. "No way! Mr. Shade, the jerk, got arrested. Was it in the news?" Daisy took out her phone and started searching.

"It's not supposed to be. The officer made it sound like he doesn't want a big uproar wherever Mr. Shade will end up being held." Ember pushed open the door and Daisy saw Mrs. Vintl on the other side of the room looking out the window.

She turned when they walked in. "Oh! Ember, Daisy, excellent. It's such a nice day, I think we'll do a bigger project today. Most of the class has gotten their notebook to float with a weight on it. I want to see if anyone can lift their platform. I was hoping you could watch and give pointers, Ember. You seem really good at figuring out what is going wrong with everyone's magic."

"Oh, yeah, that sounds great. What can I do—"

"We." Daisy interjected. She wasn't about to sit around and do nothing, especially with how tired her friend looked.

"Right. What can we do to help?" Ember shot her a thankful glance.

Mrs. Vintl stared at them as if mentally working something out. "If the two of you can set out the platforms, that would be great. You know where they're stored. I'm going to open up the roof."

Ember scrunched up their face. "Why? What's that for?"

"It's stuffy in here today. I think we need some fresh air. And, if someone can get some lift today, I'd like to see more than ten feet."

Excitement surged through Daisy. For a moment, the image of herself on a platform soaring through the clouds distracted her, and she shimmied in place. *Gods, I'd love to fly.*

The setup was easy with two of them. Daisy couldn't imagine Ember doing it alone. But together, they got the job done quickly. Afterwards, they sat and waited for class to start. Daisy spent a few more minutes on her phone, but people started coming in before she got very far.

Simon walked up to them. "I can't believe you'd stoop so low as to fabricate a video."

What a jerk! And to think I used to think he was smart. He's just an idiot willing to follow anyone who will say what he wants to hear.

Ember shifted their eyes up, but didn't otherwise move. Then they pulled out their phone.

Ha! Take that Simon. Neither of us care what you have to say. She smirked but tried not to make eye contact with him.

With a grunt of annoyance, Simon sat opposite them. "Did you hear me?"

Ember grunted, sounding a lot like their dad. "I did, but since I don't know what you're talking about, I figured silence is golden."

Daisy chuckled but kept her head down.

"Haven't you seen the arrest video of Mr. Shade?" Simon demanded.

Ember shivered. Then they shook their head. "Which is it—have I seen it or do you think I created it? Though either way, I don't know what you're talking about."

This was too much. He obviously wanted to make trouble and if Ember hadn't told her, Daisy wouldn't have known anything. She tilted her head. "He was arrested?" She debated blinking to look more innocent.

Simon narrowed his eyes at her, and she shrugged, looking down at her phone. She unlocked it and finally nodded. "Oh, yeah, here's the article." She scrolled so Ember could see the words flying across the screen with her. "And look, there *is* a video. Is this what you were going on about?"

"Of course not! That's a legit video. I'm saying whatever got the cops to go there in the first place. People are saying he killed humans and witches alike. That can't be true."

"And you think this is all *my* doing?" Ember scoffed.

Simon shrugged. "That or someone you know."

It was too much. Daisy glared up at him. "You need to get your head out of the sand and stop being so selfish, Simon. See the bigger picture. Who are these people you speak of? Why put all the blame at Ember's feet? Why would someone who hid for years do something that could land them and their family in jail? Are you nuts? I've spent my life thinking you were smart, but now I see you just want to follow anyone who will say the messed up things you're thinking are correct, no matter how far-fetched they are or who gets hurt in the process. Gods above and below, wake up! There is more to what's going on than Simon Trahous. People are getting hurt—including me at one point—regardless of whether you believe it or not."

Applause broke out and Daisy realized most of the class heard them. For his part, Simon looked gob-smacked.

Ember shook their head. "Class is about to begin. Simon, you have a choice. Get over yourself and your messed up beliefs or stay away from us. Scratch that; stay away from me no matter what."

"During class?" he asked, sounding shocked.

"During everything. I don't need your constant negativity, accusations, and lies being tossed at me all the time. You've always said you're better than me at this, as well as most classes, so why would you want me near you during class? Just grow up, Simon."

Daisy smiled at Simon in the sweetest way she could. "That goes for me as well. Someone as smart as you shouldn't be so ignorant."

As Simon stared with a slack-jawed expression, Ember and Daisy slipped away to where the class usually gathered. The teacher's office door was still shut. It didn't take long for her to come out and call everyone else over and start class.

Mrs. Vintl explained the lesson quickly. Everyone had done the exercise before; it wasn't new. Afterwards, everyone dispersed to their platform.

Daisy sat, excited at the idea of flying and sad that she'd probably fail. *Stop it Daisy, this is exactly what you spoke to Ember about last night. You can't achieve your best if you go into it expecting the worst.* She took a deep breath and tried to imagine herself in the clouds once again.

The teacher continued to speak. "This is a hard lesson. Though the probability is that no one will succeed, it's possible we'll have a breakout star." *Me! I'm going to be that person.* "I'll say that again, I'm not expecting anyone in here to fly. Your grade isn't based on the platform rising, it's based on your effort. My advice is, at the beginning, to keep your eyes shut. Try to block out as much extra stimulation as you can."

Daisy shut her eyes and focused on the air currents around her. She thought about the exercises they'd been doing with the paper and tried to expand it. The theory was sound: make the air under the platform dense enough that it could lift the wood.

I'm not lifting me, just a really big piece of paper ... that's all. I can do this. Come on, Daisy, you're a star. Lift the platform.

The leather straps bit into Daisy's hands, grounding her. As much as she wanted to fly and imagined being in the clouds, she also needed to remember she was in class.

"Daisy," Ember said softly.

Shock traveled along Daisy's spine. *Ember's never spoken to me during any of the lessons since she began helping in class. What am I doing so wrong that she needs to speak to me? Am I that much of a dunce?*

Her friend's voice continued, soft and soothing. "Relax your body, like all of your muscles. If you can, let go of the straps and place your hands flat on the platform at your sides."

Relax. Daisy squeezed the handles one last time while breathing in, then slowly exhaled all her tension, spreading her fingers to place on the wood. Her body slouched slightly as she imagined the air currents pushing up on the platform in the same way they did the paper.

"Okay, good," Ember said, voice calm. "Relax your shoulders, drop your chin, and for all that's good with chocolate, breathe."

Following Ember's words, Daisy almost laughed at the idea of chocolate. *Gods! Chocolate sounds amazing.*

"Don't freak out," Ember said. "Do *not* tense. Just ... open your eyes."

Daisy did. She gasped and her platform dropped as she *did* stress, but then she did another breathing exercise, and the platform began to level off and rise again. "Oh, my gods, is this for real?"

Ember's smile took over their face; their eyes danced. Daisy hadn't seen their friend look so happy in days.

Mrs. Vintl came over and took Ember's place, appearing just as pleased.

Chapter 44 - Can't We All Just Get Along

Ember

It wasn't until lunch that Ember finally watched the video. Throughout the day they'd heard rumors. People spoke about Mr. Shade being a brute and a bully. Some questioned all of Infinite WISDOM.

Olivia was the first to join them at lunch. "Have you seen the video?"

"I haven't. I mean, people have been talking about it everywhere I go, but classes have been a marathon today.

It's like the teachers have been wanting us to focus on school and not the greater world around us." Ember chuckled.

She handed Ember her phone. "Just watch."

The video showed the front door of a fancy mansion through a gap between low-hanging tree branches. A stylized plaque—is that a coat of arms?—next to the door with a W in the center that looked similar to some of the items Ember had seen in captivity let them know it must be the Wells' home.

Did one of the security people take this video? Maybe someone loyal to the Wellses and not Mr. Shade? Was Mrs. Wells wrong that all of her people had been fired? Did she have someone loyal to her after all?

The lead police officer who'd come to Ember's house stood outside the door with two other uniformed officers with him.

The person holding the phone whispered, "I saw three unmarked cars on the backside of the property. The two cars with these three officers drove in after checking in with the front gate."

Then the video zoomed in. After a few seconds, the front door opened, and Mr. Shade stood there. He stood tall, back ramrod straight, wearing an elegant evening robe and smoking a cigar. The light behind him was brighter than the porch light, making his face look ghoulish. "Officer, how can I help you?"

"Mr. Shade, we'd like you to come to the precinct with us."

He scoffed. "No, I don't think that will be happening."

"Look, I don't want to have to do this here, but I will if I have to."

Mr. Shade's face hardened. "Do what, Officer?"

"Mr. Tad Shade, you are under arrest for the death of multiple humans—"

He chuckled and waved his hand with the cigar.

His utter disregard for human life made Ember's blood boil. *He's such a megalomaniac.*

"—and at least one witch. A—"

"What?!" Mr. Shade bellowed, cutting him off before any names could be listed. "That never happened."

The officer went on to read Mr. Shade's rights as the uniformed men cuffed him.

At the end, the officer said, "The cuffs we've placed on you will stop any magic you may try to use. Since you are a practitioner of void magic, this should be something you're used to."

Mr. Shade continued to yell his innocence as he was manhandled to a car. Once the car started to move, one of the house servants shut the door and turned off the front porch light.

A moment later, the video ended.

With a shake of their head, Ember handed Olivia her phone back. "Well, that was ... wow."

"I know, right? He laughed at harming people, like that was no big deal. His only protest was at hurting fellow magic users. What a monster."

By the end of the video, the rest of the table had filled up.

Felix shook his head. "I thought the police were going to ensure a private arrest. I guess they messed *that* one up."

Tansy leaned forward. "Wait, you knew that was going down?"

Felix sighed, his face drawn with dark circles under his eyes. He looked as tired as Ember felt. "Yeah. I was over at Ember's last night. Mr. Shade had kidnapped their cousin. We'd just gotten him back before the arrest."

Tansy's eyes widened and she nearly choked on the fry she was eating. "Ember, your life is like a movie. Do you get any downtime?"

"I wish," they murmured. *This is probably why Mom and Dad spent all those years in hiding ... so they could get some peace and quiet. Then again, accidents always follow phoenixes. Our involvement was bound to happen eventually, and if I'm honest, this is better than denying who I am all the time. I like letting my friends know about me.*

"So, how did you get your cousin out?"

"Yeah, Ember, do tell." Ambrose put her tray on the table, joining their group. "Please explain how you got my mother and your cousin out of the cells beneath my house last night. I've been trying to piece that together. I was home while they were rescued and didn't hear a thing."

Everyone gaped at them, but Ember wouldn't be distracted. "What are you doing sitting here? Don't you have your own friends?"

"They're all crying over Mr. Shade and Cress. It's turning my stomach. I just ... *can't* with any of them." She waved a hand.

Olivia's face contorted. "So you thought you'd sit with us? We've never been your friends."

A shiver ran down Ember's back and their upper lip twitched. *I can see why she wouldn't want to sit with the other group, but why here, why us, why me?*

"This makes a statement without speaking a word. By just sitting here, I'm telling everyone I don't support anything that man did. Not anymore. He may have been living in my house, but after what he did to the humans and my mother—" chin lifted, she met Ember's gaze— "I'm with the phoenixes."

Chapter 45 - The Royal Trifecta

Ember

Ember trudged from the school, wondering what the rest of the week would bring. It was only Tuesday. *Can I make it to Saturday? Do I want to know what the weekend will bring?*

Daisy dashed down the stairs, catching up with them. "Ember, are you busy?"

"I mean ... no? I was just going to go home and collapse on a couch. I can't remember the last time I could just ... I don't know, do nothing?" Ember smiled weakly at Daisy. "Why, what are you thinking?"

"Well, we discussed your mom helping me with air magic and then ... well, you know, things happened. Then *more* things happened. And, gods above, *more* things happened. I was hoping I could come over today and we could work on the flying thing. It was really exciting and class just ... Ember, it was so amazing."

Daisy's exuberance was infectious. "Okay, yeah. Come home with me. Let's talk with Mom."

Before they took three steps, Olivia approached. "Hi, you two. Where are you off to?"

"Ember's place, why?" Daisy's eyes practically glowed with her joy.

Olivia shrugged. "I was hoping Ember and I could work on our Magical Creations. I know we're ahead of most of the class, but some of what we do is so tricky. I mean, it's fun, but hard. I want to actually learn it before Mrs. Hewett moves on."

Ember and Daisy exchanged a quick look and shrugged. Then Ember said, "Why not come with us? We're planning on doing some magic practice anyway. Since Mom will probably be working with Daisy, you and I should have time to do our thing."

"Really? I won't be intruding?" Olivia lifted her shoulders and ducked her head as if trying to make herself look smaller.

Daisy laughed. "Of course not. Now come on."

During the short walk, they talked about what would happen now that the leader of Infinite WISDOM was in jail.

Once they got home, Ember pointed Daisy and Olivia towards the kitchen. "Daisy, get a snack for us. I'll be right back."

Ember went off to find their mom. She was in the backyard with Dad and Vatra. They quickly filled everyone in, and Mom followed Ember back into the house.

Back in the kitchen, Daisy had gathered chips and a bowl of salsa. She and Olivia were already eating, waiting for Ember to return.

Mom joined them as Ember went to get sodas for everyone.

"Hi, I'm Ember's mom. You can call me Sadie, or Mrs. Savita. Either is fine with me. You are Olivia?"

"Hi, Mrs. Savita. Yes, I'm Olivia. I'm in Ember's Magical Creations class."

"If I may ask, which proficiencies do you have, Olivia?"

Olivia's cheeks turned a light pink. "That was so bold. People are usually more circumspect about that."

Mom smiled. "Life's too short, don't you think?"

"Probably," Olivia agreed. "Um, well, I have fire, like Ember, though she's a phoenix. So is that their proficiency or an innate ability?"

Mom's smile widened. "Oh, I like you. That's a great question. For Ember, it's who they are. What else do you have, my young scholar?"

"Oh, right! Mind and void magic." Olivia shrugged. "The school doesn't really teach anything for the void proficiency; it's how I ended up in Magical Creations with Ember. There aren't many students who have it. I don't know of any other students who have it, actually. If I'm honest, I wish I had something better. I understand Mr. Shade had it, but he was the only other person I knew of—besides my dad—and I'd rather not be like that criminal."

Mom leaned back and considered her. "You have the Royal Trifecta, did you know that?"

Olivia leaned forward. "The what?"

Daisy's jaw dropped slightly. Ember just wanted to know what it was Mom was talking about. This was all new to them.

"Magic can come in many combinations, obviously. Years before the War of Peace, when magic users and shifters were unknown to the population at large and the two groups, mostly, got along, they understood each other better. They didn't socialize much, but there was respect."

Mom looked over at the stove. "Ember, can you put on a pot of water for tea? The pot on the counter is full, it just needs to be moved to the stove and the stove turned on."

"You want me to do that ... from here?" They shifted their eyes to Olivia and back to Mom.

"I do. You brought a friend into our home and I'm tired of hiding. Do you trust her?"

Ember was better at calling a cup or mug to themself than shifting something over a foot, but this was a test, part of what they had to learn. Move an object, turn a knob, have control from afar. The kitchen wasn't large, and Mom wanted Ember to practice.

Across the table, Daisy's eyes widened and she practically vibrated. Olivia just looked confused.

Pulling up their magic, Ember did as Mom asked. The pot was a bit askew when it landed, and they were pretty sure the stove wasn't on hot enough.

Ember jerked their head to Olivia and saw her mouth hanging open.

Mom nodded. "Your control still isn't where I'd like it to be." She shrugged. "Okay, go and fix that, but if you could get me a mug of tea and warm it up the old fashion way?"

"In the microwave?" Ember asked, teasingly.

"No, your other magic, if you please."

Olivia found her voice. "Was that spatial magic? Like, for real spatial magic?"

"Yes, dear," Mom said gently. "You aren't the only one with a rare magic inherited from a parent. Now, as for the Royal Trifecta, back in the day, many more people had void. When someone with void magic got upset, they'd throw a bubble over an area, nullifying anyone else's magic." She leaned in. "It was rather obnoxious."

Ember returned with two mugs of peppermint tea, one for Mom and one for themself. "Anyone else want some?"

Both Daisy and Olivia raised their hands. Ember slid their mug to Daisy and headed back into the heart of the kitchen for two more mugs.

"People with mind magic," Mom continued, "soon figured out that the void bubble didn't stop the majority of what they could do. The bubble stopped physical magic, not mental."

Ember returned with the last two mugs of tea.

"Then, there's Everfire." Mom said, a tightness in her voice. "A void bubble will convert it to regular fire, and within your own bubble, you can use your fire magic to extinguish it. This is a very powerful ability. In the past, magic users with your three proficiencies were sought out as protectors. You could shield your mind, you could stop wild magic, you could even protect against the deadliest fire known. Power, Olivia. You should be proud of what you have and train hard to be the best."

"I try, but I don't have anyone who can help me with the void magic." She shrugged. "Dad was never taught, so he doesn't know much of what can be done with it. I try to excel in fire and mind magic. I'm hoping to be invited into both elite clubs next year."

Mom nodded. "I'll see if I can find you a void magic trainer. I may know someone. It isn't a specialty that should go untrained."

Olivia smiled. "I didn't expect this when I came over! Thank you, Mrs. Savita." She turned to Ember. "No wonder you're so skilled. You have so much help at home."

A warmth filled Ember at the idea of keeping fewer secrets from their friends. They also loved that their mom wanted to help guide both Daisy and Olivia into being stronger witches. With all the bad that Infinite WISDOM had brought, it was nice to find some good.

Mom turned to Daisy. "As for you, I want to see this combination of magics before we get to the flying. Both Ember and Felix were going on and on about it."

Daisy blushed. "Okay, that would be ... yeah, really great. And Ember, I didn't show you the one I'd like your thoughts on."

"Sounds good to me."

The group headed out to the backyard to work on magic. Dad and Vatra, who had remained outside when Mom came in, watched. A cool breeze sent chills down Ember's back as they watched Daisy form water arrows and try to make them fly. None of them flew as well as she wanted them to.

With a few small fixes, Ember helped their friend. By the end, Daisy's arrows flew swifter and hit their marks. Then, Daisy moved to a platform. She could hover a foot off the ground with control. Mom created a schedule for lessons that would have them meeting regularly.

While Daisy practiced with her arrows and then flying with Mom, Olivia and Ember had created an opaque fireball each. They debated doing more, but the steps involved were complicated and watching Daisy fly was more fun.

Vatra sat up suddenly. "Ash, check this out." She handed her phone over.

Dad started to grumble under his breath. "Did someone let the damn man out? Does he have people with mind magic who messed with the whole damn police department? Who is running this circus?"

"Dad, what is going on?"

"It's Infinite WISDOM. They're having an event tomorrow at seven at night. Who would do something so asinine?"

Chapter 46 - A Present From Our Leader

Ember

Ember walked around the Air Magic class, watching the students work. At this point in the lesson, no one really needed their help. They tried to ignore the students talking with their friends about the Infinite WISDOM event that night. All the speculation hurt their head.

I just need to make it through this class, and I can sink in my seat for the remainder of my classes and hide.

During their circuit of the room, Ember neared a group they usually avoided because it included Xander. The students all excelled in air magic and never asked them any questions. In the beginning, before Ember had pegged them as the top-tier practitioners, they'd asked if any of them had questions, and the students only mocked Ember.

It was less stressful to avoid them.

Although Xander and his cronies seemed destined to become the leaders in air magic, Ember knew they could make them better, but it wasn't worth it. If they didn't want help, that made no difference to Ember. Every student in the class knew where to find Ember and that they were more than happy to give aid. If these students thought, as a group, they were better than them, so be it. Ember would smile and agree.

When Ember was nearly past the group, Xander stepped away from the center. "Ember, do you have a minute?"

Every muscle in their body tensed. Of all the students Ember wanted to say 'no, I will *not* help you' to, it was him. What had he done, except beg for help, then blame Ember for every mistake he'd made? So unlike his sister Zahra; he was a real piece of work.

With a big sigh, Ember forced a smile. "Sure, how can I help you?"

He grabbed for Ember's wrist, and they pulled their arm back, "What are you doing?" Ember hissed.

Xander's eyes widened, then he lifted both hands, darting a look over his shoulder at his friends who were tittering. "Just ... can we talk?"

With a force of will, Ember unlocked their jaw. "Does it have to do with class? With magic? *Air* magic?"

His head jerked back and forth. "No."

Ember spun to walk away. They heard Xander's friends chuckling.

A few steps from the group, Xander caught up to them. "Wait, hear me out, please. Just ... please, a word or two."

Eyes shut, Ember took a long breath. When they opened their eyes, they saw the teacher watching them. "Fine. What do you want?"

"Not here. Can we go over there ... you know, away from everyone?" Ember nodded and he led them to the side of the room.

Ember locked their jaw shut. Once they were separated, they crossed their arms and waited.

"Look, I know I've been ... unfair. I said you took Zahra's spot in Ring of Fire, and you didn't." He shook out his hands. "You helped her to get into the club, and well, look, I'm sorry I yelled at you last week."

Ember was glad their jaws were so tightly pressed together. They weren't sure Xander believed what he said, but Ember was ready for this 'talk' to be over. With one last smile—or was it a sneer?—they moved to take off. "Thank you for that."

"Wait," he snapped, then shook his head. "I mean, wait." The second time he said it, his voice was modulated to be less jerky, though he still sounded like he was reciting from memory. "I'm not done. I want to thank you for helping me with my fire magic. I should've been appreciative and not mean when I tried to skip steps. My burns were my own fault, not yours."

I wonder who coached him to say that. Zahra? His parents? None of this is how he normally speaks. I wonder if any of this is how he actually feels. Or if this is because he's worried about my influence now that I'm in Ring of Fire.

"Well, I appreciate your words." Ember didn't say, 'thank whoever made you say them.'

He nodded, then walked back to his friends, who still snickered.

Ember released a big breath and continued their monitoring of the students. *Well, at least once class ends, I don't have to see him again until next Monday. Thank the gods!*

The rest of the day slipped by without much fanfare. Students gossiped and discussed who they predicted would be running the event that evening. When Ember saw Ambrose in classes, lunch, and after school, they witnessed other students harassing Ambrose, but she ignored them all.

Ember and their friends ignored Ambrose, preferring not knowing than speaking with her about it during the day.

At lunch, Ember enjoyed their food. When Tansy sat, she said she saw Ambrose heading off in the opposite direction.

Daisy's eyes narrowed as she gazed at the cafeteria doors. "Do you think she'll still swing back and try to join us for lunch again?"

Tansy shrugged. "No idea, but I won't miss her air of superiority."

"Though I agree," Olivia gazed at each of the group in turn, "no one deserves to feel completely shut out from any group or bullied."

Ember hated feeling bad for Ambrose, but they had to agree. "I just hope things settle down and she finds her own safe haven of friends."

Felix slid an arm around them. "Agreed."

Ambrose didn't join Ember and friends at lunch. Ember didn't see her anywhere in the cafeteria. Though they didn't miss Ambrose's touch of intense loathing she brought to the group, Ember did worry where she ended up. No one deserved to feel completely shut out.

By the end of the day, Ember just wanted to get some rest before the big event that night.

At five-thirty, Felix and his parents came over bearing pizza. Everyone ate and tried to guess who would be running the show. It was similar to the gossip at school, but more fun because this time it was family.

"My guess? The guards. They watched so many of Mr. Shade's speeches, they figured, how hard can it be?" Ember snagged another slice of sausage and black olive pizza.

"No way," Felix said, his plate full of Hawiian-style pizza. "My guess is it's whoever recorded that video. That person obviously was on the grounds and knows what's what."

"Good guess," Felix's mom said. "I'll give you points for that, but I'm guessing he was one of ours. Why would he hold a meeting under the name of Infinite WISDOM? Why not Julia, Ambrose's mom? She went home as soon as Tad was arrested. She could've found something she wants to share with the public. She's smart. I could see her spin something to help end the movement."

"Whoa." Ember leaned back. "Like, would she be taking it in the same direction, following what's been going on, or taking things in a whole new direction? Because ...

just whoa. That would be crazy. The followers would *not* go for something new."

"Maybe." Felix's dad shrugged. "You never know. Mindless followers are called mindless for a reason."

By the end, they were no closer to an answer.

They piled into the cars and drove to the event location. It was easy to see where to go. Being so late and winter besides, there were huge lights all over, lighting the stage, the gathering area, everything. The event site was probably visible from space.

Despite the stage and spectator areas, there weren't many vendors about. There was a stand selling doughnuts, another with hot drinks, and one with souvenirs. Other times, there had been dozens of booths.

Giving the locals twenty-four hours is not enough time for everyone to gather to get their ducks in a row.

By seven, the place was packed. Ember was shocked at the number of people. They leaned over to Felix. "They must be here to see if Mr. Shade's going to show up."

Dad shook his head. "I called the police station. He hasn't been released. Whoever it is, it is not him."

Relief slammed into Ember. It hadn't occurred to them to ask or even how worried they'd been that Mr. Shade would somehow make an appearance.

Someone, a kid, maybe twelve, came out onto the stage and set up the microphone stand and a table. The table was a new prop. For that matter, it had been ages since any of the speakers had used a microphone.

A man came out carrying a box. Ember began tapping Dad's arm. "Dad, Dad. That's ..."

"I know what it is, Ember, but does it have ... ?" His voice trailed off as they both watched the box intently.

"It did when it was in the room with me. Could he have secured more? And who would be carrying it so cavalierly into a crowd this big?"

Vatra slid over. "Mr. Shade had it last week. I don't know who that is, but this isn't good."

Dad reached over and got Aunt Nuri's attention. They stared at each other for a few moments, then both nodded. Dad turned to Mom. "We'll go shift. If things go south, we'll need phoenixes."

Ember got out their phone. "Should I text ... I don't know." They thought for a moment. "Olivia has void magic, would that help?"

"Her magic isn't trained, love," Mom said. "I wouldn't want to put her in any danger."

"How about the person you knew who could train her?" Ember's mind worked furiously, desperate to find a solution.

"He's out of town. He said he'd come visit next week to meet her." Mom's face was hard, and she sounded distracted as she gazed at the people around them.

"Right. Okay. Well what about—"

"Good evening, everybody," the speaker began, cutting off any chance to plan. Ember hadn't even seen them walk out.

Ember narrowed their eyes, focusing on the person on stage. "Who is this person?" they muttered.

"Cress's dad," Felix whispered.

"My name is Brian Walsh," the man continued, "and I am an associate of Tad Shade. After our benevolent and fearless leader was arrested ... on trumped up charges, I might add, I searched his office and rooms to see if there was anything I could bring to you, his people, to show you his concern and devotion to you all." He paused for effect. "Anyway, on his dresser, there was this ornate box. A note atop the box read, *'For the people.'* To be honest, I haven't opened it yet. I thought, to be fair and true to all of you, we could open it together."

Oh, gods, the idiot is going to kill everyone! A lump formed in Ember's throat.

Ember turned to Felix. "You have to go, like now. That's Everfire. If he takes off the top ... just go."

Felix blanched but nodded. He gathered his parents, and they all began weaving their way out of the crowd. There was no way to tell everyone. A stampede of panicked witches could be just as dangerous as the Everfire, but Ember saw the trio whispering to a few people they knew as they headed out.

Mr. Walsh walked over to the moonstone box and rubbed his hand over the stone. Ember shivered, remembering how odd the stone made them feel. They had the bracelet on, but they'd grown used to that small amount. Whenever they came in contact with a new source, especially one that large, their whole body felt ... off.

Mom said, "Ember, we're going to combine our magic. I want you to flash a wall of fire as a blind while I move the box."

A chill traveled down their body. *Spatial magic in front of all these people?* "Are you sure?"

"It's the only option we have." The stress poured from Mom.

Ember's fire was about to fly when Mr. Walsh backed away, rubbing his hand on his pants leg. "Before we get to the box, I want to remind you all, Infinite WISDOM is about bringing magic users ... witches, together. The idea that Mr. Shade would harm even one of us is just wrong. He had nothing but love for the life around him. He wants for all of you to cherish the life around you."

"Even the humans?" someone in the audience yelled.

Mr. Walsh was no public speaker. He was so out of his league that his eyes bugged, and he rubbed his palms on his jeans once again. Though the thought of violence disgusted Ember, they had to smile at the question.

As Ember gave Mom a bit more time to prepare her magic, they formed the size and shape of the fire wall they wanted to create. Not only did Mom need to pull away a box filled with Everfire, but she also had to decide where to send it. Audience members grew restless while Mr. Wash rattled on.

Focus, Ember! We have to save as many people as we can from this maniac! Remembering their goal, their heart began to pound faster.

Mr. Walsh squeezed his hands into fists. "Why, um, I think, if you dig deep into your heart, you will know the answer to how you should treat fellow beings on this planet."

A voice, coming from another area of the packed audience, yelled, "Just open the damn box. It's probably empty and if you're the only speaker, you're wasting our time."

There were shouts of agreement from different areas of the crowd. Ember shivered with dread at the thought of him opening the box and releasing Everfire.

Just don't!

Mr. Walsh's eyes widened, and he backed up a step. He stumbled, but didn't fall. Finally he nodded. "Right, the box."

Mom nodded. Ember lifted both their hands. Then a group of ruffians slammed into Ember and Mom. "What are you doing, phoenix? Trying to stop the presentation?"

Around them, people glared.

Ember's old fear at being named and seen for what they were washed through them, and they hesitated.

On stage, in a final attempt to win the audience over, Mr. Walsh reached to open the shimmering, iridescent box.

Ember and Mom collapsed to the ground in defeat before pushing the brutes off them and getting to their feet. Ember yelled, "No, stop!" But it happened too fast, the top fell to the stage with a clang.

In a flash, the fire consumed Mr. Walsh.

Chapter 47 - Dreaming Of More

Ember

Ember watched, horrified as the Everfire consumed Cress's dad, the table, part of the stage, a bit of equipment, and anything and everything it touched. It hadn't grown beyond the size of a large man ... yet, but as it consumed, its size increased.

All around, people screamed, frozen in terror. Ember ran forward, pushing their way through the mob hoping to escape. Desperately, they tried to think of anything that they could do to contain the destruction.

The audience was full of witches. Water came out of nowhere, a tidal wave trying to combat a flame that had grown to the size of a recliner chair and growing with everything it ate.

The fire roared, doubling in size.

More screams erupted all around and the scent of smoke and burning wood filled the air.

"What's going on?"

"That's not how it's supposed to act!"

"What kind of fire is that?"

"Devil fire!"

Someone—or several someones—tried to use air magic to 'blow it out' but still the fire grew.

Ember and Mom pushed their way forward. "Can't we make them stop? They're making it worse! It was containable before."

"I know, love. I'm thinking. Everything is getting warm. It's consumed a quarter of the stage, the table, and that idiot man. Thankfully he's the only person."

Ember shivered. "And it was fast."

Mom shook her head. "That's the only thing fast about Everfire. It moves slowly. Okay—" Mom was cut off as a wood structure grew around the fire ... thaumaturgy. It was quickly consumed, the fire growing, nearly reaching the edge of the stage.

"Mom, can we create an air bubble?"

"With its current size, I'm not sure. We'll have to work together."

Ember trembled. It had been years since they'd done anything like this as a training exercise. "Right, okay. We can do this."

Mom turned to face them. They'd made it almost all the way to the stage, and Ember tried to ignore the chaos around them. "Yes, we can. Focus and follow my lead."

Clasping hands, Ember felt Mom's magic and intertwined theirs, trying to match the harmony. They combined their spells, Ember letting Mom mold both wells of power to try to encircle the Everfire. Once the air shimmered fully around the fire, they lifted it up in a swirling sphere of air. Sweat broke out on Ember's back, but the bubble held.

The fire fought them. Needing more power, Ember tapped into their fire. *Thank you, Daisy, for giving me this idea!*

They had to keep all the people safe.

Around them, Ember heard gasps.

Felix ran up next to them. "You didn't get it all. There's a lick of fire still burning on the stage."

Ember shook their head and wanted to snarl. Why had he come back when they'd told him to flee? There was nothing he could do here except get burned. "I don't know what we can do, this is taking everything we have."

The fire jumped out over the stage, approaching the audience. Fire witches came up in droves, trying to dissipate the danger, spitting mad that Ember and their mom were in the way.

"Give way to the experts, *air witches.*"

"You're merely containing the problem and not even all of it, move aside."

But as their fire failed, they slunk away with their proverbial tails between their legs.

Why do they think it would work now when it didn't work before?

Then Olivia ran up, breathing hard. "Mrs. Savita ... Royal Trifecta ... right?"

"Yes, child." Mom breathed hard as she and Ember kept pushing magic out, fighting the Everfire that wanted to feed.

Olivia took long, slow breaths and lifted her hands. Ember saw the power as it left her friend and shot towards the last of the Everfire. A dome appeared, containing the living fire.

Matching white phoenixes swooped down from the clouds.. Ember grinned in relief. Dad and Aunt Nuri had returned.

People in the crowd gasped and yelped.

The words danced in the air above the crowd near Ember and Mom. "Sorry we're late. Traffic."

They collected the fire in the air ball and were off before they knew Olivia held more in a void bubble on stage. Ember began to tremble as they dropped their spell, a wave of fatigue washing through them. They couldn't imagine flying with that awful package for six hours, but necessity and all that.

Then they focused on the more important matter of the remaining Everfire. Olivia strained; her whole body trembled. "I don't know if I can access my fire while holding this down."

Ember shook their head. "I can help."

They started to reach out, when Ambrose bumped into them. "You have to trust me, Ember, and follow my lead. We have a chance, you and me, to fix this, but you have to trust me. Do you trust me?"

"Um ... no." The mere idea was ludicrous.

Mom narrowed her eyes. "Just do as the girl says. She's been through a lot. If she has a plan, she's the only one. Look around, Ember, it's chaos."

Though the massive fireball was gone, people hadn't left. Most still milled about, talking in groups, staring at the void bubble, and the remaining fire it contained. There were tears and some people embraced.

Ember pursed their lips, frustrated. "Fine. Olivia, how long can you hold that bubble?"

"Maybe five minutes? ... I think."

A silky smile slid onto Ambrose's face. "Perfect. Come on, phoenix."

A sense of dread slammed into Ember as they allowed themself to be pulled, of all things, onto the stage, the part that hadn't been destroyed, with her ... Ambrose. *Gah!*

Ambrose picked up the microphone. "Good people of Feniks." There was a pause as she waited for everyone to gape at the two of them. There were murmurs.

"It's Mr. Shade's girl."

"It's the phoenix."

"Why are they together?"

"What's happening?"

With her typical aplomb, Ambrose began, "That was a horrible occurrence. Thankfully, the phoenixes have come to clear away the Everfire."

Someone in the remaining audience yelled, "That was Everfire? The phoenix's death blaze?"

"Yes," Ambrose confirmed. "This has been Mr. Shade's plan and intention all along. But you can see, with the help of the phoenixes and their friends." Ambrose waved her hand. Ember felt the push of her magic as she extinguished the last of the fire under the void dome.

Relief washed through Ember as the last of the fire that could consume the world was finally gone. *Thank the gods for my friends ... well, Olivia. I can't believe Ambrose used that as part of her show ... Well I can, but...*

It occurred to them that Ambrose was still speaking. "We've crushed this hidden agenda. Thank you, Olivia, for your help." Olivia bowed her head and slid behind Mom.

Ambrose took a moment to search the faces in the crowd. "When I was asked to join Infinite WISDOM, a group whose goal was to put themselves above humans, I was focused on the part where witches were in harmony and supporting each other. Then I spent night after night with Mr. Shade where he spoke of all of us, human, shifter, and witch alike, as cattle. I tried to stop him, but then he locked my mom in a cell."

Unlike Mr. Walsh, Ambrose knew how to work a crowd, she put the pauses in all the right places. Ember watched as everyone listened, taking in the story, word by word. They would've been more comfortable as part of the audience, not up on stage with Ambrose.

"Mr. Shade used his void magic, much like Olivia did just a moment ago, to tame Everfire. Unlike Olivia, he didn't do it to save lives, but instead to put it in that box. To use it as a weapon. A weapon to take down anyone he saw as an enemy—human, witch, and shifter alike. His definition for 'enemy' was pretty broad."

The murmurs in the crowd grew, and Ambrose's smile widened.

"I want to speak with you all about Infinite WISDOM. The original talks I gave discussed building a stronger community. I would like to go back to that: helping *all* of us grow stronger together. In my view of this movement witches and phoenixes, shifters *and non-magic wielders* should all work together. Because at the end of the day, *we're all human.*" She said that last bit louder and let the words hang over the crowd. "I think we've forgotten that part."

The applause started slowly, building to a roar as the crowd cheered.

"In my opinion, this is what Infinite WISDOM could have been, should have been, and with Ember, our famous local phoenix by my side running it—together, under the advice of FB coalition—I believe it's what it can become. WISDOM - witches, including shifters, dreaming of more."

Ambrose elbowed Ember in the side. Suddenly they realized they were on stage, too. People were watching. Forcing a smile, they gave two thumbs up.

Chapter 48 – Twelfth-Year

Ember

Fotia sat next to Ember eating bacon and eggs with a huge smile on her face. "I can't believe this is really happening." She sipped her coffee. "I know it's been a couple of weeks since the start of the school year, but it's still so unreal."

Vatra sat across from her. "To be honest, neither can I. Your dad and I never thought we'd see the day the three of us would be looking for a second home outside of

Sarafina Landing. We plan on spending most of our time back there, but this can be a vacation spot, of sorts."

"But we won't start looking until this weekend, because I'm really busy this week, right?" Fotia asked, waving her fork at her mom. "I mean, not only do I have my testing tonight, but adapting to classes is crazy."

"Yes, daughter, we know. Everyone knows. Probably the whole town knows."

Fotia's eyes lit up with her joy and she laughed.

Ember checked the time. "Okay, it's time to go."

They both cleared their dishes and gathered their bags. It was beautiful outside with blue skies and a warm breeze. Despite Fotia's excitement at home these past few weeks, she'd seemed stressed on the walk to school. The two cousins had only been in school together for three weeks, but even after such a short amount of time, Ember loved having their cousin at Feniks Secondary school. The last year had seen so many changes, but this had to be one of the craziest.

They saw one of the Infinite WISDOM signs in a yard across the street. An infinity shape with a cauldron on one side and a phoenix on the other. Underneath were the words: *Together we're stronger.* Ember smiled.

Fotia bounced a bit before shaking out her hands and rattling off, "Okay, so, we start off in history class, then we have our proficiency class. But since I'm not magical, I just do fire every day. Usually, I observe to learn what witches can do and sometimes help. Then math. After that I meet you for Spanish class and then it's time for lunch."

Ember wrapped an arm around Fotia's shoulders. "Breathe. I don't know that you actually took a breath in all that. You're doing great."

"I know, I just ... I still can't believe I'm going to school with you and not that you're going to school with me."

A lightness filled Ember. "Well, after Ambrose thrust the two of us as the faces of the new movement last spring, Mom and Dad realized if I suddenly disappeared it may slow progress down. I think Aunt Nuri had a lot to do with the decision, too. Anyway, we have years and years on this planet. What's one more before heading back to Sarafina Landing for school?"

"And to the short-lived, each year is so much more ... " Fotia nodded. "Noted."

It wasn't as if they hadn't discussed this before, but any distraction before getting to school helped Fotia to relax. Once they arrived, everything seemed to fall into place.

At the lockers, Daisy met up with them. "Hiya, Fotia. I brought you a travel mug of coffee. Somehow Ember only needs their mug or two at home. I'm not sure how they survive."

Drooping onto the locker, Fotia's eyes widened. "I know, right? And thank you! I wasn't sure I would make it to class."

Daisy laughed, and linked arms with Fotia. "Come on, let's go. Ember will meet us there once Felix shows up. I see Ambrose down the hall, and I have no desire to interact with her."

A shiver ran down Fotia's body. "Gah! Agreed."

Ember watched them leave as Ambrose approached, face set in a determined glare. Despite all the time and work they'd done over the last few months, not much about their relationship had changed. *It's like a point of pride with her. Then again, what isn't?*

"Phoenix, we need to meet during study hall on Friday in the library to work out some logistics. You can't just dilly-dally your time away with your friends. We have an organization to run."

Before Ember could respond, Ambrose spun on her heel and walked away.

From behind, arms wrapped around their waist, and Felix's voice, low and amused, whispered, "Yeah, *Phoenix.* No down time for you." Ember turned to give him a hug. He continued. "Think she's unwilling to say your name because then she'd have to admit you two are partners?"

"I don't know, but I'm super curious what she's going to do this afternoon to get into Ring of Fire, assuming she's one of the initiates."

"You don't know?" One of Felix's eyebrows shot up.

"Nope. I just know that there are twenty potentials. Last year only twelve made it after the second wave ... so, who knows. Oh, and I know that Olivia and Fotia will be there to try to amaze."

"And you're the only one there in a robe?"

Ember smiled. "Yeah, usually at the fall initiation, there aren't any students since everyone has graduated. Mr. Tine offered me the leadership position and the robe comes with it. I said we could wait until the fourth meeting, which is standard, and vote. I have a lot on my plate right now and don't really need that, too. I did tell him I'd run the first few meetings."

The two walked to class. "You do know that all but guarantees you'll end up as the leader, right?"

"Nah, Ambrose will be there. She'll assert her own superiority. I really prefer these meetings when they're *not* at school."

Felix scoffed. "So, in these meetings you have with Ambrose that aren't at school, do you include your aunts? Is that why they're better?"

"Usually. The ones here are about creating an outline of what 'we' want done. Then we have the larger meetings with the adults. When she mentioned being under FB's leadership, that wasn't just clap-trap; we're kids and the adults know what they're doing. Ambrose is obnoxious, but she does know how to get into a position of power. She's also utilizing her mom, who, for the record, is freaking smart. I'd work with Mrs. Wells any day of the week."

The bell rang as Ember and Felix got to class. Ember took a deep breath and cleared all other worries from their mind. It was time to just be students.

Thank you for reading Veiled Phoenix!
Please leave a review online.

Check out my website to find all the links to my socials and find information on my next series!

Coming Soon:

- Pebble's Story

  o Xenagogue

  o Yugen

  o Zephyr

About the Author

Huckleberry Rahr is a mathematics instructor at the University of Wisconsin-Whitewater. She spent many years teaching math around the Midwest and in Papua New Guinea with the Peace Corps. Her parents  instilled a love of reading from a young age.

She grew up with lesbian moms who had a huge collection of women authors with heroines as the protagonist. Her favorite genre was fantasy and science fiction, that is, until she discovered urban fantasy. What her mom's library lacked were books with characters that looked like her family: diversity in background, gender identity, and sexuality. She decided if she couldn't find that series, then she would write it.